2,00

SELECTED STORIES

By the same author
FUTILITY AND OTHER ANIMALS
THE AMERICANS, BABY
COAST TO COAST (ed.)
THE ELECTRICAL EXPERIENCE
CONFERENCE-VILLE
TALES OF MYSTERY AND ROMANCE
BETWEEN WARS (script)
THE EVERLASTING SECRET FAMILY AND OTHER SECRETS

AUSTRALIAN CLASSICS

SELECTED STORIES

Frank Moorhouse

ANGUS & ROBERTSON PUBLISHERS

ANGUS & ROBERTSON PUBLISHERS
London . Sydney . Melbourne

This book is copyright. Apart from any fair dealing for the purposes of private study, research, criticism or review, as permitted under the Copyright Act, no part may be reproduced by any process without written permission. Inquiries should be addressed to the publisher.

This selection first published by Angus & Robertson Publishers, Australia, 1982

© Frank Moorhouse 1969, 1972, 1974
© in this edition Frank Moorhouse 1982

National Library of Australia
Cataloguing-in-publication data.

Moorhouse, Frank, 1938-
 Selected stories.

 ISBN 0 207 14563 6.

 I. Title. (Series: Australian classics (Angus & Robertson)).

A823'.3

Typeset in 11pt Garamond by Setrite Typesetters
Printed in Hong Kong

Acknowledgements

Some of these stories were originally published in *Balcony*, the *Bulletin*, *Chance International*, *Hemisphere*, *Pol*, *Southerly*, *Squire*, *Thor* and *Westerly*.

The drunken man in "Becker on the Moon" quotes a stanza from a poem "Does Grass Grow on the Moon" by the late Elsie Carew.

The italicised narrative in "The Machine Gun" is a loose adaptation of parts of "Che Guevara's Diary", published in *Ramparts* magazine, July 1968.

Contents

The story of the knife	1
Across the plains, over the mountains, and down to the sea	13
The first story of nature	16
Lou shouted "hey!"	24
Walking out	29
The train will shortly arrive	36
Futility and other animals	52
The second story of nature	57
The third story of nature	70
Dell goes into politics	78
Becker and the boys from the band	86
The machine gun	95
Becker on the moon	104
A person of accomplishment	111
The Coca-Cola kid	123
Soft drink and the distribution of soft drink	133
The St Louis Rotary Convention 1923, recalled	145
Jesus said to watch for twenty-eight signs	161
George McDowell does the job	168
George McDowell changes names	175
Business no picnic	180
Rules and practices for the overcoming of shyness	190
The enterprising spirit of the Anglo-Saxon race	199

The story of the knife

"THE KNIFE was in the duffle coat—with the methedrine and *Herzog*."

"Shit."

"Someone might have taken it by mistake. They might return it."

"Oh yes."

"I'm sorry."

"It's not your fault." She stood before him, contrite, perhaps a little frightened. Her youth showed when she faced him defensively.

"All things pass," he said. "That's folk fatalism. Perhaps the time of the knife is over." The time of the knife. She did that to him. Twenty-year-olds were always saying things like that. The knife was stolen. There was nothing portentous about that. In fact the duffle coat was stolen—the knife just happened to be in it.

She had moved over to the refrigerator and taken out a flagon of dry white and was pouring a glass.

"You want some?"

"No, I'll have a scotch—with two ice cubes."

"I'm sorry."

"I'm not blaming you. It doesn't matter."

She went about getting him the scotch, running water on the ice tray to free the ice.

Then without previous hint, quite unpredictably, she said: "Roger, I think our time together is finished. I think it's time I moved out."

Well.

He first thought to argue against it and hold her. Then he let go to a feeling of resignation which was stronger. She was probably right. It probably was finished. If she *felt* it was over then perhaps ipso facto it was. It wouldn't shatter him. But weren't twenty-year-olds too much. They always *knew* and they acted so biblically as though life was a series of mystically revealed events. A time for every purpose. They woke on a morning and were able to feel and believe that from *that* day "things would be different" or something. Anne, he thought, Anne, when you're twenty-eight you'll be sure of different things. You'll be sure that life is confusing, you'll be sure that you can't be certain, and you'll know that life doesn't change but goes on in eccentrically undulating cycles. He caught sight of his thinking and was embarrassed by it.

She put the scotch in front of him.

"If that's the way you feel, Anne."

She sat opposite him on the other side of the table.

"I've been ignoring signs, Roger. I think our feelings have changed. It's almost as if the knife marked something—symbolically. It was a symbolic thing."

Twenty-year-olds were *too much*.

His indifference left him without a reply. Now that they were living in the city their affair was certainly flatter. But pleasant. At the cabin where there had been fantasies, it had been a digression from their mainstream, a suspension from routine, and other things.

It was cold living in the cabin above the gorge. Perry had left a Portagas stove but the gas had all but gone and they were conserving it.

"I could light a fire in the middle of the room. Underneath the matting it's cement."

"You'll smoke us out," she said. She was painting, an army blanket around her shoulders. She had on his navy blue polo neck jumper he used for sailing. Her knees were drawn up to form an easel.

He drank from his glass of claret. He dipped his finger in the claret and wrote her name on the table. He dipped his finger again and sucked it. He liked sucking. Sucking nipples. Sucking her fingers. Sucking cocks? No, not that. He couldn't come at that.

"I'm going to buy a knife tomorrow," he announced.

"Great."

Her sweet typical reaction. Why did she think it was "great"—as though she was expecting him to buy a knife?

"Do you really think it's 'great'?"

"Yes, I want you to have a knife."

He smiled. Oh, the sweetness of it. He moved over to her and kissed her hair. He knelt and hugged her hunched knees.

"It's a man's thing," she said, her hand on his face. "You're my man—down here anyway. I just want you to have a knife."

"I'm not buying a sheath knife."

"You'll know what sort of knife to buy."

He rested his head on her feet. Times such as these, when she spoke with female authority, when she acted with such sure emotional touch—these times made him swell as a man. Her touchings, her words, her movements, the way she handled food, the way she cut an onion, the way she painted, and the way she washed herself.

Was he playing with manhood or something? Or was she playing with womanhood? Or was it just a part of the thing they had going between them? How could she know, at her age, what she did to him? She'd had a kid but that was a mistake and it did not make her a woman. She was just twenty. She was playing it by ear and it was all so right. But perhaps it was his private fetish. Should you tell the other person that they were catering for a fetish? Was a secret pleasure dishonest? But Christ, feeling this way wasn't a fetish. This was the way he should feel. Like man, it's the real thing. It's the real bit, man. Like you wouldn't want to know.

Next day they walked the four miles to the store along the track to where it met the bourgeois asphalt of the town.

He told the girl in the shop that he wanted a knife with one long blade, a short blade, a can opener, a needle, a pair of tweezers, a screw driver, and a bone handle.

She handed him one to look at.

"No—I'd like to look at that one," he said, pointing to a black bone-handled knife. She handed it to him. He opened up its implements—fanned out like a sun god. He half knew then that this was the one. Anne stood silently while he compared it.

The black bone-handled one had everything except the screw driver. But it was the one.

"I'll take it," he said to the shop girl.

Anne came up against him. "It's a splendid knife," she said, and ran her finger along its body. She picked it up and held it against her face before the assistant wrapped it. "It's a knife for all seasons—a knife for the backwoods."

The shop girl looked at her.

3

"I'll skin animals," he said, "and defend you and cut ropes and carve wood."

The shop girl looked away.

Outside he unwrapped the knife. "It's a good knife."

"Yes, yes, yes," she said, putting her head against him as they walked away from the town, off the bourgeois asphalt and along the track which became wilder and then tenuously reached the cabin.

He made a strap for the knife. He found a leather strap hanging from an army water bottle in the shed behind the cabin. He cut a length from it which included a buckle at one end. The leather had dried but he rubbed it with oil. On one side it was finished and on the other rough. The oil he rubbed into it gave it back some suppleness. He tapered the free end and bevelled the edges. He used steel wool to clean the rust from the buckle until it was a dull, smooth metal gleam. He oiled the buckle. Giving the strap another application of oil he hung it in the shed until the afternoon.

In the afternoon the leather was alive. It had regained its full suppleness and a sheen. He slapped it on his thigh. Threading the strap through the lanyard loop of the knife he then buckled the strap through his belt. It hung about eight inches.

He went into the cabin.

"Look."

"Oh fine—it looks so fine."

She came over to him and handled the knife.

"When I'm down here I'll wear it out like this. In the city, I'll put it in my pocket."

"Yes, wear it all the time—in the city too—it should go with you everywhere."

Next day he carved her name in a tree.

"It doesn't hurt the tree does it?" she asked.

"A tree doesn't mind being cut with a real knife for a real reason."

He first cut away the bark to reach the wood of the bole—thigh white.

He carved: "Roger and Anne loved in this place." He felt that the phrasing "loved in this place" carried the correct interpretation of their affair—more a passionate affection limited in time than a deep important love. He hoped Anne understood it that way.

One day they went to the shoreline and with the sea swirling around their legs they prised oysters on the sea-pocket rocks, snatching them between the onrush and retreat of the sea, eating them from the knife blade. The knife hung from its strap around his wrist, the leather strap dark wet from the sea.

"God," he said, wiping his face with a dripping hand, "oysters—the sea—and you."

"And the knife," she said smiling. They kissed with the knife caught between them, hard against their chests and the sea surging around their knees, cold and uniting.

They drank wine that night with some methedrine until they both burned brightly.

"You don't talk about everlasting love," she said, "and that's what I like about the way we are."

"Don't you believe in everlasting love?" he asked. He was always intrigued by the way she catalogued herself.

"No I don't—do you?"

"I don't know, Anne—I think probably some people can have everlasting love."

"Really passionate everlasting love?"

"Everlasting in the sense that it is sexually and in every other way alive—and goes on for years."

"How many people do you know who have it?" she asked disbelievingly.

"Perhaps one or two couples—that's among my friends—but then, my friends are not prone to everlasting love. Not that they don't try."

He saw some who had tried and failed—Sean, Robyn, and Jimmy and Jeanette, Anderson and Sally and saw them in frozen stances of pain or anger or disillusion.

"Love lasts for as long as it's there and it's too fragile and vulnerable to last for long," she said, "and I'd hate for us to pretend. I think that's sick—when people pretend."

He doodled mentally. "What's wrong with pretended love in the absence of anything better?" he asked her and himself. He was playing with her.

"I should hate that."

"In the case of compassion, isn't it better to pretend to compassion than to express your indifference?"

"No, *non*, no, it would be better to be true to your feelings."

"Even to appear cruel?"

"Yes. Because it wouldn't be as cruel as the pretence."

"But sometimes you can be so neurotic that your true feelings—the way you want to feel—can't get through—when you're all hung up. Why not act the way you want to feel, until the hang-up passes."

"Once love is gone it never comes back."

"What about when you're angry—you mightn't feel loving then but love hasn't gone. Or when you feel hopeless—that passes and love comes back."

"Real love is always there and it never goes away."

They sat thinking in the fast methedrine silence.

"I don't want you ever to be false to me," she said, "and I don't think that we are neurotic."

He didn't usually talk like this about these things. The methedrine allowed him—his words breaking out like fowls through a broken fence.

They listened to the lute music, sitting cross-legged facing each other, with the methedrine singing through them.

"Soothe me," he said.

He lay his head on her lap. She put her hand down his shirt and rubbed his back.

"Come to bed," she said, "where I can properly soothe you."

They moved over to the bed in the corner of the cabin. The lantern burned a soft temple light. They undressed each other and stood naked, their hands touching each other. They kissed. Naked, he held her breasts and she took his penis in both her hands, holding his testicles tight. He became submissive to her touch. She responded, pulling him down gently to the bed, leading him by his swelling penis. In the lantern light the logs of the cabin wall rippled up to the roof. She held him tight in a kiss. He moved his head down to her breasts. She stroked him—pressed him against her breasts—nuzzled his hair. Then they petted in an erotic calm.

Then she whispered: "Give me your knife." He did not hear her clearly and shifted his head. "Give me your knife," she whispered. With an erotic trembling he reached across to his clothes beside the bed and unstrapped the knife from the belt and gave it to her.

In the lantern light he watched her strap it around her naked neck. The black bone handle of the heavy knife hung down between her young heavy breasts. She looked up at him, holding out her arms to him. She took him to her, pulling him over on to her, the knife coming hard against her skin pressing hard into her breasts. They rolled hard with the knife between them, clamped in a kiss. He felt the bucking and rearing of desire. They writhed and he felt the pleasure of the knife hurting. Swept by her deft sexuality. The knife like another penis. Her penis? Or did he have two? Or was it their penis? They rolled with the rearing desire.

Then he pulled back away from her, looking at the black leather strap and the black bone knife hanging from her neck against the soft white skin. The knife had left its imprint on her breast. She was his girl with his knife strapped to her. In the flickering of the lantern he grew dominant. He moved to her aware suddenly of how much bigger he was than she. She stared at him, her hands on his thighs, and then lay back wide, the knife lying against her body. He reached down touching her breasts and touching the knife. He pushed down on the knife tenderly hurting her, and then came down on her, entering her. She was his woman and the knife she had strapped to herself was his knife. She was his sexual liege, she lay back and wrapped her arms and legs around him in a gesture of total surrender.

"Have me," she said, lying there wide, the knife biting into her.

Later he went to piss. He stood cold, shivering in the winter damp grass. The knife was in his awareness but he did not bother with it intellectually. It had played a part in a wondrous pleasure. He went back into the cabin, wiping his wet feet on the blanket. He huffed out the lantern.

Crawling in beside her he again felt the knife between her breasts, as he held to her for warmth. They both lay electrically awake but unspeaking, the methedrine humming through the wires of their minds. They remained embraced throughout the night. He felt the knife during the night but did not wonder about it. They slept and made love again sometime early in the morning, sometime before dawn. They slept some more. She took the knife off sometime after that. In the morning when the sun was up the knife was beside them on the floor.

When he rose he strapped it back on to his belt.

That day they built an outdoor fire from stones and an old iron grid, carrying sand from the beach for the fire bed.

On Friday they went to a party in the city. A packed, three-storey terrace house. People they both knew. In jeans, drinking from bottles of beer and in one room the clandestine sweetness of pot. The constant, heavy rock beat. He moved restlessly from room to hallway to stairs to room. He knew that she was in the front room, or at least that was where he sensed she was. He wanted to talk to her but he resisted. They had not come to the party to do that. He imagined her talking in her tough guarded manner. The heavy, constant rock beat followed him from room to room. They were from another place and he felt it. They had detached themselves from the city for a while and re-entry was not a simple matter. He felt a distance from the city. Perhaps it was the distance he enjoyed in a mild sort of way. He was not alien. It was that the experiences and the tempo of their life at the cabin would not mesh with the wild agitation of the party. They were disengaged. They had been living alone and their social reflexes were slower and they weren't ready to change back yet.

Sally Fith came to him as he stood in the hall. Before, in the city, he had wanted now and then to get off with her. They sat down together in the hall.

She asked him about the life down at the cabin.

"It's a good life," he said, "but I'm frightened to say how good or to talk about it for fear the gods will take it from me." People stepped over them and around them and he felt as if they were sitting undiscovered while people passed by looking for them.

"Painting?"

"No—I've done a little sketching now and then. Essentially I'm doing nothing. I went there to do essentially nothing."

"Money?"

"Haven't bothered to calculate—we're still eating. Anne looks after all that."

"Is she hung up about the baby?"

"She doesn't talk about it. It's gone—finished. I think she'd talked it all out of herself before she met me."

"Anderson's around somewhere," Sally said tiredly.

"So what? He's finished with her. Is he finished with you?"

She gave her bitter wry smile. "Ex-husbands never finish with you. And Anderson always keeps sniffing around his old bitches."

He wanted Sally at times but she frightened him. She was older and had an analytical toughness. She wasn't aware she frightened him and therefore could not ease him nor could she turn the fear to a sexual excitement.

He felt his knife.

"Look at my knife," he said to her, pulling it from his pocket by the strap.

"A knife?"

"Yes, for hunting and carving."

"You don't hunt."

"I don't carve either—except I carved our names on a tree. In a heart with an arrow through it."

"How romantic."

He tossed the knife in his hand with short tosses.

"Are you and Anne having a serious thing?"

"Not really...not in the 'I am in love' sense but perhaps in other ways."

"The old ambiguity—you 'love' her in *your own way*—your private definition. But of course she thinks you 'love' her in *her way*."

He tightened. "No it's not like that—it's all understood. We understand the situation." He was uncomfortable. He didn't like to talk about his life in this analytical way. "Perhaps sometimes—I'm speaking hypothetically, not about Anne and me—sometimes ambiguity might be useful. Perhaps it's needed sometimes so that two people can get what they want from an affair."

"Roger! You're capable of the most miraculous rationalisations."

"I wasn't speaking about Anne and me. We understand each other."

"It'll be the first relationship in the world where both people have."

"God I hate the word 'relationship'—you and the others use it all the time."

"We have so many..." she said drily.

"I want to show you my knife," he said again, opening out the blades.

"It has two blades, see?" He cut the floor.

"Why did you get it?"

"It has a needle, tweezers, a bottler opener, a can opener, and a corkscrew."

"Ooooh," she grinned.

"If you don't appreciate it I'll put it away," he said with mock injury.

"No—go on—I'm fascinated," her chin rested on her hand—one finger on the side of her face—she was looking at him, not the knife.

"I can see that you're not interested."

"I don't feel anything about knives."

"I felt I needed one." He closed it up.

"Probably an important male symbol. Painters always doubt their masculinity."

"For God's sake!"

"Just an impression I have."

He didn't want analysis. This always got between them before they could get off. He remembered then, the love-making with Anne and the knife. Sally could tear that apart with Freudian zeal. People were always unloading heaps of analysis on to his mind. He never knew what to do with it.

Sally put her hand on his neck, her fingers under his ear.

"You don't need any symbols, my sweet," she said. "Let's go upstairs and find a bed." She took his hand and kissed the side of his face.

He nearly took the easy way out and went but he sensed that it would be one of those unfortunate fucks where indifference on his part would cause it to finish messy and cold in an uncomfortable shared bed. And there was Anne.

"No Sally, not tonight. I don't feel good." He realised that he probably couldn't have anyway. He felt as closed up as the knife.

"What are you doing this morning?" Anne asked, her mouth against his ear.

This morning. He rolled over and looked through the cabin window and saw the morning. An empty day before him. A free day or an empty day? He see-sawed.

He lay back, his fingers behind her neck, in her hair.

"I'll clean my knife," he said. "Today, I'll clean my knife."

"I'll watch."

He smiled at her. "You just want to watch me clean my masculinity symbol."

She frowned, puzzled. "Who said that was what it is?"

He laughed and didn't tell her.

"It's just your knife," she said. "It's nothing more than Roger's knife."

He rose, warmed some water and washed.

After breakfast he looked in the shed where he'd seen a whetstone. He took some oil and cotton waste and steel wool and went to sit on a flat rock in the sun.

He used the steel wool to clean off the rust which had formed from the oystering. He made the steel clean, cool, and smooth to touch. He cleaned out the grit in the blade slots with a match stick twirled with waste. He oiled the knife lightly, rubbing the bone handle until it gleamed.

She lay on a blanket nearby in the sun and watched.

He spat on the whetstone and sharpened. He started at the

circular smearing of the spittle and carborundum, whirling like a universe. After a while he tested the sharpness with his thumb and by slicing a blade of grass.

He oiled the joints, opening and closing the implements until they clicked free and tight and snapped out firmly. Finally inspecting the knife, he held it for a few seconds in his hand enjoying the weight of it and the shape, enjoying its existence. Then he buckled it back to his belt.

He looked at her lying on her back, her knees up, her dress bunched around her hips, her legs apart to allow the sun to warm her. She was smiling to him. He let the knife fall to his thigh and wiped his hands on his jeans. He went over to her, kneeling down beside her and taking her in his arms. They made love in the sun on the grass.

A breeze made it too cool to stay there after they had finished and they went inside. She made coffee with milk.

"So, my sweet girl, the knife is gone. And you are going too." Outside the city stood around, as if watching.

She drank down most of the glass of white wine.

"Yes, I'm going," she said. "Does it hurt you?"

"Yes, I'll miss you. It hurts." He was careful not to overstate his feelings.

"But you weren't ever involved in it. It was a passing thing for you. Everything passes, you say."

"All things pass."

"All things pass. I think we can have something better now between us, on a new and different basis, something less restricting on you, and because of that it will be freer and better."

Twenty-year-olds were *too much*. At times like this they were just *too much*.

"Why? Because it will be non-sexual?"

"No. It needn't be that—if you still want me—but because we won't be living together and constantly around each other—you won't have to take me into consideration."

He looked at her. She looked away.

"We can still go to bed together," she said, without looking at him. "If you still want me."

He said nothing. He sipped his scotch. Should you sip it? Should you throw it down like in the Wild West?

"You know what happened?" she asked.

"No...what happened?" he poised for a surprise.

"When I found that the knife and the coat had gone—that very minute—it began to rain from a sunny sky."

Oh, no.

She came over to him and kissed him on the forehead. Then she went to the sink. She threw the dregs of her drink out and rinsed the glass, standing it upside down on the sink to drain.

"I'm going to get my gear and then I'll go."

He nodded. There were things he could say and some he wanted to say but he didn't. He had subsided. He shouldn't become mixed up with twenty-year-olds. With twenty-year-olds one was a father. A teacher. An oracle. A psychiatrist. A model. A priest. A reference book. A mentor. An ever-present refuge in times of real or imagined strife. It was tiring. Not because they took much which was of value but because of the demand from them for these roles. They gave you gifts—verbal and material gifts were constantly being laid at your feet. They were all undeserved gifts. Undeserved gratitude was the sourest of human profferings. One of the most difficult to turn away.

She came back down the stairs.

She was crying.

She came over to him and kneeling down beside the chair she put her face on his arm.

"I don't want to go, Roger. I really don't want to go."

He put his arms around her and said: "Sweet girl."

"I don't want to go."

"Don't go then—don't go."

"I was being stupid. I wanted to test you or something," she cried. "I couldn't leave you."

He looked across the kitchen at the Ajax, the Fab, the Lux, the Steelo. Outside the broom, the bucket, the tray, the brush, and the mop.

"Don't cry. You stay. We'll go on as we were."

"I won't bug you," she said. "I'm not possessive. I won't get like this again, I'll just be here when you need me." She held to him tightly and cried.

Twenty-year-olds were always softer and more susceptible than they pretended. And they didn't believe a lot of what they said. He'd forgotten that. You forget things for your own purpose. Anyhow, what the fucking hell.

Across the plains, over the mountains, and down to the sea

"IT WAS THE ROAD on which Cindy and I had driven. We drove from a long way inland on a hot day to the coast. We drove the car on to the beach and swam naked. It was that road in the dream."

"Was this trip of special importance to the affair? What was its significance?"

"Oh yes. Yes, it was a climax. It symbolised everything. It symbolised the leaving of a hot, dusty and choking marriage for the clean, free sea."

"I want you to describe the trip and I want you to free-associate on the dream."

How do you describe to a psychiatrist when you are blocked by overlapping grief and jubilation. Grief from having lost perfection, and the jubilation from having had it. God, we loved then. It may have been neurotically doomed but God it felt right. I feel tears about it now. But I do not want to cry. Cindy released me. I don't mean from marriage—I had left that myself—but from a living numbness. She was coming alive out of childhood and I was coming alive out of this numbness from an anaesthetised marriage.

The marriage wasn't bad in the hostile yelling way. I've told you about the marriage. We could never admit to each other that there was anything wrong with the marriage because we were supposed to be perfectly suited and had to live out all our private proclamations about how superior our marriage was to those around us. We had to live out our marriage propaganda. And I left my wife then, not understanding why, and Cindy left me later not understanding why.

At the time of the trip Cindy and I had been together a month. We had to go inland, where a friend's book was being launched.

"You use the word 'inland'."

"Yes."

In-land. Within-land.

"Oh yes—I see."

Well, at the launching we drank champagne, toasted, danced and cheered and sang. It was the first book by the first of our friends to publish a book. I remember holding Cindy and feeling the fire coming from her hot body. Everything was hot and delirious. It was a raging "inland" heat during the day and like the heat of the hot coals at night.

"Tomorrow we go home. We'll drive that 360 miles straight to the sea," I said.

"Yes. Please. Let's do that," she said. She could be as bright eyed as a child.

"We will rise early at daylight and drive to the sea, across the plains, over the mountains, and down to the sea. I know a road over the mountains off the highway which is shorter."

"Yes, we'll do that. We'll swim naked."

Drunk, we made love in the motel. I tasted the salty sea juices which came from her. I sucked them from her to my parched river bed. Those juices left a taste that I can never swallow away. They were of the whole world.

We rose to a squinting hot sun. We had fruit juices, grilled lambs fry and bacon, and very cold milk. We ate in bed. I saw Cindy's teeth against the milk. Very white, perfect. Then we showered together and we made love in the shower under water, standing up.

The day was very hot and we sweated as we packed the car. With bad love the packing of the car is the greatest irritation of all. For us it was the best of all games.

We drove then along the blue highway. There was a shimmer by ten. The bush had that screech of hot insects, as though burning to death. And there was a smell of scorched foliage and drying mould. Cindy looked at the shimmer of the highway and said: "The road is dancing with us." She said the sticking bitumen was a-kissing at our tyres.

We talked about how love was not our word. Not the word we would use. We would escape its fouled-up connotations. We wanted a new word for what we had. We celebrated our feelings by eating peanut butter sandwiches from a country store. They tasted as no other sandwiches have ever tasted to me. And we had a can of cold beer.

We reached the mountains by two. They were cooler but still the sun was hot. They had more moisture. I supposed they were protected by the thicker growth. It was cooler because of the moisture. I drove on the winding road over the mountains. Further on I knew the shorter road which went to the coast. It was a stony and unsealed road with trees which touched overhead. The road jumped the car about because of the speed we drove over the stones—we were impatient for the sea. It is not a well-known road, no other cars passed us. It was our road. We saw the sea from the top of a rise in the stony road. Cindy squealed and pointed and hugged me. For all the driving she smelled as clean as the shower.

We drove down the last of the stony road with the dust choking up through the car. Bouncing, we came to the sealed road and the coast.

The car sang along after the stones. We drove fast to the sea, across the grass and on to the deserted beach. It was about four. We pulled the clothes off each other. Damp with sweat. Her body was just out of adolescence. Breasts only slightly larger than my own. We ran naked into the sea. Holding hands, into the cold sea. I remember the sea, cold and swirling around my penis. I felt enlivened.

It was as if the journey had been a *passing through*—360 miles across the hot plains, over the moist mountains, through the tunnel of trees, and down to the sea. We had been together a month then. It was the leaving of my stultifying marriage for the clean free sea.

But do you know something—and it is this which upset me so much since I saw you last. Cindy and I have only been separated two years. The other night I was talking to her at a party and I told her that I had dreamed of the trip. She smoked in her new careless way and said, "What trip?" I said the trip from inland, over the mountains, and down to the sea. We made it. Remember?

"No," she said, "I don't remember it."

I went out of the party and on to the balcony of the house and wept.

I'm crying now.

"That's all right. When you're ready, we'll analyse the dream."

The first story of nature

ALTHOUGH SHE wanted to become an historian—or, as she sometimes told herself, a serious thinker—she led an impulsive sort of life and was glad that she could. She was glad that there was still *some* of the child in her, that she hadn't frozen into a stiff Apollonian. That would come, she guessed. Her impulse to act would be slowed down and increasingly restrained by questions of whether it would be wise. Had she considered alternatives abcdefghijklmnopqrstuvwxyz? Was she succumbing to the seduction of mood? Didn't she have responsibilities? All these sorts of questions. Or perhaps people never became coldly rational but simply replaced impulse and spontaneity with habit, patterns of living, and styles of life. But rational questions raised their frowning heads at her even now. She could act on impulse, but sometimes, say in the morning while showering or riding the bus to university, she would find herself face-to-face with one of the frowning questions. They frowned like her father. Even thinking like this now after having made an impulsive decision was a sign that the frowning person in her was working against the giggling person—against her decision to live with Hugo. But she had expected it to come. Perhaps all this meant was that she was becoming an intellectual—becoming aware of herself. She would not let it bother her.

"And how old are you?" Hugo had asked, his Nebraskan accent a melody.

"Sweet twenty."

"Do you think age difference is important? I'm exactly sour

thirty. Do you think that will bother us? Do you think love is embarrassed by age difference?"

Before she could answer, he went on: "I do not. Love is a rapport fed by an exchange between two people. From you—the insights of youth—from me, the experience (be what it may) of the twenties. Love is a caring and what does age have to do with that? And love is having children and we have bodies that will do that. Where then, may I ask, is the problem?"

Answering his own question with overwhelming definiteness, he said: "There is no problem."

The Nebraskan accent was a Hamelin piper. And his words, too. But that was not the important thing about him and that was not in any way the thing which made her do it. She felt that Hugo seriously wanted a "cohabitating relationship"—strongly and without nonsense. And she wanted it. She felt that she had made adequate allowances for her infatuation with him and that the decision was basically rational. But no, the decision to live with him had been impulsive. The analysis came afterwards and was a summary. What she probably meant was that there was nothing foolish about going to live with Hugo. It offered her things—experience and a close human relationship etc.

When he had turned to her during the film and said, "For God's sake, Cindy—let's live together," she had replied, without thought or resistance, "Yes."

"We don't know much about each other," she had said, meaning it not as hesitation, but as a way of saying, "Isn't it wonderful that not knowing each other doesn't matter—we have rapport." She told herself that "knowing" people wasn't a test in which a certain number of correct answers had to be given.

She hesitated before the word, she feared it had an avalanche of implications. "...love...I guess, is rapport," she said to him.

He said they would have a lifetime to find out about each other. "Even then we will not know everything."

She was determined to be certain about this. Certainty was lacking in everything else. But she accepted this. Uncertainty she supposed, was a natural state for anyone who thought. But in a human relationship one could find certainty.

"Are we having only potatoes?" she asked. He was cooking the meals until she had become "acclimatised" (as Hugo put it) to him and his house.

17

"Yes. With lemon juice—baked potatoes with lemon—with butter—with pepper and salt. Delightful." He spoke with exuberance.

She hid a hungry disappointment.

He continued, like a salesman: "Simple, wholesome potatoes. I like simple wholesome cooking. I've done a list of my favourite dishes. Of course, you'll have yours, too. I argue that there is too much confusion of flavour and too much spicing in modern cooking. I like the meals of the pioneers and peasants."

She watched him serve, caught helpless by a new situation. Her disappointment went. A bowl of baked potatoes—a beautiful dark wooden bowl—two wooden platters—a pile of coarse black bread—two sliced lemons, yellow—and deep yellow North Coast butter. He made a side salad.

Her eyes liked it. And her mouth, she ate the potatoes and found their taste for the first time. She was able to savour them. After, they ate mixed, unsalted nuts.

Hugo was "primitive" in other ways. He ground his own pepper, coffee, herbs, flour, and baked a type of bread, and extracted fruit and vegetable juices by a special process, and ate only unrefined sugar.

As a chemist he knew about the properties of food. "I will teach you the real arts of cooking," he laughed. "How to really use food. Do you know why our teeth rot out, our hair falls out, why we get ulcers and cancer? It's because of our over-refined diet. Old Henry Miller had a delightful essay on it. I'll hunt it out for you."

"My parents' teeth haven't fallen out."

"They will—or perhaps they escaped as children."

He said that modern food manufacturing was criminal.

He must have partially indoctrinated her because she felt guilty when she threw away the raisin sandwiches she'd made for lunch—at Hugo's direction. She ate two meat pies instead. The guilt came from feeling that she was betraying Hugo—or betraying herself by not being able to openly resist. Then the guilt dissolved to resentment. She did not follow the resentment because it led down an overgrown track. She laughed it off saying, "You're becoming *so* self-analytical."

Usually she did not mind the natural cooking which Hugo taught her. Now and then she cooked him grilled steak with onions, chips, eggs and fried tomatoes and he complained about the fats or she cooked him something from *Cooking Greek Style* and he joked that she was killing him with spices.

Hugo and she fished in the harbour and he talked of hunting and fishing trips in the Nebraskan forests and once in Canada, before he'd fled the USA as a "nuclear refugee".

"We'll go hunting one day and in the evening you can cook the food we've hunted and then you will really come to know the natural life."

"I've always had a repugnance for hunting, for killing animals."

"You'll get over that. It's OK if the food hunted is eaten. For sport—no. But hunting is at the very heart of natural existence."

She had hurt a boy to come impulsively to live with Hugo. Bobby had been seeing her at lectures during the first year and taking her to film screenings, buying her coffee in the foyer, and having lunch with her on the grass. Nothing about love had been spoken, but in the second year she had bought her first pills and after a few timid circlings they had slept together—clutching each other and trembling—his elbow pinning her hair to the pillow—both sweating with tension. Still, it was good. It was exploratory for them both and she accepted it as that. She was relieved also that the "first time" was behind her. Perhaps this had been a big part of the satisfaction. She remembered little else.

She had not told Bobby about Hugo at first although it happened so quickly and there was so little to tell. Over coffee in the foyer she had told him she was leaving Betty and Jill's flat to live with Hugo. Bobby had been upset and told her that she was being stupid, had stood up and abruptly said that he had to go.

She had shrugged and said that there had been nothing between them really, she hadn't pledged herself. She felt irritated by unreasonable guilt.

Hugo's way of life was a second crossroad taking her in yet another direction, and taking her further from her suburban upbringing. She had moved a long distance from baked Sunday dinners, cold meat and salad in the summer, and Chinese food in saucepans from the Dragon Restaurant on the corner, once a week. She was not of the suburbs anymore. She had known that when she left home to live with Betty and Jill, when she stopped reading *Women's Weekly* and found her way, lost and unguided, in Betty's *New Yorkers*. She was not dramatically *alienated* but she was bound in her own direction. She was glad that she could expose herself to

Hugo and that she had flexibility to go in a way that was different.

Yet there was the resentment and the confusion which was the overgrown track. Without vanity, she saw herself as an intelligent, independent, and unneurotic girl (certainly not as neurotic as Betty—or Jill). Yet some of her reactions to Hugo were uncontrollable and they battered her—as though he was holding her fists and hitting her with them. She kept her reactions secretly held down because they were foolish. The reactions were mainly from housework and cooking and his attitudes to them.

She had been doing the housework while he was out, as she preferred to. He had returned early.

He said, kissing her, "It warms me to see you cleaning the cave."

She gagged an outcry which rose in her.

"Hygiene is essential for survival," she said standing behind her mock rationality. "I was just finishing up." And she put away the cleaner leaving the work uncompleted. Two hours later she recognised that she had felt degraded by him. By him seeing her doing the work and by his remarks.

They were drinking beer from his twenty-ounce Mexican pewters. It was the time for what Hugo called "looking over the day".

"I think we should share cleaning the house," she said, aggressively.

He drank a large mouthful. "I agree, I agree," he said, and then, pointedly, "we do."

He in fact did more than she, but she disputed peevishly and on a technicality. The toilet.

"I know. I want a clean toilet. I think it is important and I appreciate the work you put in on it," he said. "I simply cannot come at it—it bugs me. I have a thing about toilets." He gave a big shrug.

She had a thing about toilets too but did not let it into the conversation. It was opposite to his. He had an aversion to cleaning them: she had a compulsion. Tiredly, she acknowledged that her mother did too.

He gave her, from time to time, kitchen efficiency lessons. When he did she switched off into a hostile buzz. She couldn't receive them and usually didn't apply them. He seemed to know more about the kitchen than she did.

"I come from a family of boys," he said, laughing at her

sarcastic query, "and I lived as a bachelor for three years. Two training schools."

So he tended to cook and clean more frequently and better than she. She read during it, closed-down by her weird tension, seeing the print and not the words. When she did cook she slopped and burnt and when she cleaned she did so secretively and without patience.

Hugo's comment about *him* hunting and *her* cooking returned to her often. She would have an angry inner dialogue. She was not a squaw. Yet when he had said it she had felt a warm emotional touch and had roughly and intellectually pushed it away. She was going to be an academic, not just a woman—and never a squaw. She was a woman biologically—because she had a vagina. But she did not feel "womanly" whatever that was. She was not going to be socially conditioned to some *Women's Weekly* idea of woman. She was going to be an intellectual with a vagina—like de Beauvoir.

Then came the remark.

Hugo liked her for her simplicity.

"I like your simple clothes and I like your graceful ways. I know precisely how you will dress our children and how they'll imitate their mother's grace."

The remark reminded her. "Talking of children, have you seen my orals? I left them on the ledge in the bathroom but they're not there."

He looked at her solemnly. With hard Nebraskan authority he said, "I threw them away." And then smiled directly and warmly at her.

She was amazed. Struck.

"You what?"

He turned the book he was reading face down on the table.

"I threw them away. They outraged me."

She shook her head.

"I hate contraceptives," he said. "I hate to think of your body being twisted by chemicals."

She was having difficulty composing a sentence. She said something like: "What!"

"I want children," he said loudly, gesticulating the expression "So-what-the-hell-is wrong-with-that?"

"You must be out of your mind," she said.

"Love goes bad between people when they don't want children," he said. "Contraception is a rejection. A rejection of me as a father. It's hesitancy." He talked quickly.

She remained standing at the bathroom door, toothbrush in her hand.

"But—I've got a year to go at uni—we've never even discussed it. It's unbelievable." She was rigid with anger.

"Love implies children," he said, buttressing his words with a heavy definiteness. "Children are the other part of the natural equation."

"What crap. What crap. What shit."

"No. It's true."

"I don't give a damn about children. You threw away my pills. You authoritarian shit."

She remembered other things he'd done. Theatre bookings without her consultation. Things like that.

"You didn't ask me whether you could use them. You didn't tell me you were using them. Who imposed on who?" he shouted.

"For God's sake only a fool wouldn't—you're—you're like all men—you think we can be used for your—fantasies."

He didn't move his hands from the table where they lay palms down in front of him. As though he was about to rise. He began to colour.

"So children are a fantasy. You're hung up—hung up on modern crap about independence. You think being independent means being neuter—you're hung up, Cindy."

"You monster."

"Having children means being a woman. That would scare the living shit out of you."

"I don't want to be a woman," she yelled, sensing the bad tactics of the admission. "I mean I don't want to be that sort of woman. Your sort of shithouse, servile woman."

He seemed to collapse in a hopeless way.

"You're sick," she yelled.

He raised his hands in a gesture of futility. He stood up. He reached out to her with his hands. His eyes followed hopelessly behind. He tried to take her in his arms. She pulled away and went to the bedroom. She heard him break down. Cold and frightened she piled some of her things into her wicker basket. *He had tried to force children on to her.* In the kitchen he was sobbing at the sink with his back to her. She left the house, saying: "I'm going." *It was male domination.* And she was humiliated by the demoralising power of the things he had said. But they were crazy things. *His attitude was authoritarian. He resented the independence that the pill gave her*. She wouldn't become involved again—she would have lovers—but not the involvement of domesticity. *One didn't have to have children*. In a mental skip she was nauseated by the thought of the sexual act. Instantly she expurgated the nausea from her mind. She gathered her principles and theories around her like bedclothes. She almost ran down the street in emotional panic. Wondering where to go and wondering about the mess of it. "I had no alternative," she said, and she herself heard how positive and how desperate it sounded and the sound frightened her. Oh shit, Oh Christ.

Lou shouted "hey!"

I WAS IN THE Fortune of War Hotel wondering how I got to be twenty-three. I could remember being eighteen and nineteen and then it became sort of vague. I couldn't remember being twenty or twenty-two and I didn't feel different now I was twenty-three. It was odd because when you had a birthday people always said: How does it feel to be such-and-such an age. I thought that perhaps after being young all the years felt the same. Beside me, Lou and Paul made part of the noise which filled the pub. They were saying something about how it was smart to spring the truth on someone in a difficult conversation. They were saying it was smart to admit you were wrong now and then because people trusted you. I had fallen out of the conversation, or they had pushed me out, about a middy ago, but I was still being dragged along by what I heard of what they were saying. People seemed to curl in and out the bar, like smoke, bringing in new smells. Hair-oil smells, sweat smells, dry-cleaning smells, tobacco. Then there were the smells of beer, spirits, and the rest. I wasn't feeling sick from beer but I wasn't feeling very well either. I remembered that Marj never admitted she was wrong in a conversation. I supposed that came from being an infants' teacher. You think of funny things when you're drinking and I thought about whether Marj would wash my underpants when we were married. I couldn't imagine it. We'd been going together for nearly two years and I bet she'd never thought of my underpants once. I laughed aloud. I often thought of hers. Lou and Paul looked around at me and then went on with their conversation.

Then I watched the man in the blue suit with an RSL badge on his lapel. He was weaving through the smoke and people towards us. Towards me. I said to myself that I must be the type that bar flies always picked to bite. It must be that some faces are sucker faces and the bar flies can pick them.

He reached us soon after his words.

"Got enough for a brandy, mate?" he said, and then he reached us. The others didn't hear him and I looked blankly at him sideways from my beer.

"Got enough for a brandy—for an old Digger and a good trade union man?" he said. He looked nearly drunk and had a beggar-smile. His suit was a Salvation Army handout, for sure.

"Christ!" Lou said as he heard the bar fly. He didn't say it at the man but he said it because he was irritated by the man.

The old man continued his spiel and Lou and Paul turned around.

"I served in the war in New Guinea, mate. They were bloody hard times and I thank the Christ that you won't have to go through it."

I reached into my pocket for money but Lou stopped me by putting his hand on my arm.

He said: "What's this crap about trade unions? You're on the bludge."

I could tell that Lou was going to put the knife into the man.

"Look, mate," the old man said, screwing his eyes narrow and steadying himself with one hand on the bar. "Look mate, you want to know why I'm a trade union man do you? Well, here's why." He cleared the phlegm from his throat.

"I was the best hatter around the place. I made hats with the best of them. I've made top hats for Members of bloody Parliament. Then the Depression came. You're too young to remember that—but I remember. Too-bloody-right I do. We went on strike, see—the hatters' union—thought we'd get things our way a little. See, we didn't know how big this Depression was going to be. Everyone said it'd be over next week. I was a union rep, see. A good tradesman but a good union man. I could ask my own money in the trade but I was for the union. We was out for fourteen weeks. Lived five of them on bread and dripping. You've never tasted that, I'll bet. But things got worse and when the strike was finished there was no jobs for them who helped organise the strike—or for a lot of others too. A lot of us were out of the industry on our backsides. I worked as a labourer when I could, digging ditches on relief and filling them in again. Built a swimming pool at Parkes too. Always thinking that things would pick up. I still put meself down as hatter on all the bloody forms I had to fill in. I was a tradesman. A man with a craft. Here I was digging filthy drains and carrying boxes. You can grin—smirk away—you're only young. I see you don't give a damn. Well, when things picked up general the hat trade never did. In the thirties everyone wore hats. Now? No one wears hats. The nearest thing I ever got to the bloody trade again was in army stores during the war. I never got back to my trade and labouring ruined my health. You can't learn a new trade after twenty bloody years. You try taking up a pick and shovel after working in felt for twenty years." He looked down at his hands.

I looked at Lou who was grinning and I couldn't stop myself grinning. I felt bad about it and tried to hide it from the old man. But he saw us.

"Christ," he said at us with disgust. He shook his head and said quietly to himself, "Jesus Christ."

I dug twenty cents from my pocket. The man looked at it and then looked at me.

"Stick it up your fat North Shore arse."

He pushed himself off from the bar and weaved away.

Lou turned to me and said: "You didn't fall for that yarn, did you?" He laughed again. Paul laughed with him.

"It sounded true," I said. I leaned back on the bar.

"It was all bull," Lou said. "Ten-to-one there wasn't any such bloody union. Anyway, a man can always earn a living in this country if he wants to." He took a drink of beer. "The whole bloody army from the last war seems to be on the bludge." Lou was a salesman. He ordered another round of beers although I didn't want one. I didn't see what Lou would know about unions, or hats, or the last war. I still felt sorry for the man.

Three days later I was sitting at work feeling what my father would call "disorientated". I had begun to feel this way when composing a sales letter which told people of a great new deal our company was offering on trade-ins. It didn't seem that good to me. And I couldn't keep my desk orderly. Our "good deals" made me think about Lou and Paul and their conversation about winning arguments by admitting you were wrong now and then. I thought about doing this in the sales letter: "Dear Customer, This is a lousy deal we are offering you in appreciation of your past patronage." I grinned and thought of giving it to the sales manager. I thought about the Digger in the pub and the hatters' union. I wondered if the story were true and how I could find out. I would like to prove Lou wrong just once. Just once. I knew a man who lived across the street from us who was a history teacher at the university. I'd talked to him about lawn mowers while we both mowed lawns on Sunday. He seemed the sort of person who might know. I decided to ring him. I was uneasy because the sales manager could hear through the glass partition and he didn't like personal calls.

The university put me through.

"I'm the son of Mr and Mrs Wake across the street. You know, we were talking about mowers last Sunday."

I told him I wanted to know about the hatters' union and the Depression.

"I'm surprised to hear you're interested. Is it for some sort of assignment—technical college or some course?"

I told him it was for a bet.

He said the story sounded plausible but he didn't know details. He gave me the name and telephone number of a man at the Trades Hall who would know. We finished and he said in a friendly way, "Till Sunday."

The union man was fairly cold when I told him what I wanted. I said that it was a university assignment.

"As far as I remember about half the hatters lost their jobs over a period of years up to and after the war," he said. It sounded like a speech. "I was not actively associated with the hatters' union but we of the Federated Textile Workers' Union had connections with them and I was a personal friend of the late state secretary. It was always a tight industry but it's a good deal tighter today. A little like the blacksmiths."

He pretty much backed up the old man's story and that made my day.

I met Lou in the bar next day and told him. He laughed louder and longer than I felt was necessary. I thought he must be laughing while he thought up what to say.

"Jesus," he said. "You're not still worrying about that drunk."

I asked him if he had been bulling about the man.

"Of course I bloody was. What would I know about hats? Can't you tell bullshit when you hear it?" He laughed again.

Maybe it was my mood from the office which was still with me. "Disorientation." It was at first. Then it was the way Lou laughed and what he laughed about. It was because what he laughed about was so like everything we had laughed about for so long.

Then it occurred to me as I stood there in the bar that I was feeling very tired. Tired in a way I'd never felt before. I didn't feel like talking. What Lou said was true. I couldn't tell bullshit when I heard it. And then, I hadn't really thought about bullshit until Lou put it to me that way. How do you tell bullshit? The old man hadn't been talking bullshit. Lou had. How do you tell bullshit?

There was a lot of bullshit around. At work for instance. That bullshit letter.

I put my glass down and puffed out my cheeks. I tried to get an idea of what to say or what to do but the only word which came in my mind was "bullshit". I was feeling very odd, to say the least. Sick in the head as though my brain wanted to vomit. I picked up my glass again and then I realised that Lou and I were both in the bullshit game and making a living at it. The old man was fair dinkum and had to bludge a living. I thought: "That's bloody funny, that is." Then the glass started to slide down my fingers on its moisture. I just let it slide. It dropped out of my hand. Down to the floor and beer splashed like an explosion on our shoes and trousers. I looked down. The glass wasn't broken. That seemed bloody funny too, for some reason.

I still wanted to cry but not only from the eyes.

"What's the bloody matter with you?" Lou said, angrily brushing the beer from his trousers.

And then I gave the glass a tremendous kick and it shot across the bar floor and smashed against the wall between a man's legs.

Lou shouted "Hey!"

I pushed past a few people and ran. I ran out of the bar and along the street for a block or so.

Since I ran that day two months ago I haven't been back to the pub, to work, to Marj, to Lou, or to anything.

Walking out

HOW, IN BED EARLY Thursday morning, do you explain to your father and your mother who you have lived with for twenty-three years, that you do not want to go to work and that you do not want to see your friends? How do you explain that you'd rather not see them, too? How do you explain that the idea of working and the idea of seeing your friends makes you feel sick in the head? How do you explain that you want to lie down somewhere on your own?

So I lay on my back in bed early Thursday morning knowing that the clock was ticking towards seven o'clock and that at that time my mother would call me, saying "Thomas, Thomas," as if she worked by the cogs and springs of the clock. Some mornings I thought that if I stopped the clock Mother would stop.

I didn't know why I wanted to lie somewhere by myself, like a sick cat. It didn't sound reasonable to say to anyone. Having something strange to do or say always bothered me and I would rather shrug out of it if I could. But this time I wasn't going to do that. I told myself that when I stopped work I could loaf about. And this was just what I wanted to do because I'm a lazy bastard at heart. Reading was one thing I hadn't done much of since school. Always other things on. I liked a good story — something like *Peyton Place* and I wouldn't mind reading *Lady Chatterley's Lover* if I could get hold of a copy. There were a lot of movies I wanted to see.

"Thomas, Thomas," cried my mother. I looked at the clock: seven o'clock — bang on. This morning I was fresh when I heard her call instead of dull.

I propped up on my elbow and looked around the room. Pennants of school football.

A pile of magazines — *Playboy* hidden at the bottom. In the cupboard I knew that there was a box of broken toys. The wardrobe was full of clothes. On the door hung a camera bag and camera worth $250 — it used to be my hobby. A speargun leaned in a far corner partly behind the wardrobe. I knew my mother had pushed it behind the wardrobe because it frightened her. It was worth a few bucks too. A window overlooked our lawn where I had spent the last ten years of Sundays mowing. There was a picture on the wall of two nude boys warming their arses in front of a coal fire. On the dresser was a big flagon nearly full of cents and two cents which was once a saving for a car and then for going overseas. When Lou had decided not to go I had pulled out. Now it was for the marriage. Marj always put money in it when she came over.

Marj. I wormed back in the bed away from thinking of her. I guessed she was part of it all. Part of my mother and father and work and Lou and the whole lot. We'd had beaut times, Marj and me, but Christ she drove me up the wall at other times. Then I realised that I had not let the thought about her driving me up the wall come into my head before, or if I had, I more or less pretended that I hadn't seen it. I'd hidden away from the idea. The more I thought about Marj the more I realised that she was a silly bitch. She knew every-bloody-thing. I loved her though, I guess. I told her I loved her every time we went out. It seemed that it always came out when we were kissing and loving up. That's when it always happened. Perhaps I didn't really love her. I nodded to myself in bed and felt relieved that the idea of not loving her had come into my head and stayed. My brain had never really let in ideas against Marj before. My brain keeps telling lies. No, it wasn't always like that — I hadn't been game enough to ask my brain direct questions. Of course, I'd known my brain was lying but I'd been too weak to stop it. It was easier to let it use me and my mouth. Easier to stay in the rut of a lie, like driving. I'm two people, I thought, one of me is a liar and the other is a coward. What a splendid combination. I lay face down in the bed and enjoyed condemning myself.

When Marj and I would be talking or sitting about at home she would often start saying how it would be nice to live in this suburb or that suburb and she would would cut plans of houses out of the Sunday papers. Now I knew that I'd never really believed that I'd live in one of those houses with her.

We usually had a fight if we were sitting around with nowhere to go. I used to listen to the way she talked with Mother too. Some of the things didn't mean anything. I think they only talked to let each other know they were still in the room.

We'd never had any real sex either. Just playing around. When I did get her to use her hand she would always say after that she had been carried away. She'd lie there looking depressed and sinful as if something putrid had happened. And she wanted to wipe her hand as quickly as possible. Other fellows' girls would be in it. And then there was her makeup. I couldn't understand why she wore makeup so thick. I thought she looked all right without it. She would only laugh when I mentioned it. She'd say: "Oh, you're a boy and you wouldn't understand." I thought it was supposed to be worn because it pleased boys.

I heard Mother coming along the hall. She looked her gray head in.

"Time to get up, Thomas. Father's up."

Father was always up. How could I tell her? She would be puzzled and scared. Father would come. He would ask what all the nonsense was about me not going to work. He'd be quivering around the lips.

"Are you all right?" my mother asked, puzzled by the way I was looking. She came into the room and peered down at me, putting her hand on my brow.

"You have a temperature," she said.

"I'm feeling sick," I said. "I don't think I'll go to work today." And then I felt wild for having said that instead of saying what I really wanted to say.

"It could be the flu—it's going around."

"Yes, I think it's the flu," I said, and rolled over away from her—tired from knowing how easily I bullshitted.

"I'll bring you your breakfast in bed. I'll get something from the chemist when I go up the street later."

"I'm not hungry."

"You must eat. I'll bring you a poached egg," and she straightened the bed clothes and left.

I had to clamp my mouth to stop from shouting at her that I didn't want a fucking egg. I was racked with the feeling that I wanted to jump up and run out of the house in the same way I'd run out of the hotel and away from Paul and Lou. Again I had the same feeling throwing up inside me. I had smashed my beer against the wall of the pub and run out. I smiled as I saw it all and Lou and Paul standing with amazement on their faces.

Now that feeling was coming again. I wanted to get away from the endless bloody conversations which tried to make me do what I didn't want to do. They just beat me down until I said yes for peace and quiet. Plans for me to settle down when I didn't want to settle down. Get up in the morning when I didn't want to get up. Writing letters at work that said things I didn't want to say to people I didn't want to say them to. Bullshit letters. Poached eggs I had to eat when I didn't want to eat them. I felt they were dragging me by the legs over a gravel road. But I was going to kick my way free. I wasn't going any further with them.

Father was at the door.

"What's the matter with the young lord?" he boomed. He was dressed for work. Blue suit. Shoes spit polished, army style. He was doing his tie as he stood there. Chin pointed up.

"Feeling a bit of Thursday sickness?" he said.

Mother was behind him. "He's got the flu, I think." My father laughed. "That's what I call the typists' sickness. They have flu a day or two every month." He laughed. "Never seen a man with it yet." He laughed some more.

"Father, you're naughty," my mother said, leaving the room to cook my unwanted poached egg which I would stuff down my unwilling neck.

"When you take sickies they find out that you're not wanted," my father said, walking down the hall to the bathroom. "You'd better watch out," he shouted. Chuckling, chuckling, chuckling.

Oh Christ, not one more day of this. I was twenty-three. Not one more day of this.

Then, depressingly, I knew that I was weak. Weak as shit. I wouldn't do it. Before going to sleep I had the idea of getting a flat. I had my pay for the week and $800 in the bank. I could live for a fair while without working. Bugger it, I thought, I will do it. I got up and went to the kitchen and picked up the *Herald*.

"You get back to bed," my mother said. "You can't be very sick if you want to read the paper."

I stuck my thumb at her in the hall where she couldn't see.

As I was about to get into bed my father appeared at the door of the bedroom again.

"Come on son, you're not sick."

I turned to him. I felt weak standing in my pyjamas in my bedroom filled with things which made me feel as young as a boy. My heart beat fast. Answering Father back had always been difficult.

"I'm not going to work today," I said, quiet and strong.

"What?" he said, although he heard me.

"I'm not going to work today."

"But you're not sick," he said.

"I know," I said, almost firmly, "but I'm not going to work today." Shaking a little I lay down on the bed and spread the paper out and pretended to read it.

"You're a damn fool," he said angrily. "You'll find out that playing around doesn't pay off." He walked off. I felt as though I had won something. But I wished I'd told him what I really felt.

I heard him say to Mother: "He's no sicker than my big toe."

My mother said something about me not having had a day off sick for years. No, I thought, not even when I was as sick as a dog. My father had always talked me into not letting the firm down. Shit.

I saw that there were plenty of flats advertised in the paper. I ate the poached egg almost gagging on each spoonful. I heard my father taking his careful steps along the path to work. I heard my mother washing up and singing. Heard her ring the office and tell them I was sick. Heard her carpet sweep the lounge room.

At about eleven my mother went out to shop. I showered and dressed. As I was doing my hair I started to whistle and I felt strong in my clothes. I felt free because everyone else was at work and that I had my own plans for once and my day was my own for once.

I put on my transistor and the blare of the music scared away a spider of uneasiness on my stomach. I looked at my face in the mirror and picked a pimple. Noticed dandruff in my hair. Still from about three feet away I looked almost boyish. I noticed the skin under my jaw was starting to droop. Jesus, a fellow would be old before he knew what happened to him.

I took my bank book and looked at the figures $800. I kissed it. I packed an airline bag with a few casual clothes and things I would need. I found my sheath knife at the bottom of the drawer. I put it in because it was somehow good to have. I decided not to take any aftershave lotion. It smelt of going to work.

I looked around the room to see if there was anything else I wanted to take and as I did I felt weakened and pushed down by the memories in the room. I turned up the transistor and the music scared away the memory spiders too. My eyes read a framed saying on my dressing table:

"This above all: to thine ownself be true, And it must follow, as the night the day, Thou canst not then be false to any man."

As I read it I thought it was a beaut saying. It was bloody true. I thought that I would take it with me. It was a twenty-first birthday present from my uncle, who was a Rotarian. I read it again and a bloody strange thing happened. I read half way through it and as though someone had scrambled the words it didn't make sense. I tried to read it again. I knew what it meant one minute and the next I didn't. Or had I known what it meant at any time? I tried to work it out. I supposed it meant that you had to tell yourself when you were bullshitting. If you did this then you wouldn't bullshit to others. But this wasn't right. Sometimes a thing was bullshit at one time and not another. I told Marj I loved her when we were loving up and I meant it. But this morning for instance, it had been bullshit. It was hard to catch yourself being honest. Sometimes I'd be talking and something true would sneak into my head and I would see it but not take any notice. Then it would be gone. Even when I knew I was bullshitting it didn't stop me being false. I was a bullshit artist and I wrote bullshit letters. I was false to every bloody man. I laughed. So I left the saying where it was on the dressing table.

In the dining room I felt weak and knew I could never face my father or mother. So I told myself I was a coward and wrote:

"Dear Mum and Dad, I've decided to do a thing which is pretty strange. I'm leaving home for a while. I'm going because I want to be alone. I want to work things out. I'll ring you. If Marj calls will you tell her I'll be seeing her soon. Love, Thomas."

I propped the note on the fruit bowl on the mantelpiece of the dining room. I had to go over the reasons why I was leaving again to get my legs to move. I remembered my dry cleaning and wondered if I should pick it up. I remembered that Lou would call for squash on Monday night. I thought about the housekeeping money and pulled out four dollars. I wrote on the note: "P.S. Here is the housekeeping money. I'll pick up my dry cleaning."

I took an apple from the fruit bowl, picked up my bag, walked through the kitchen and outside down the path. The front gate had an enamel plate on it saying "Beware of the dog" but we hadn't a dog for ten years. My mother said dogs caused too much grief. They were either hit by cars or they ran away. Ran away, I thought, and grinned. Not only dogs.

Chewing apple, I walked along the streets of hedges, trees and lawns. I looked at the lawns and gardens and thought about the work involved in them. If there were 365 lawns and gardens in the street it would mean that about a hundred years of work would be sweated away every four years. A hundred years of life. But no more of my sweat would go to fertilise the lawns.

I was feeling free but nervous. It was no use lying to myself. Unto thine ownself etc. I was nervous because I didn't know what I'd be doing tomorrow or the day after or the day after. Perhaps I was feeling lonely already. I thought about Marj. What would I say to her? Then I laughed because at that moment I realised that I had no intention of seeing her again. I was walking out on my job, my parents, my girlfriend and every bloody thing. I was cold inside my stomach as though it was raining there. But I wasn't going back. Of that I was sure. I'd left all right. I laughed aloud and then the bus came along loaded with silent, hunched people.

But in the bus I knew that I had been laughing to hear myself. Like Marj and Mother. Making noises to show myself I was still there.

The train will shortly arrive

THE TRAIN WILL *be arriving at Eden in approximately five minutes. Would passengers wishing to alight from the train at Eden please move to car five. The train will stop at Eden for approximately one minute. Thank you.*

In the rocking train toilet he tried to do *something* with his hair. He smoothed it down with water. He sighed. They were just going to have to put up with it. It had been trimmed and shaped. It wasn't as though it was *scruffy*. It was just *long*. He pulled a face at himself and began to move unsteadily along the corridor to his seat. No one would look twice in the city but at Eden...

"Your stop next," the bore next to him said, in case he'd forgotten.

The train stopped, and stood making those impatient steaming noises. "All right, I'm getting off, don't rush me," he said. He looked around for his mother or father although his mother had written to say they couldn't meet the train because they had visitors. He went to a cab drowsing at the curb.

He got in. *Rylands Cabs for fast reliable service. Radio controlled. Twenty-four hours a day. Telephone Eden* 2343. He gave the driver the address. The driver knew it.

"You'd be Fred Turner's son—young Bernie—," the driver said, screwing around to look at him.

He nearly denied it for no particular reason.

"Yes. I'm home on a visit."

The cab driver gave him another glance. Glanced at his hair, his sunglasses, his bracelet and then started the cab.

Satisfied?

"You've changed. I remember you as a kid. You wouldn't remember me."

"I do. I remember you but I don't remember your name."

"Jack Ryland. I run a couple of cabs."

Jack Ryland pulled a card from the upholstery trim above the driver's seat and without looking passed it back to him.

"You were a tough little bugger."

What a lie.

"But that'd be going back to when you were about ten. What you be now? Around thirty?"

"That's close enough." How coy.

They drove up the drive of the house. Ryland helped him out with his bag. His parents must have heard the car and they came out to the front porch. His father peering through his reading glasses. Why did he always, but always, wear the wrong pair? His mother was wiping her hands on her apron.

His mother hugged him and they kissed. He shook hands with his father, who said hullo to Ryland.

"Your boy's changed, Fred—I mean he's grown."

Oh, for God's sake get off the *changed* bit. His father looked for bags to carry—anything to distract him.

Inside he was introduced to the visitors who were sitting in the lounge room drinks in hand. They struggled to be interested. He felt the dull private alcoholic humour of a group which had been drinking together for some time. He felt the group stir alcoholically in an effort to fit him in.

"Bernie's been overseas. We haven't had him home for years."

He took off his sunglasses.

"How nice for you," one of the women visitors said, then gave a smothered giggle and said: "I mean that he's home again." The others giggled.

"What'll you have to drink son? We got everything." His father opened the stocked drink cabinet which was lined with mirrors and lit up when the door opened.

"Let Bernie wash his hands dear," his mother said.

"No, have a drink—first things first," his father said, looking to the visitors who laughed accordingly.

The cabinet's range had expanded. Before it had been rum and sherry. The store must be prospering.

"Come on dear," his mother said to him, picking up her sherry. "I've put you in your old room." She guided him out. How much sherry was his mother drinking these days? And how much rum his father? His mother led him off.

"I'll have a gin and dry," he said over his shoulder to his father. He saw his father stare at the cabinet with just the slightest hesitation. "I have some Black and White." For a second he felt like accepting it, to please his father, as a gesture of something, but he didn't. "No, gin and dry would do nicely, thanks Dad."

Out in the hall his self-consciousness slipped away. They were all dull and boozed and he felt clear control. He'd reached a stockade of superiority.

Sherry in hand, his mother led him to his old bedroom.

"You wash and put your things in there while Daddy gets the drinks."

She noticed the bracelet. "What a lovely bracelet, Bernard." He flushed.

"Oh, I bought it... for the trip. My blood group's engraved on it," he lied. He twisted it around nervously and moved off to the bathroom.

In the bathroom he was at the mirror again. He rubbed under his eyes and for a cruel second saw age looking at him.

He came into the lounge room to hear his mother say: "He's been working at one of the private schools in Sydney—Grammar..." His mother turned to him as he entered.

"Your drink is on the cabinet," his father said. "Hope you like plenty of ginger ale."

He didn't but there wasn't much he could do about it now.

"No, that's fine."

"I've been telling everyone about your new position," his mother said.

"Not really new—I've been there six months now."

Someone asked him how he liked it. He said that conditions could be better.

"We teachers are becoming worse than farmers with all our complaining and carrying-on," he swizzled his drink.

"You deserve better dear," his mother said. "Education is so important." And with that the conversation left him. They talked bowls, business, with the women talking across at each other and the men talking across at each other. Now and then it would all link up coming back together on the same subject. Now and then his mother would make a reference to him or seek his opinion or give him an explanation—lacing him back into the group as best she could.

He went to bed after dinner, bored and slightly tense.

In bed he missed Mervyn. He ran his hands down his body, aware of his masculinity. He took his penis and it grew rigid in his hand. He longed for Mervyn. Mervyn was probably lying in his bed doing the same. In their flat. How long would he and Mervyn last? Another few months? They had both been with girls. Pathetic attempts. They got along. But there were the days when he said: "Go *away*, Mervyn. Fuck off. Leave me *alone*." Those days of deep angry depression about God knows what. But didn't all people feel that? And there were the days of glorious fun and loving nights. Of waking to feel Mervyn close and hard. Of the delightful relaxation together in front of television after hectic times. The relaxation and pleasure of showering and then going to Mervyn's bed. Of putting his head on Mervyn's chest. The shouting rows were worth that. The flowers they grew together. He remembered Mervyn teaching him how to garden.

He was careful of the sheets. The climax exploded away some of his tension. Immediately after he had a glimpse of his father— distant and puzzled—and of his mother, so unsurely and clumsily devoted, and then they passed from his mind with the tension.

Cum was messy after lonely masturbation. With someone there was usually affection and cum was a binding thing and a tangible expression of it. No, that was bullshit. It was sometimes true—but not always true of those drunken promiscuous nights. Sometimes it was then the mess of spent desire. Sometimes it was the mess of guilt. If the guilt anxieties were troublesome then the "tangible affection" baby, became "tangible guilt". Which one wanted to wipe away quickly.

He awoke to the early morning ABC news.

He'd forgotten the early rising Saturday mornings. The big morning at the store.

His father and mother, alcoholically sour, were probably not talking. He knew his mother would bring a cup of tea and shortbread biscuits. He didn't want to get up. All through childhood he had been made to get up, except now and then when his father and mother fought about whether he should be made to work in the store and his mother won. This morning he would not get up.

His mother brought him the tea, and kissed him good morning.
"I'll stay in bed," he said.
"Yes, do that darling. No need for you to get up. Father's in a foul mood."

He drowsed, leaving his tea to grow cold on the bedside table. Later in the morning he arose, ate his breakfast alone, put on his sunglasses and strolled up town.

Saturday morning in the country town. People stood on the sunlit side of the street at the gutter's edge talking about yesterday. Children ran slow messages. Young people swaggered on their bicycles propped against walls. A few early drinkers stood at hotel doorways with their first-of-the-day beers calming the jumping nerves and taking away the bitter taste of last night's sweetness. The adolescents out of schoolclothes flirted with tough aloofness in laminex milk bars. In the Red Rose, the New York, and the Paragon. He'd taken tense girls there after Saturday night movies at the Kings or the Victory for cold milk shakes and later when older, to the coffee shop for sophisticated black coffee and sophisticated raisin toast. He'd liked double dating with Peter best. Mainly because it was reassuring to have male company when one was so unfamiliar and ignorant about girls. But he had liked, or perhaps loved, Peter. He'd not been fully aware, and could not have admitted it, and it could not have been advanced. Only later when they were about twenty and he was beginning to recognise and admit his sexual nature had he recognised what he felt about Peter and it was then too late. Peter was tough and could never have been approached. But there had been a timid, guilty, mutual masturbation at about sixteen. Amazingly spontaneous at its beginning—a sexual urge forcing itself awkwardly, but strongly, through their conventions and inhibitions. It had been at Peter's home. It was left undiscussed. They both feigned sleep immediately after. He must have been staying with Peter that night. Peter's parents were probably away. It had never been repeated and never mentioned. He had dreamed of Peter and thought of him while masturbating in the years since. Had Peter thought of him? He doubted it. Peter had married a Catholic. Of course, Peter hadn't been the first. There had been a younger sexual thing—unselfconscious and pubescent. Of a different nature. Before girls. Girls had been necessary for Peter and him. Necessary for all of them then, for status at school and for curiosity, and so that they could say "I love you" for the first time and feel the first breast since infancy. But oh the tension of it.

He went into the Red Rose and ordered a banana malted. The taste of it made him shiver with memories.

He sat in a stall and watched people as they went by on Saturday business, some he vaguely knew. Some he'd seen fifteen years ago walking by on Saturday mornings as they did now. God how comfortable. Knowing that you'd be doing that on Saturday morning, every Saturday morning. Knowing that there was nothing hostile, hysterical, or dangerous to face in the journey through Saturday. Or perhaps there were horrors in that Saturday journey for some. As they went down the sunlit street some must have feared creditors, had to face forbidden people they desired, face people who held grudges. But weren't his Friday nights and Saturday mornings also ritualistic? But they were frantic—frantic rising late on Saturday morning, frantic hangovers, and hungover shopping with Mervyn at the supermarket with all the other frantic Jews and camps and bedsitter girls. He smiled and wanted to be back in the frantic ritual. It wasn't all *that* depressing and at least one knew one was *alive*. But it didn't have the...blandness...of the country town Saturday.

A man came into the milk bar. No. A boy came into the milk bar. In his mind the man was a boy. The boy, Harrison Bryant, was about thirty—in his mind he remembered him as a soft boy of eleven. The boy had coarsened into a man. It frightened him a little. He could hardly see a trace of the soft boy. Bryant's hair was cropped up to the crown. He had fattened at the waist. His belt pulled tight was his only attempt at control. His clothes were the characterless light greys and fawns. A singlet formed a vee across the neck of his sports shirt. Harrison Bryant's hands seemed frightfully wrinkled. He looked down at his own in shock. But he could not see them as someone else would see them. They seemed as they had always seemed—young and vivacious—if hands could be vivacious.

Harrison Bryant wore rubber thongs. He abhorred rubber thongs—ugly, common, and probably harmful to the feet. The thirty-year-old Harrison Bryant was buying a packet of cigarettes and with cupped hands had lit one, dragged on it and emphatically expelled the smoke in a relieved gust, as a smoker who was overdue for a cigarette. He had a gold metal watch band. Against the sun-bleached white hairs of his arm it was the only feature resembling the male attractiveness of youth.

Should he speak? It would be unbearable. But it was intriguing.

And wasn't he there for *that* sort of thing—to see some of it again. He wasn't sure whether he wanted to see it all again. But wot-the-hell, archy.

"Harrison," his voice came out light, almost camp. He roughed it up. "Harrison."

Harrison Bryant turned around and saw him. Quickly taking the cigarette from his mouth, smiling widely, he came over. "Bernie, for Christ's sake, it's been a long time." He came over with his hand out. They shook hands. The last time we touched, he thought, was when we were eleven and your hands were on my penis and my hands were on yours. Remember?

"Well, bugger me," Harrison said. "Where you been hiding yourself? Christ, you've changed." Harrison's eyes made appraisal.

"I've been overseas," he said. The appraisal sent a fizz of agitation through him. He wished he hadn't spoken. He pulled out a cigarette.

"Have one of mine," Harrison offered.

Never.

"No thanks, Harrison. I've got to like these."

"Fussy—nothing but the best." Harrison grinned aggressively.

"I don't smoke that much," he said. Calm down. Calm *down*. Harrison moved into the stall opposite him.

"Been overseas?"

"Yes, Europe."

"I was going to work in New Zealand but I don't suppose I'll be going now. Four kids and another on the way—what you think of that? Married?"

"No," he carefully ashed his cigarette, calmer now, "but it sounds as if you've been hard at it." What a coarse expression.

"All my own work—unless the milkman slipped in," Harrison laughed. He smiled involuntarily at the sheer corniness and pride.

"Where do you work, Harrison?"

"Cut out the 'Harrison' bit—Harry—everyone knows me as Harry. You'd be the only one who'd remember that's my real name."

"I like it," he said. Oh shut up.

Harrison laughed nervously. "I'm at the Golden Fleece service station. A fellow called Simpson runs it—you wouldn't know him, he's from Melbourne. I do a bit of panel beating and work the bowsers—you know."

He nodded.

"It's not the best job in the world. I've got ideas about starting my own panel-beating place or getting a station, but you know." Harrison smiled a lost smile.

He nodded. "Who'd you marry, Harry, anyone I'd know?"

"Betty Harris—don't think you'd know her—she would a been a year behind you at school."

He didn't know her.

"You'll have to come up and see us. We got a Housing Commission place up in the new part."

"I'm only up for a day or two."

"Perhaps next time then."

"Yes."

"Anyhow, what you been up to?"

"I teach. At Grammar."

"Posh school."

"Kids are the same anywhere." Except some have richer parents. Which makes all the difference.

"God you've changed. I mean from what you were at school." Harrison laughed, again nervously, in case he had said something wrong, partially realising what he meant, realising what was different.

"We've all changed," he said, defensively.

There was a silence.

"Ever feel like leaving the old town?"

Harrison tried to consider the question. "I was thinking of moving to Goulburn. Wife's mother lives there. But it's not a bad old town."

Another lapse.

Then Harrison asked again: "What do you do for a crust?"

He tried to answer it as a fresh question, rephrasing his answer to avoid embarrassment.

"Teach school."

"Oh yeah—I asked you that." Harrison stubbed out his cigarette uneasily.

"How's Jimmy Hagan?"

"Don't see much of Jimmy. He's on a farm near Captains Flat. He comes back now and then but I don't see him much. At the football sometimes."

"He always wanted to work a farm."

"He's share farming or something."

Harrison went to take out another cigarette but remembered

that he'd just finished one. He played with the packet.

"It's hard to realise that we were in infants school together and grew up together," he said, watching Harrison's face.

Harrison laughed and shook his head as if trying to deny it or shake away the embarrassment of his childhood. It was impossible to know if he remembered the sexual game they had shared. He kept shaking his head and laughing. "It's funny how you grow old."

"We're not *that* old yet." Let's not talk about *age*.

"I see your mum and dad about the place. Your dad drinks in the saloon bar down at Cassidy's. That's where I drink. I see him in the saloon bar after work some days."

"Who do you drink with? Any of the boys I'd know?"

"Sonny Buckley—you'd remember him. Lyle Bates? Used to be real fat?" Harrison warmed to safer talk.

He nodded. He remembered them. He remembered them as kids he'd played football with. Who for years seemed to wear a football jersey or football socks whether they were playing or not.

"Why don't you come down and have a drink with us? They'll be down there about now. We all get down there Saturday mornings."

Curiosity tempted him but his discretion grimaced.

"No thanks, Harrison...Harry...I have things to do."

Harrison didn't repeat the invitation.

Harrison stood up and said that he had to go and to call in if he was up around the Commission area.

Harrison left the milk bar.

He'd left too. His mind had gone back to among the lantana and grape vines grown wild where he and Harrison had crawled and made a hide-out and where one day, on some forgotten pretext, they had taken off their clothes, lain together and fondled each other's penis to erection. This had occurred—how often? Each time had been initiated by some pretext which even at eleven they had needed to justify the innocent, curious, and affectionate reaching out to each other. Then the first ejaculation—Harrison—and the amazement of it. Harrison had called it "spunk" and seemed to know something about it. But there had been fear and boyish bravado and a need to understand it. They had looked in *Pears Cyclopedia*, Arthur Mees' *Children's Encyclopedia*, and the book *Enquire Within Upon Everything*, and dictionaries. They looked for all the taboo words they'd ever heard—penis, prick, cunt, shit, spunk, and masturbate. The dictionary had told them that spunk meant courage. All the books together left them in a mocking darkness. They didn't touch each other after that—as though the signs of manhood had frightened them away from each other into the "proper" sexual distance for men. He'd been frightened too, of losing his courage.

He remembered their young, hairless, vibrant bodies. His penis stirred even now. Oh God, ageing was miserable. And foolish. An unbelievably foolish process.

Football matches came back to him. Rising on cold, frost and mist mornings to travel by bus to football carnivals. The vigour, and the bodies. The closeness of the team. The beautiful smell of the bodies in the dressing room spiced with the smell of liniment. The male heat of the bodies before and after. The dressing room had been an exciting, male place.

He dug and ground the sugar spoon deep into the plastic sugar container on the table, angry about ageing. The anger drifted away leaving the grim, impotent acceptance.

He thought again about Harrison's abashed reaction to him. How obviously different from other men he must appear and how he sometimes forgot this. Perhaps he'd never quite accepted that he was. Perhaps he had pretended that if he wanted he could conceal it. That no one need ever know. But it wasn't like that anymore. And it wasn't that he had changed. He hadn't *changed*. He'd simply unwrapped himself. That was that.

Drinking a banana malted in the Red Rose and thinking of the ghosts of childhood princes—princes who had become toads—was a disturbing game. Exciting oneself by remembering pubescent experiences was saddening. Next thing he'd be panting after twelve-year-olds and that would be *the end*. The End. Grammar School scandal.

He dragged himself out of the stall. The milk bar was agitated now by loud adolescents who moved restlessly between the juke box and the street. "Juke": of African origin, he'd told his class. He tried to buy his brand of cigarettes but couldn't and settled for Craven A.

He strolled along the sunny side and around the post office corner. A former primary school teacher came towards him erect with the same ageless authority he had twenty years ago. Was *he* like that to *his* pupils? Existing in the limbo especially allotted to school teachers. He felt like speaking but it would be meaningless for them both. Young people were always so aware of their own identity but for teachers, they were simply part of a straggling procession. The teacher passed with his shopping bag.

There had been a teacher later in high school, and a seduction. He remembered the playground stories about the teacher which had come first, and which had kindled him. The breathless, fearful desire which he had felt when first alone with the man in his office. With the inevitability of mutual desire he had become the teacher's special boy—first for his messages, then for his special conversations and then for his special pleasure. The conversations between them had quickly become personal with the teacher asking about his dreams and about his father and mother. Then the fondling. They had been sitting together at a desk one afternoon when the rest of the school had gone to sport. He remembered being asked to report to the teacher's office instead of going to sport and he felt again the wild excitement which had trembled through him.

They had sat at the desk reading figures from a sheet with the teacher checking them off. He had known it would happen. The teacher's hand came down on to his leg. Firmly then caressingly. His body seemed to silently hum changing then to a silent, low urgent moan but the only sound was the sound of his voice intoning the figures. Trying to control his breathing which wanted to break into grunting or panting. Up and down the columns of figures. The teacher's hand working up slowly and warmly towards the screamingly rigid penis. Up his leg to the fly and then firmly stroking the penis through the trousers. Then in the fly and down in through the underpants. When the hand reached his penis and gripped it he had wanted either to bury his head on the teacher's shoulder in erotic surrender or to run run run away from the embarrassment and guilt which swirled way down under the desire and excitement—an excitement ten thousand times as intense as anything he had ever felt before, with Harrison in the childish bushes or with Peter in the furtive bed. The tickling and caressing brought out the first thrusting of a new feeling—the trembling ecstasy of male touch and sexual submission.

He did nothing for the teacher. He did not look at him. He had stopped reading, suspended in the intensity of the hand on his penis. Then the teacher coughed and the hand withdrew and the fly was zipped. Why did he stop? The unejaculated penis subsided in cold disappointment. Why did he stop? The reading began again. His voice took hold of the figures, up and down the pages. Why did he stop? Then the smile and the gathering of the lists when they finished. The gathering of the pencils and the thank you and the teacher's squeeze of his shoulder. Why had he stopped? His legs were unsteady as they had been on rare occasions since when a certain pitch of sexual intensity was reached with strange boys in strange ways in strange flats. Why had he stopped? The brightness of the playground, empty except for the sound of singsong rote learning somewhere from a defaulters' class. He had gone to the toilet and locked himself in a cubicle to cry against the wall from utter frustration. He had been close to rage and couldn't masturbate. He just cried and beat his hand against the terrazzo wall. Why had he stopped?

God, he'd been so attractive then. So golden, so smooth and so sexually hungry. Soft clean blond hair and clean finger nails—one of the few boys who had clean nails—and not only because his mother insisted. His fully-grown eyelashes and a physical movement light and without conceit.

There had been three other times with the teacher, again wordless and never as blindingly intense and again never to ejaculation. Why had he always stopped? The sexual occasions with the teacher were flashes from the grinding school year. His place as special boy for the teacher had ended when he left at the end of that year to go to another school. It ended with a dull shaking of hands and pleasantries with him hating the teacher for having always stopped. Their friendship was cracked. He could not straddle the distance between them because of the inadequacy of youth. If only the teacher had not stopped and had spoken to him, tenderly, and coaxingly, he could have had him and gone on totally for years. He would never have opted for another school or gone to teachers' college. He would have stayed at that school to be with the teacher.

He stopped feeding the fantasy. Still alive after all those years. He was now away from the town's shopping centre and moving towards its outskirts where it was circled by bush. The teacher had obviously been blocked and hung up. Probably scared to death. Ejaculating would have demanded something, perhaps would have advanced it all further than the teacher was prepared to go. He wondered about himself. Would he one day begin to fondle favourite boys in his classes? He blanched at the risk and was relieved to see an ethical qualm, large and strong, standing in the way.

He had reached the streets which were half sealed with tracks at the edges for horse traffic. He then came to the end of the sealed streets where only kerbing and guttering had reached. The beginning of the bush. Houses had marched along the new streets with plumbing, cement footpaths, and kerbing running alongside.

The bush had been a place to go. It was, he remembered, at first a frightening place in which one did not go far. Each foray required a mustering of courage which, because of the gang, had become a forced courage which had taken them further than they wanted into unknown territory. But over the years it was explored and then roved. Familiarity came and the bush offered up its facilities—caves for hideouts, trees for lookouts, creeks to swim in, bamboo for blow pipes, berries to eat, and places to lie quietly concealed. There had been birds to kill although he never had—always firing blind hoping to miss. If the others had known that! But perhaps they all fired to miss.

He crouched on a rock and smoked. He had smoked for the first time in this bush. With Jennifer. What was her other name? Sims? Smoking had given him something like a sexual feeling. It wasn't clear. He remembered the dizziness and the forbidden excitement. She had been the only girl among them. He had kissed Jennifer later, around about puberty. It had been in a dark room and he could not see her. Somehow he had found her hand and then felt her lips against his, moist and moving, like some alive animal. His first kiss. Tinged with nausea.

That had been his childhood—sweet uneasiness. He rocked forward, his legs hunched under his chin.

He became aware of his bracelet which had slid down over the back of his hand. "From Mark." Given before Mark had returned to the States on his wandering from girl to girl and from boy to boy. It was not in memory of Mark that he wore it. Their affair had been brief, passionate, but socially difficult because of possessiveness. The bracelet was a reminder of his sexual identity. His sexual identity bracelet. He put it to his mouth and tasted the cold silver. The cold silver of his youth.

"My youth was nothing but a storm, tenebrous, savage,
Traversed by brilliant suns that our hearts harden,
The thunder and the rain had made such ravage,
That few of the fruits were left in my ruined garden."

He threw up his metaphorical eyebrows. His life didn't warrant poetry.

He glanced back through the thin bush to the Commission houses. He saw a sagging woman in woollen slippers hanging washing on a sagging line. Outside another house a man in overalls lay beneath a car, as though submitting to some sexual machine.

Was that woman Mrs Bryant? She was straightening up, bracing herself against her pregnancy. A child crawled around her feet. He let himself believe it was. Made himself feel a devious and superior sexual connection with the woman. But I was there first, darling, he thought, and I was there when it was beautiful and Harrison was fresh and sweet. She had picked up the child and was dragging the clothes basket towards the house.

He jumped from the rock and began to walk back towards the town.

Children. What about children? Sometimes he wanted them. Teaching them wasn't close enough. Did he want to mother a child? He remembered a strange night when he had gone to bed with Terri and she had wanted a baby. They talked about her and Mervyn and him bringing the baby up together. He'd loved the fantasy. Mervyn would kill him if he found him thinking like that. "Let those thoughts loose, sweet, and God knows where you'll end up—in the clinic at Rozelle—and hospital visiting is such a bore." He smiled. For Mervyn certain thoughts were taboo. He wondered if Mervyn could really control his mind as well as that.

Mervyn had bought him a Siamese cat. "You need a family to look after," Mervyn had said. He'd bought himself an alley cat to prevent the Siamese cat from becoming snobbish and spoiled. He wanted to see Marlon, the Siamese cat. He missed Marlon. He wanted to stroke him and have him give back a purring warmth. God he needed that purring warmth all of a sudden. He preferred Marlon to James Dean. James Dean whined and had no pride. Like all alley cats. Like alley boys, too.

Perhaps he was ready for a Big Affair. With Mervyn? They hadn't talked *that* way. But perhaps it was getting to be *that* way.

For Christ's sake why was he going in for the introspection bit? Why didn't he just let it all happen—if it was going to happen? Why did he pester himself all the time? Why didn't he leave himself alone—stop picking at his mental nose? It was the damn homecoming, of course. But even at other times he was always picking at himself. As if to see if he would fall to pieces when prodded. Why did he bother? Everything was OK. He was a bloody good teacher. He had Mervyn, he had other friends, he had the garden, and his colonial cedar furniture. And they were always doing things.

Everything was OK. Everything was going fine. He walked up the curved green cement drive to his home. He hoped that his father would have lunched and gone to bowls.

He went inside. His father was still eating. His mother had waited for him.

"What did you do, dear?" his mother asked, putting his lunch in front of him.

"Walked about—up the street—up to the bush."

"See anyone you knew?"

"Only Harrison and a couple of others—from a distance."

"He's married with four children."

"So he told me."

"What did you do today?" asked his father, putting the newspaper aside with effort.

"Bernard has just been telling you," his mother said before he could reply, "if you'd only listen."

"You didn't come into the store—should see the extensions," his father said.

"I went up the street and looked around the new Commission houses," he answered his father. They both knew he wouldn't go near the store.

"The town's growing," his mother said. His father began to read the newspapers sideways.

He ate his lunch.

"Something wrong, Bernard?" his mother asked.

"No, just thinking," he said. "Beautiful salmon."

"You seemed quiet all of a sudden," his mother said.

He would have liked to think that his visit home resolved something or other. But that was Young Thinking—to want to resolve everything simply by doing something dramatic. And really that hadn't been the reason for going home. Perhaps it had confirmed something about himself or his parents or something or something.

Mervyn was at the platform exit. "Oh come let us adore him! Really!"

Mervyn took the bags.

"How were the mater and pater?"

"Oh, you know...."

"Well, you've done the Right Thing—now you needn't bother till Christmas."

"I really don't think I could bear to go down again. There's *nothing*. And Mother comes to the city fairly often."

They walked to the taxi rank.

"How are Marlon and James Dean?"

"Marlon's been restless and moody—missed you dreadfully. Kept prowling around looking for you in such a possessive way."

He smiled.

"And James Dean is very happy—hasn't missed a meal. Absolutely without any feelings."

"Alley boy." They laughed at their joke.

They waited for a cab.

"I met my first love again—after fifteen years—nineteen years."

"How devastating. I never think of you having a First Time."

"He's gross—and married with four children. Lives in a *Housing Commission* area."

"Of course."

"He's not camp. I mean, he's never been camp. It was just kids' stuff."

They got into the cab.

Any cabs in the vicinity of St Mary's Cathedral—a Father Henderson for Vaucluse—thank you one-oh-nine—he'll be outside the main entrance. Someone for O'Sullivan Street, Rose Bay...

The traffic and buildings of the city gently ingested him. Mervyn laid a hand on his. He let the city take him. Its browns, blacks, and greys dressed with the red-amber-green of traffic lights and the mechanical dance of purple and orange neon.

Futility and other animals

SHE SAW IT for the first time when they were unpacking at the cabin in the isolated gorge country, and she said: "Why do you have a gun, Daddy?"

"For the security that might be in it." ... Was it wrong to talk about security and insecurity with an eight-year-old? "Insecurity" is what you'll call it, he thought, when you are thirty-four and compulsively hiding your head under the blankets of your bed during an emotional gust.

"But why, Daddy?"

"The gun? I've told you. It is a comfort to me like your old dolly is to you. See, if any wild animals come to the door I'll point the gun at them and they'll go away."

"Are there wild animals around?"

He remembered a pot-high talk over a fire on a beach where he and Jimmy had slept for three nights, escaping the city's emotional magnetic field which had pushed and pulled both of them.

"Having a gun is political, Jimmy."

"But what about your non-violence and all that? Where does that all fit in?"

"Having a gun isn't being militaristic or aggressive. Or being a thug. Having a gun is like having a vote. Or a say in things. A vote is for times of social stability and a gun for times of social disruption or upheaval. A man defends himself with an argument when confronted with an argument and with a gun when confronted with a gun." He said it like a part in a play.

And for a moment the pot made him feel the gathering of dark, dangerous times and upheaval and chaos and shooting. He could hear the shooting. Then dissolving into a drifting calm.

"With a single shot .22? Ho Ho Ho Ho," Jimmy said.

He heard the Ho Ho Ho Ho of Jimmy and smiled and loved him and giggled.

"A shot...single 22," he thought. "I was nearly shot single at 22."

He had found the note after coming from having lessons on the harp from Waterhouse. His usual Wednesday night lesson with Waterhouse. How had he come to want to learn the harp? He had tried but never mastered it. Worse, he had never extracted any sense of beauty or skill from it.

The note had read: "My dear, dear Perry, I was going to wait to tell you and then couldn't. I have gone over it in my mind for weeks and hidden it from you and feel so guilty. But I can't face you—not after how beautiful it has been now for eight months and not after how much it has meant for both of us. Anyhow, what it has meant for me. That sounds corny. And this note is all disjointed but so am I. Parting isn't everything and what we've got from living together is good in itself and lasts beyond us. As you will know, I've gone to live with Daniel. I didn't 'get over it' as you said I would. I'm desperately in love with him. I love you—but in a different way. Leave me for a while and then I will be able to talk to you about it all. Oh, my sweet. If only it could have gone on truly, but it's ending without becoming stale and that's good. Margot."

He had thought about this happening. But having thought about it in no way whatsoever helped him take the emotional pain which stormed him. He lay on the bed. Cried. Searched for sleeping pills to kill himself but found only three. Saw her toothbrush in the bathroom as though she was still with him. Lay thinking over the times together—the first time they had acted together, their trip in the canoes. His mind stabbed away with memories. He took the pills to stop that.

In the savagely lonely morning he tried not to wake. He wanted to crawl back to sleep but his body wouldn't take any more.

He rang Daniel's room and Daniel said he thought that Margot didn't feel like talking to him.

"Well, I bloody well want to speak to her so for Christ's sake put her on or I'll come around there and smash your fucking door down."

Margot cryingly confirmed all that was in the note and he cryingly reiterated his love. Oh, his love.

He had gone then to a sports goods store and bought the first rifle shown him by the assistant who wanted to talk of range and sighting. Who was nonplussed because sales talk wasn't necessary. Who wrapped the rifle so carefully with a packet of .22 bullets.

He had driven tear-blinded back to the flat. Carrying the parcel, he had been aware of the weight and balance of the rifle. The first awareness that morning of a thing outside himself.

In his flat he found Marylou.

"Margot phoned me last night and told me about it. She said I might be able to help. She's distressed about it happening this way." Marylou suggested getting drunk.

Before Margot, he had had an affair with Marylou and had been with her once or twice while living with Margot. Margot didn't know that. Oddly enough she had been a sweet, close friend to them both.

He had even laughed on that picnic. He got drunk, took some tranquillisers and passed out in the car while Marylou drove him to her flat where he lived for a month or so. The rifle lay unopened on his bed for that month or so. He had been aware of it while getting his clothes and stuff for his stay with Marylou. He had thought of it being there for when the pain came back beyond his endurance.

"Daddy, I asked you if there were wild animals here. *Talk to me.*"

"Yes, darling, there are wild animals down in the gorge but they won't hurt us as long as we have the gun."

"But what if they come in the middle of the night while we are asleep?"

He had married Robyn and taken on the role of father of her child. She had found the rifle in his flat shortly after she had moved in.

"When did you get this, Perry? What in heavens is it for?"

He had forgotten about the rifle.

"A man should be able to feed his family—should be able to hunt. It's basic, primitive—good. It's fashionable to be primitive, you know."

"Yes, I must say that a rifle is a very primitive. Tell me. That's not the reason. Tell me."

"It is. We face extinction unless we know how to preserve ourselves in a primitive environment. We're forgetting all the old skills and crafts but if we have to go bush to avoid the bomb or invasion or something we'll need them."

She hadn't believed him and kept asking.

He'd told her, feeling that it was probably necessary for the openness of their marriage.

"I bought the gun to shoot myself," he said. "I had a broken heart."

When they had talked away the incident and Robyn had digested this new thing about him, she had said: "Well, you're not ever going to be heart-broken again, my love, so why not get rid of it? Guns scare me."

He had said he would, but had not intended to and did not.

Chris had gone to the cliff edge and was looking into the gorge for wild animals, bending, hands on knees.

"You be careful, Chris."

There had been a time before his marriage when he had lost his way psychologically. When he had been swept with futility. Where it came from he did not know. From the gorge? He had walked out on a minor role at the Royal. He had stopped drinking at Watsons. He lay staring at the river. Sleeping fifteen hours a day. Saying what does it all matter?

He had loaded the rifle one day in the time of his deepest angst. The only time it had been loaded since its purchase. He had looked down the barrel. His patient servant. He had ejected the cartridge. Reloaded, ejected, reloaded, ejected. The cartridges spun across the room from the kick of the extractor. He had lazily symbolised it: saying, like human beings who fire their lives and are then ejected. Something like that.

The futility or angst or whatever it was at that time had not gone far away. It had come back, making him stumble after two years of marriage. Robyn had tried to help but he had been alone in a mental pit. He felt those around him looking sympathetically down at him, unable to help him rise. He wondered if he would ever fall down again, and if so, whether he would rise up. Robyn had thought that it meant he didn't love her or Chris. "If you loved you would not find life to be futile." But in time he had convinced her otherwise. He did not know if this had been honest. Futility came from a life which was ungratified. At these times especially, but at other times too, Margot was alive in his mind. It was that word love which he thought he should look at again soon. Futility was a wild animal all right, and the gun was a way of scaring it. It could be a way of killing it for all time. Perhaps it was best when used only to frighten the animal away.

"I said, what if they come while we are all asleep?"

"Well, Chris, if they come in the middle of the night I will hear them because they make such a frightful noise and I will get up and frighten them away."

"But what if you're not here."

"But I will be here."

He gave Chris a lantern to carry into the cabin and he carried the rifle and the Portagas stove.

The second story of nature

SHE HAD BEGUN love-making with a passionate relief. It had been held off because of the visitors. Now the others had left, including Anne, his girlfriend from years ago. As the door closed they locked together, the cigarette smoke was still scattering and the beer dregs were not yet flat.

Standing, they kissed into each other, burning brightly with the sexuality of the beginning but eager with physical impatience—the physical impatience which would eventually swing them past completion, leaving the pleasure behind, to be contemplated for the short while and then forgotten. Their urgings took them further on. They leapt the forced pauses—the pause between standing embraced and moving to a lying embrace—the pause after rolling while they kicked off their shoes—the pause after intertwining, to pull off their clothes.

Their skins seemed to adhere where they touched. Their feet frictioned fire into each other. Their hands inflamed their hair. Their pushing stomachs and then the joining.

On and off during the time that they moved away from the closed door and towards the open bed, she was aware that she could become pregnant. She had not begun taking her pills that month and he didn't know. He would assume that she was. It wasn't till soon after he had entered her that she told him, finding strangely that she herself did not care and that she wanted him also not to care. He smiled and did not falter and went on, probably not from decision, she thought, but from the irresistibility of arousal.

This was the first time like this. She had furiously cared at all times before this and had never taken a risk—not for years—no, not ever. The problem flickered around outside her mind, just outside her concern. She saw that it was kept away from her by the heat of a kind of pleasure and the pleasure was that of feeling unconstrained. She was partly able to marvel at it as it happened and it was as though she was no longer drugged down or as though her legs were no longer tied. It was, she struggled to believe, a foolish, foolish reaction. But she was overcome by it and could not move to stop it. She was overcome by it and the loving. All her thoughts then, on this and her feelings about it melted into her immense feeling for Roger, laying her wide open and then closing her around him with the thudding and the burning and then the hot stillness.

They lay there, he looking away and slightly out of breath. She lay there, internally drenched. He dribbled slightly from his mouth, bodily slack. Her foot was caught in a twist of the blanket. She eased herself free and soundlessly scrabbled for cigarettes on the table beside the bed. And so it was a bed. And so it was a table. And then the room and the house were there.

"Want one?"

"No. Not yet."

She heard a woman's voice some distance away outside say: "No, it was the twenty-fifth." Somewhere she heard a toilet flush and a dog yelp. She moved her legs and it was moist and cold between them. But there was some warmth there with it. Like the lick of a dog. He rolled off and away. He scratched his head and then his balls and said: "Oh, bloody beautiful girl."

She kissed his tit and said: "Yes?"

The interchange went nowhere into a silence and then she said: "Fucking is all now."

She moved her leg and pulled up the blanket because she was cool. He didn't want blanket because he was hot. Incompatibility. Incompatible bastard. Bastardbility. "You are sometimes incompatible," she said tiredly, smiling.

"*We* are—you have to have a *we* to have incompatibility." He licked her navel under the blanket and inside her there was a stirring again like a whirl in her. A very little whirl.

"So, no pills," he said.

"I was going to tell you. I was going to stop for a month or so. They say to. The doctor said to. But I didn't tell you, didn't get around to it. It's kind of late. We should have done something."

He smiled at the ceiling and did not say anything.

"You mad at me?" she asked.
He shook his head and kissed her.
"It was odd," he said. And then added: "It was a kick."
"Yes," she said, thinking. "It *was* a kick."
"At least you are being very *was* about it."
"It has to be a *was* thing," she said, without much force.
They lay. She smoked.
Inside herself she began a rationality dialogue...

Women are freer now because they control contraception and it is premeditated contraception and they can be free of the fear of pregnancy and unhampered by devices and totally relaxed about it, but it means a daily sexual routine, a medical regimen, and it's a policing of the body and now suddenly I've broken the regimen and lost the freedom and am exposed to pregnancy and I feel a new freedom, a new free feeling, and it comes from being exposed to pregnancy and giving up control of my body and becoming reliant on a man to care for me, to be my... hunter and my soldier...

Mentally she slapped herself, shocked at the words which had come from her...

Irrational and mawkish and sickening. I am still for free loving and against conventional marriage and remain firmly so, and yet I see an involved relationship and its mutual dependence and I am not frightened. I may want other lovers but other lovers would be for passing pleasure and not for sharing of the dependence—and I think perhaps I'm just saying that, and will not want other lovers at all. The mutual dependence and that kind of relationship is a track down which only two can walk comfortably. I was different years ago. With Hugo. What would poor Hugo say about me now? Poor, emotionally deaf Hugo, grabbing when he should have been feeling, poking when he should have been touching...

"We're a bit neurotic," she said.
"More than a bit," he mumbled.
"Will we always be?"
He didn't answer.
"Perhaps our way of life is a sort of group therapy," she said.
"It probably makes us worse—sometimes."
"We couldn't be much bloody worse," she said, trying to make her cigarette smoke reach the ceiling.
"It's the nine-to-five people in the suburbs who are the happy ones," he said.

"What makes you say that?" Her sentence jumped from her mouth and stood astride his statement. What he had said was something that she was frightened was true. She had met it before and had not dealt with it. It was something she had put away.

"What they want and the way they live fits together. No conflicts. It all fits with the way they were brought up. They don't kick against it and it doesn't kick against them," he breathed out.

It was a long thing for him to say.

"But us," he said. "Sometimes we're arrogant and sometimes we're lost."

"You're oh-so-wise all of a sudden."

"Instead of emotional security we have only theories," he said, making a movement with his mouth in appreciation of his own succinctness. On the wall he drew with his finger an invisible picture of them both.

"But we have good times," she said.

"Yes."

"And we could have children and family and do good work and have a free sort of life as well?"

"The children would be sick, too."

"But they'd have their good times, too," she said.

They lay side by side, fingers touching. She smelt and liked the drycleaning of the blanket which had yesterday come back from the laundry, cleaned after two years of use. She thought how she was comforted by the blanket and how warm it was, and how woolly, thick and clean.

"Anyhow, what's this about having children?" he asked.

Was it a neutral enquiry or was it cautious?

"Nothing," she said, sensing that this was untrue...

Sometimes I feel desperately isolated, sometimes I feel inadequate and failed. Perhaps I should have married and had children. Sometimes I feel that by going to university and becoming a lecturer I have wasted my life and avoided the real living. Avoided fulfilment. Sometimes I plunge into these feelings and they do not go for some time. But I would have simply been running away from demanding life to the hideaway of marriage where I would have been unchallenged and unthreatened. But I do not have a brilliant mind. I have no saved money and have no beautiful possessions and I move restlessly from flat to flat. I sometimes feel that I have wasted time, for all I have done. I am growing old. Sometimes I don't feel these things but feel elated and glad and I observe and listen and am breathlessly interested in living and painfully absorbed and I do feel acute enthusiasm and I am not preoccupied then with my feelings of mediocrity and misdirection. I have ideas and I see things clearly and see people perceptively and am out of myself. And then I feel other times drowningly involved with Roger and our living together. Sometimes we yell at each other. That was something I couldn't bear once because I wanted harmony. I didn't find harmony of that sort and I don't care much about it now. Why did I enjoy fucking without contraception? Why don't I care about it anymore?

She softly began to quote to him: "I stand in the whirlpool and tell you I don't know and if I did know I would tell you and all I am doing now is to guess and I give you my guess for what it is worth as one man's guess. Yet I have worked out this guess for myself as nobody's yes-man and when it happens I no longer own the priceless little piece of territory under my own hat, so far gone that I can't even do my own guessing for myself, then I will know I am one of the unburied dead..."

"Who's that?"

She made to answer but he said: "No, let me guess. It's Sandburg, Sandburg the simpleton."

"You know because I always quote from Sandburg, and you can't abide him—incompatibility again."

"He's too simple."

"It's good to be offered simplicity now and then."

"Give me a cigarette."

She passed one to him.

"Well, what were you guessing about?" he asked, "and what is your guess?"

"About why it was so good."

"The fuck?"

"Yes—wasn't it good for you?"

He didn't answer immediately.

"I've already told you," he said. "It was a kick."

"A special kick?"

"Yes—a special kick."

"Why was it a kick?"

He shrugged.

"I know," she said defensively. "It's all sentimentality and emotional stuff from my upbringing coming up to the surface out of the murky depths of my unconscious. Just because for once I don't take the pill, I regress."

They lay in silence. She wanted him to contradict what she had said.

"I think it's more than that," she said after a while.

"What?"

"We are frustrated, repressed parents."

"Well," he said.

"We're at that age. Perhaps we are on the threshold of a new experience."

"Mmmm," he said, softly, gently mocking.

"Do you ever feel like being a father?" she said, clambering atop of him, pinning his arms to the bed. "Answer me," she said in a loud tough voice. "Do you want a baby?" She watched his eyes and mouth and then yelled victoriously: "You do—you want a baby, I can tell. The bum artist wants to be a daddy," she gave a rebel yell.

"All right," he said, "don't get excited. I sometimes fancy myself as a daddy—but it's only fancy."

"It might be in my belly now—that fancy."

"That was a bit unplanned."

"You never told me you wanted children."

"You never really indicated an interest in the subject. On the contrary, it seemed to be very much out."

"That," she said, laughing at herself, "was yesterday."

She sat on his chest, thinking. "My baby?" she asked.

"Who else?"

She bent down and affectionately rested her head for a few seconds on his chest. Then she rolled off him, concealing her fast breathing.

"We're too selfish to have children," she said, without endorsing her words. She was excited.

"Perhaps we're too childish to have children."

"And we have other plans."

"Do you fancy yourself as a mummy?"

"Only now, for the first time," she said. "First time in my life." Then: "Perhaps it's a passing mood," she added.

She watched flashes of their life, with its boredom and its drinking and their tense friends and she wondered if she was changing. It was not a really representative set of impressions. She tried to see another life but no other offered. "Perhaps we could live in suburbia," she said. "It'd be unneurotic." She didn't believe it.

"You don't throw it like that—and who wants to? This is our way."

He was being certain. He was so often noncommittal.

"Yes, I know. We-should-learn-to-live-the-imperfect-life-graciously-as-is-our-lot." She said it with tried acceptance.

He didn't comment but lying face down on the bed said in a muffled voice: "So you want to have babies," and laughed into the pillow.

She pouted and moved away, interrupted in her mood, offended by his flippancy and his accuracy. He looked up and grinned at her pique. He tickled her and she screamed first with irritation but collapsing into pleasure of it. They rolled, giggled, and fought.

They lay panting.

Getting her breath: "Well," she said, "I think having kids is a good idea. Women can keep their freedom and still have kids. So there."

"What an interesting change of position," he said. "I begin to suspect you've been corrupted, Cindy. Catholics?"

She ignored him and said: "Why was it so good, Roger? I mean this time? Not that it isn't always superb."

He turned to the wall and with his finger traced a new picture of them both. "You're the one who reads all the books," he said.

"I guess they'd say that I was fulfilling my true biological function and conforming to the values of my upbringing and therefore felt totally free of guilt."

"Sounds very academically correct."

"It's sad."

"What's sad?"

"That what we believe seems to change our emotional life so little."

"As long as it makes some difference."

"It all sounds like surrender, doesn't it?"

"It's not only the squares who want to have children."

"Fucking without pills or anything must be different because of a lot of things. I mean it's alien to the sex act, isn't it? There's nothing intrinsically good about contraception. I mean, is there?"

"We talk about everything too much."

His old theme. "Pooh. I could say you draw things too much. It'd be just as stupid."

He smiled. It was an old argument.

"Are we still going to France?" she asked.

"Of course we're still going to France. We haven't had a baby yet, for God's sake."

He clutched her around the body and bit her back. And they made love again, rollingly, and softly, and quickly. She came up from it with a leg hanging over the edge of the bed, conscious that it was dark outside and that she could smell the cooking of cabbage drifting from some neighbouring kitchen.

Murmuringly she said: "Again—and you do it again. Now we will have two babies."

He grinned and stretched, clenching and unclenching his hand.

"You never do it twice," she said. "Not since Christmas and then it was the champagne—a champagne erection, that was."

"It's the new, hot, fertile you."

"I've never thought of myself as fertile."

"You have a fertile stench."

"Is that good?"

"Fine by me."

She lit a cigarette. He took it from her. She lit another.

"You know something, Roger," she said seriously. "I've never felt this emotional urge before in my life. Never. Not with Sean. Never with Hugo. On the contrary I was dead against it with him. Did I ever tell you about him and the pills?" She raised herself on her elbow. "He wanted children. Did I tell you about what he did?"

"You've told me about Hugo the hunter and Hugo the man who ate nuts and berries but never about Hugo the pill."

"He threw them away."

"The pills?"

"He wanted me to have children so he threw away the pills one day."

"What did you do?"

"I walked out."

"What was his problem?"

"He said that children were natural and the pills were unnatural and we were to have babies as they come—if we loved each other. I was only twenty."

"Catholic?"

"No, he was Lutheran—but an agnostic. Just wanted to have children all over the place."

"Very odd men you involve yourself with," he said, getting out of bed. "I'm going to have a leak."

She wandered back to the affair with Hugo, carefully uncovering memories left untouched for seven years...

"I want children," he said loudly, gesticulating the expression So-what-the-hell's-wrong-with-that. *"You must be out of your mind,"* she said. *"Love goes bad between people when they don't want children,"* he said. *"Contraception is a rejection of children—a rejection of me as a father of your children. It's hesitancy."* He talked quickly. She remained standing at the bathroom door, toothbrush in her hand. *"But—I've got a year to go at uni. We've never even discussed it. You've never mentioned it. It's unbelievable."* She was rigid with anger. *"Love implies children,"* he said, buttressing his words with a heavy definiteness. *"Children are the other part of the natural equation." "That's crap. Crap. What shit." "No, it's truth." "I don't give a damn about children. You threw away my pills. You authoritarian shit."* She remembered other things he'd done. Theatre bookings without consultation. Things like that. *"You didn't ask me whether you could use them. You didn't tell me you were using them. Who imposed on who?"* he shouted. *"For God's sake, only a fool wouldn't—you're—you're like all men. You think we can be used for your—fantasies."* He didn't move his hands from the table where they lay palms down in front of him. As though he was about to rise. He began to colour. *"So children are a fantasy. You're hung up—hung up on modern crap about independence. You think being independent means being neuter. You're hung up Cindy." "You monster." "Having children means being a woman. That would scare the living shit out of you." "I don't want to be a woman,"* she yelled, sensing the bad tactics of the admission. *"I mean, I don't want to be that sort of woman. Your sort of shithouse, servile woman."*

She opened the window and hung out, her breasts pushed against the sill.

Shivering, Roger clambered back into bed.

"You're wet," she complained. "Don't men dry their penis?"

She stared at the backyards, at the corrugated iron bonnets on the backyard toilets with their ribald saw-tooth grins and the clothes lines like crazy cats-cradles.

65

"Hugo would like me now—steaming with fertility. Is that sexual? Does that sound sexy to you?"

"When I thought of you steaming with fertility it felt sexy. I felt pretty good when I held my cock just now—out pissing."

"Because of the babies and all?"

"Perhaps," he was uncomfortable about the admission and she noticed, and let it go.

"I told Hugo I didn't want to be a woman."

"What in God's sake did you want to be?" he asked with surprise.

"I wanted to be an intellectual with a vagina."

He guffawed and she blushed.

"Well, bugger me," he said. "Why don't you make some coffee, *woman*."

"Is that a big male order?"

He gave her a loving push.

"But I've realised that we have to come to terms with our background and the way we've been raised," she continued with lament. "We're just not free."

"Make some coffee."

"You shut up." She lay back for a few seconds of protest and quiet sadness about what she'd said but this worked itself into a relief of self-recognition—something she was coming to accept. She rose and pulled on his duffle coat, freeing her long hair from under its collar, and brushing it a few times. She went barefoot to the kitchen. She sat on the table with feet on a chair as the water boiled, the coat hauled around her, too long at the sleeves and with shoulders which drooped down her arms. "I've been rescued from the sea and pulled aboard a ship and a sailor has given me his coat to keep me warm in the freezing Arctic night."

She was bodily alive. She pulled the coat apart and caressed her stomach with her hands down to her crotch and imagined a baby swelling her rounded, tight stomach. She caressed up to her breasts and handled the weight of them.

"I'm pregnant," she said impulsively at the bedroom—to try the sound and feel of the statement.

He made a snorting noise.

She put a Leadbelly record on the record player.

She wiped down the beer-puddled table.

She picked up the empty beer bottles which stood in groups on the floor, symbolising the drinking groups which had emptied them earlier.

Rooms seemed very empty after Sunday parties.

She tore March from the calendar, which was three days expired.

She put back the book *The Idiom of the People* and wondered who'd been looking at it.

She poured the boiling water onto the instant coffee and added three sugars. She felt feminine sometimes from doing things—even things as simple as that. Feminine. The word had once nauseated her. He did things for her—like unscrewing stuck lids—for all his bitching. But it was only a good feeling now and then. God protect her from being overwhelmed by it. It was a good feeling but it had dreadful, insidious dangers. It was a treacherous word. It could push you back into the pit.

She took him his coffee, carrying it as if it was full of dangers.

"What will we do the other times?" she asked.

He shrugged, sitting up to take his coffee.

"I suppose I'll have to get fitted with a diaphragm," she said. "I hate the thought." She sat hunched on the bed, pushing back the long sleeves of his heavy coat. "There's a strong smell of sperm about the bed," she sniffed. She felt secure and protected simply because she was wearing his coat. She scoffed. "I'm weakening," she thought.

"You could abstain," he said.

"Ho ho."

"You could have babies."

"We may even yet have babies, my dear, dear man," she said, sipping her coffee. "And what would you do, Roger, if I were?"

"What would *you* do?"

"I don't know what I would do. I'd probably...probably— have it." She moved her shoulders slightly as if in resignation, or perhaps, acceptance or perhaps uncertainty.

"Would you?" he asked.

"But I wouldn't get married. There's no reason for that," she said aggressively.

He said nothing.

"You haven't answered," she said.

"I'd probably want you to have it. In my present mood I wouldn't mind," he said, slurping.

She contemplated his answer with a beating stomach and then, twisting around, put down her coffee, and grabbed him, sinking down into him as though in warm mud.

"My fertile fuck," he said softly, holding her with one hand and his coffee with the other. "Watch out for the coffee."

"But what will we do? What are we going to do for the month or so—make a decision!" She demanded.

"Let's play sexual roulette for a month," he said lightly.

"It's immoral and irresponsible," she laughed.

"We've nothing to lose. We'll still go to France—might be three of us."

"It's irresponsible," she laughed. He put down his cup.

The sex they had that month was free and steaming, she thought, although she was less aware of any difference later in the month. Towards the end she remembered only now and then. She was sure that Roger responded to her vulnerability. She often made herself conscious of it, playing with fertility fantasy during the month. Roger said he sometimes remembered it and became excited by it.

At the end of the month she was not pregnant. She met her period with the same inevitability as she would the end of a play, but it psychologically halted her for an instant—as if she'd expected never to see blood there again. Disappointment flashed and then was gone. The period burst her fantasy and switched her back to her former way of life. Perhaps there was relief there too. She revived and played with the idea of going to France.

Coming from the bathroom she said to him: "Well, now we can go to France." He didn't look up from the drawing board where he was working.

"We were always going to France," he said, head down.

"I'm not pregnant," she said. "That's what I meant."

He looked up and smiled at her. "Oh that." And went back to his work.

She stared at him.

"We really didn't have to have one and not the other," he said, not looking up. "We could have both."

She was surprised.

"I thought it would be easier to travel without a child," she said, finding herself unwillingly putting the tough line.

"Perhaps," he said, preoccupied with his drawing. "We might have them over there after we've been around."

He kept on working and she watched him, with some amazement.

She realised that it had happened, simply like that, and that they both now accepted the idea of children in their relationship and she had now no disappointment or relief about the month not yielding. She guessed that the idea of children would hang around with them now wherever they were.

The third story of nature

SHE SAT CROSS-LEGGED on the bed, her thighs cradling the weight of her pregnancy. She had wanted to feel the weight from the day she knew she was pregnant. She'd wanted to feel pregnant. She did not have to imagine now.

"You'll have to keep the place cleaner than this when baby comes," said her mother, moving outside with a five-pin cluster of beer bottles, holding them away from her in a gesture of dissociation.

"You must admit that I've improved," she said, humouring her mother.

She watched her mother wipe her hands on the apron as she came inside. She watched her mother come across to her and she felt the hand on her face.

"You must look after yourself, Cindy. It's a critical time."

"Mother, I'm twenty-six."

"In some ways you're still a child. Now promise your poor old mother that you'll be good and keep the flat clean."

She almost nodded but her mother moved away from the uncertainty of her answer. Pulling on her rubber gloves her mother began to clean the bath with a righteous vigour.

"You could come home until after baby arrives. Father would love to have you home," her mother called, her voice hollowed by the resonance of the bath.

"That's out of the question."

Her mother refused to concede Roger the rights of a husband. In his casual way Roger didn't claim them and in the formal sense he wasn't a husband. What rights? The old trap again. The trap of looking for established patterns of rights and explanations. Established patterns were used by people whose relationships were too weak to generate their own living patterns. Or perhaps all human relationships were too weak to do this? Did they all require social patterns? Was it childish arrogance to think otherwise? Were social patterns congealed wisdom? Social patterns changed. And some people changed faster than social patterns. Some people were out of synchronisation. "Synchronise your watches."

"But sir, we have no watches." Were you in the vanguard or simply impatiently running on ahead—to find yourself without society—isolated and scared with other isolated and scared people?

"We just thought you might like to come home, dear," her mother said, her fangs retreating into a chatting mouth.

"Sara and I walked out of a film for the first time for years, the other day. Hopelessly silly thing it was. I'm afraid I don't understand modern films."

"What was the film?"

"A thing called 'Morgan'."

"Oh—I'd heard it was funny."

Roger had said it was funny and Ken had raved about it.

Of course, just because you were married did not mean that you weren't having a living relationship. But married people hampered themselves.

"Here, dear. Your eyes are younger than mine. What does it say on the label? Two tablespoons to the gallon?"

"Yes. Two tablespoons to the gallon. Warm water."

Relatives and acquaintances and society felt legally justified in applying all sorts of pressures to ensure that you conformed to their idea of marriage. And you tended to adopt their ideas from tiredness. Because she and Roger were not married their parents were generally wary and uncertain. They came to visit with a frightened curiosity which could change to blustering aggression. But these things didn't worry Roger. He didn't discuss them either. He lived simply by his personal tenets. She didn't have tenets. She wished she did. She had only tentative wild ideas to live by. Sometimes the ideas ran away from her.

"I'll do the toilet and then I must go."

"Don't bother, Mother. Leave it—please."

"You make a cup of tea. That would be something useful."

Her mother would clean the flat, arranging the books, dusting, organising the kitchen cupboards with clean newspaper, throwing away old food from the refrigerator. But she would not touch the bed. The bed was a symbol of her daughter's defection. Periodically her mother did this. She made these cleaning attempts to retrieve her from the degradation of her runaway disorganised life—tried to pull her back into the middle-class boat. Her mother cleaned the flat regardless of its condition. And it was always hygienic even if it was sometimes disarranged. Her mother would also buy her clothing from David Jones—clothes which were to serve as a uniform and a correction to her daughter's deviant taste. She would clean the flat and ask her to come home.

She hauled herself from the bed and to the kitchen. I'm beginning to waddle, she thought.

"Next time I come I'll bring my new detergent. It's really excellent."

"Oh?"

"Father brought it from the factory. It's for industrial use. I use it around the house."

"Roger hates the smell of detergent."

"This has a lovely clean, strong smell."

Her mother's virtue for cleanliness had become a violent, acidic thing. She turned on the kitchen tap and let the harmless water run over her fingers. She filled the kettle. One day her mother would find a detergent which would keep all things permanently and deeply clean. Her mother would bring it to her and wash out her life and bathe her in it. From then on she would never be able to again feel dirty or have a sweating fuck. But at least the soles of her feet would not be gritty after walking from the bath to the bed. That would be something.

"You'll have to tell Roger to keep things clean. It's dreadfully important when you have a baby."

"He thinks we keep things too clean."

Once he had yelled at her: "Don't try to impose your mother's sterilised existence on me."

"Yes, well, we both know how funny he is about some things."

The kitchen alliance. Her mother had in one sentence taken her into the female alliance against men—mother and daughter. The female superiority of "understanding" their men.

God knows she wanted it sometimes—not against men—but to be in female alliance. To rest upon the certainty of female knowledge. To understand by female intuition. To have a set of female tasks and female skills to handle them. But that female alliance belonged to the order and the cleanliness and stability of the home she had left. At times she wanted them too. A home unchanged and clean for forty years—changed only by accumulated decoration of the basic theme. Sometimes she fantasised that she would surrender back. Her mother did not know how close she came at times to crying "Oh, Mother" and flying back into her arms. But she did not. Did her mother want her back—an adult child? Did she want back a wayward baby? She had no place back at home, except as a visitor and then as an uneasy one. Her "place" always kept was a sepulchre for them to regret at, not a refuge for her to go back to. She was supposed by now, according to the rules, to be in her own home, working daily to imitate the cleanliness and order which becomes stability when it has been maintained for twenty-five—or how many years equalled stability? Even then perhaps it was threatened daily and one never knew when one had stability. Her mother lived in a threatened world of headlines and news flashes which said to her, "Morals are changing, prices rising, workmanship is poor, fashions are ridiculous, communists and trade unions run the country, community spirit is dead." Perhaps her mother feared daily that her prayers and her polishing and British troops would not be enough to hold back the seeping chaos. Perhaps she was nibbled by fear that others were not putting their rubbish in the Be Tidy bins—that others were not trying.

"Father's having trouble at the factory—unions again."

"What's the problem?"

"It's not the men—it's their leaders. The men are decent enough. It's the leaders who make the trouble. But for them there would be no strikes."

She could not reply. On subjects like this she choked with irritation. She didn't give a damn about trade unions but when her mother attacked them she was swept to their defence. She could feel her breathing break rhythm. Her mind fumbled.

"The cost of living is always rising," she said, ineffectually, moving a cup and saucer in a sort of physical twitch.

"They make it rise—they send the prices soaring," her mother said, looking for a broom behind the door.

"There should be price control."

"No dear," her mother used her condescending voice, kept for statements which she thought carried the wisdom of years, for eternal truths. "We had that during the war and it didn't make a scrap of difference. You have the black market then. Human nature can't be changed."

No matter how calm she tried to be her mother's tone and her arguments made her heated. She sweated in an impotent silence. Why did she bother? Was it that she felt herself attacked unjustly by her mother and therefore defended anyone attacked by her mother?

"Cindy, dear—I've been telling you all your life to heat the teapot before you make the tea. Sometimes I think you just do it to annoy."

"I don't think that in summer it makes much difference, Mother I really don't."

"It's the only way to get a good hot cup of tea."

Her baby would be born into a time when grand-daughters would not understand their grandmothers. Already mothers and daughters were having difficulty. Perhaps we were creating an orphan generation—no parents and no God. Where had she heard that—someone in the common room? She corrected herself. It was not the whole world that was alienated from its parents, only the teenagers and they for only a short time. They mostly fell back and went about imitating their parents. It was the intellectually rebellious and the neurotics who went on feeding and nursing their alienation—proceeding further in the direction away from their parents. But her daughter would be freer. Her daugher would be offered more alternatives and less censure. The following of strange paths would be easier for her and she would have a mother who—if she had not gone far along the strange paths—at least understood why some people did. Or did she understand? What was so great about nonconformity? What was so great about independence? What was so good about strange paths? Perhaps her daughter wanted a familiar path? But whatever, her daughter would not live with the emotionally gruelling voice which said, "Do you really think you are doing a wise thing?" whenever she deviated from the normal. Again, perhaps this was a useful exercise. Perhaps there was value in living with a question like that. Her problem was that her judgements were hooked to values she no longer held. This was something she could help her own daughter with. The freedom to develop values suitable for her times and her personality. How for God's sake? How did one do that? She had been tormented about becoming a lecturer instead of marrying and setting up home. She had been tormented about her sexual behaviour. Worse, she had to pretend to herself that she had no conflicts. Middle-class girls make poor rebels.

"You don't seem very happy, dear. Was it something I said?"

Was it something she said!

"Oh, I'm fine. Just thinking."

"I hope you're not worrying."

"Oh, no."

Oh, no.

"You'd tell me. Wouldn't you?"

Tell you!

"I'm very well and everything is fine." She held back her irritation and kissed her mother on the cheek.

They sat down with their cups of tea and her mother stirred hers too long.

"I don't want you worrying. Not at this time."

They chattered about her aunt and her brother. Her mother washed up the cups. Her mother talked about a road accident which had killed the son of one of her friends.

The road accident had become a folk drama for her mother— and perhaps a mortality play asking, "Why do some of us have to die this way and why do some die so young?" The road accident was the unpredictable terror in an otherwise predictable society. Everyone had their accident and their escape from death. It was the idea of chaos again. The road accident had the music of chaos—the screech, the smash, the tinkle, the scream, the groan, the high pitch of stuck horn, the siren. The siren was the way we announced the conflict between order and disaster.

Her mother was now standing in the room, her hands on her aproned hips surveying the work she had done.

"If you do a little every day you can keep it clean. When baby comes you'll have other things to worry about too, you know."

The baby would bring chaos if you weren't careful, you know. If it was not fought with order and hygiene it would cause a life smash. Her mother often treated her as if she had been in a life accident. But she saw the threat of chaos too. Perhaps she would be dragged down into chaos by dirty nappies and crying in the night.

"Please think about what Father wrote to you. If only for baby's sake. The little mite should have the protection of marriage—even if you don't want it."

"What protection is that?"

"Legal protection. Just in case something happened."

"What legal protection?"

"Well dear, I don't like broaching these things but we have to be practical. What, for instance, if Roger left you? I'm not saying that he ever would—but there's nothing holding him, is there?"

Her mother had sat down beside her and had assumed a businesslike voice. A for-your-own-sake voice.

"There's me and baby. What more can there be?"

"But if you married him there would be a legal obligation for him to look after you both."

"I resent that. You shouldn't say that." She was calmer now but emotionally aroused. "For God's sake, laws don't hold people together. They might stay together in one house, technically, but who wants that? And who wants money that has to be forced out of someone you love?"

"Dear Cindy, you must be sensible. It's not only yourself any more. There's another person to think of now."

"I am thinking of baby. I want a real relationship—not a legal document. I don't want to be able to say to baby: Look, Daddy's gone but we have this certificate and ten dollars a week from the court." Her agitation made her get up and without reason she washed her hands. But she still had mental confidence.

"It's much nicer to have things done properly." Her mother's voice changed, softened, and the fangs withdrew. There was a religious idea driving her mother too but this was not mentioned.

Her mother began rubbing at a stain on the kitchen wall.

Her mother's presence in the flat suddenly insulted her. She felt that she was being aggressed. Her mother was not offering assistance, not reaching out to her. She was manipulating her. Her values and aspirations were not being accepted—they were being attacked.

"I want you to leave, Mother."

It was sudden. She was suddenly cool.

Her mother stood shocked.

"I feel that you have come here to impose yourself. You don't like me. You don't like my way of life. And you interfere. I don't feel I can resist you any longer because I'm tired and weak. Please go."

"Cindy—I was trying to help you." Her mother put one hand on her. The other held a Wettex.

"Please go. I don't want to fight with you."

"We've never fought, Cindy dear. We've never."

"Please leave." Her voice slightly louder.

"You can't talk to me, your mother, like that." Her mother's voice became bitter and strong.

She went over and picked up her mother's coat and hat. She handed them to her.

"Get out."

"This is deeply, deeply hurtful to me," her mother said. Her voice lowered—a prelude to crying. Another way of manipulating.

She remained silent. She looked at her mother's face closely—for perhaps the first time. Saw the pores and saw the wrinkles and saw the shape. She saw it as a woman's face.

Her mother dabbed at her eyes, gathered herself, took off the apron. She came over to her and gave her a hard kiss.

"We'll think of you. You are not yourself. But when you want help come to us," her mother said, knifingly.

"Go, please."

Her mother left. She closed the door and bolted it. She felt freed. She trembled and agitation shook her. Today she had not been submissive. She listened to her mother clacking down the stairs. She thought of the hopelessly shattered links between the three generations which had been at afternoon tea.

She sat down shaking, but released. Roger would be home soon. Or would he? Would this be the night when he did not come home—the night he would be with some other girl? It would be only for a night or two—she was sure of that. Was she sure of that? He never had got off but the possibility was always there, built into the relationship. She needed Roger not to get off now, of all times. Her conventional breeding cried for conventional comfort. At least for a make-believe security. Sad she needed to make believe that she was as safe as her mother. She wanted to make believe. Even though Roger had given her the security of honesty and the implicit pledge to be the father of their child.

She sat in the middle-class clean flat and brushed her hair for Roger, still trembling. I am frightened, Mother, she thought, and I do fearfully wish there was a document which would guarantee love. And if you had asked one more time perhaps I would have gone home with you, Mother. But not after today.

Dell goes into politics

DELL lugged her bag off the Coolamon train and felt instantly grimy, and very countryfied. Her white makeup didn't seem to help, nor her Oroton handbag.

Billy Toomey, who worked on the railway station, gave her a funny smile and hullo and then her mum came over and her dad. There was the kissing and then they got into the utility.

"Gosh, we're glad you've come to see us, Dell," her mother said.

"About bloody time," her father said, friendly for him.

She thought to herself that she hadn't come to see them, to sleep in that rotten narrow bed, in that room in that shack of a house with a chip heater. She'd come back to marry one of the Lindsay boys. Perhaps. Maybe. Maybe not. Come off it, Dell.

"It's over a year now, love," her mother said. "Lovely bag you've got," touching the Oroton bag. "Always wanted a bag like that."

The utility stopped outside, the kids came out. Little Terry in his singlet, his prick bouncing, no hairs. It'll do its bit one day, she thought, kissing him. Then kissing little Marge.

"What you bring us?" they shouted.

She handed around the goodies.

"Got a young man yet?" her mother asked, as they went inside.

"No—at least not one."

"What happened to that young schoolteacher?"

"Oh him..." Kim and his politics and sex and always

wanting to be doing something different to her in bed, always teaching her, "he was a bit odd," and he was married now, teaching somewhere out this way, where she didn't know and didn't care.

"What you mean odd?" her mother said, fearfully, knowing the word had something to do with sex or madness.

"Oh, I don't mean it that way," she said.

"You were pretty keen on him for a while." Her mother made a pot of tea and put out the mixed sweet biscuits—the real treatment.

"Bet she'd like a beer," her father said, "the city girl now."

"She's not going to be drinking in this house so early in the day."

Her father laughed and opened a bottle of beer. "You have one if you want."

She had tea.

Flies in the afternoon sun, smell of old lino wearing further and further away from the doorway and the sink and the stove, rotting leaves from the fruit trees, rotting fruit. Harry Lindsay would at least be able to afford a new house. Kim had always lived in old houses. She couldn't understand it. She wanted a new house.

"What do you do, Dell?—in the city, I mean." She knew her mother was dreaming she'd gone to the city too, instead of staying in this hole. Which was the hole?

"Oh, you know..."

"Dancing, you go dancing?"

"No," she nibbled an oatcake, "only at parties. People don't go dancing."

"At least you haven't got yourself into trouble," her father said, trying to play the concerned father bit.

"You'd be the last to hear."

She looked at him, drinking beer from a hotel glass, sitting there, King of the Kitchen Table.

"What else?" her mother prompted.

"Oh, nothing." She twisted, restless, not wanting to be there. She stood up and walked to the gauze door which was still broken, and looked out across the paddock to the silos. That bloody chip heater and that bloody old bath tub in the bathroom out the back.

"You're not in trouble, are you?" her father called. Did the old bastard really want her to be in trouble? To wet his dirty old mouth.

She didn't answer. She thought for an odd second maybe she wished she was going to have a baby. That would be something.

"Answer your father." Her father had obviously been drinking and was being *the father*. Wanting to know her sex life. Fishing around. If he only knew.

"Leave her alone, Dad," her mother said. "She's scarcely in the house before you're at her."

"I'm not at her," he said. "I asked her a civil question."

They ignored her for a time while they squabbled themselves.

She climbed through the half door in the roller shutter of the service station and in the dimness her eyes were caught by an oxy welder flame.

"Put that bloody thing off, Harry," she shouted.

Harry Lindsay turned his goggled head towards her and switched off the oxy torch.

"Jesus, it's you, Dell." He pushed his goggles back on his head and, wiping his hands on his overalls, came over. "I heard you were back."

"You work on Sundays too—haven't you got a union?"

"Just doing these harrow blades for Ridley." He hugged her with one arm and kissed her on the lips. "What's all this union business?"

She pushed him away, saying, "You'll get me all greasy."

"You're pretty good on the eyes."

"Take me for a drink then," she said.

"The Royal open yet?"

"It looked open to me when I came past."

"Hold on, then." He went back to the harrow blades and chipped at them with a hammer. "It'll do."

He unzipped his overalls and pulled them off over his army boots. He wore a pair of shorts and a dirty floral Hawaiian shirt under his overalls.

"You've certainly learned how to dress," she said.

"What're you doing home, then?"

"Thought we might get married," she joked.

"OK," he pinched her backside, "why bother about getting married?"

"Get your hands off," she said, holding them briefly. "Don't touch the fruit before you buy."

They walked to the pub.

A few Holdens were already angle parked in against the ditch outside the pub.

"So you're not married yet," he said. "Aren't those city fellows paying any attention?"

"I'm not complaining—never lonely in the big city."

There were greetings and joking when they went through the Sunday morning drinkers.

"You old enough, Dell?" the publican called out, winking at her.

"Old enough for what?" one of the men laughed.

"You're too old, aren't you, Bill?" Harry said. "Shrivelled off, hasn't it?"

He brought the beers to a table and the conversation of the pub left them alone.

"Like the city?" Harry asked her.

"It's OK," she said. "At least I don't have my bloody old man pushing me around."

Instead I have everyone else pushing me around, thinking of the time she'd been with Kim and those intellectuals.

"We thought you'd never come back," Harry said, still eyeing her over.

"So did I."

She felt, whether she liked it or not, any interest she'd had in Harry was draining off as she looked at him and listened to him. She knew whatever mad idea she'd had in her head, she would never marry Harry Lindsay. But she wasn't sure she'd ever believed she would.

The Sunday pub was changed by a noisy, smiling, bald man who hit the bar with both hands and called for drinks. He began shaking hands. He used both hands, she noticed, the left one to hold the person near the elbow and the right to shake the hand.

"Who's that?" she asked Harry.

"Fuller, the local member—I hear he's got a bunch of singers from the city."

She looked him over.

"What is he?"

"What do you mean?"

"Labor or Liberal or what?"

"Labor Party."

"State or Federal?"

"I don't bloody know—he's in Sydney I guess—no, it's Canberra—how come you know so much about it all?"

"I don't know—that's why I'm asking you."

Harry had a thick head.

"I mean the State or Federal thing," he said, troubled.

"Christ, Harry, that's about the least you can know."

Harry looked as if he'd got a bee flying around him.

People were calling out to Fuller and wisecracking him about folk singers.

She looked at him and all her fury about the town and the fact she didn't have a man here or in the city or anywhere—not one that she wanted, that was—came to her, and before she knew it she'd yelled out, "Why don't you bring the boys back from Vietnam?"

"Aren't there enough around, Dell?" someone said, the bar laughing.

She almost blushed, it was as if they'd seen her thoughts—but she hadn't meant it that way.

Fuller laughed with them and ignored the question and went on talking with the men.

"Well, don't I get an answer?" she called out again.

Fuller looked at her and came over. "As soon as we get into office we'll be looking into the whole question of our Asian commitment."

"You don't sound so sure about whether you're going to bring them back."

"It's not a simple matter to withdraw from a war like this."

"Sending them over there and putting them in gaol when they don't want to go seems pretty simple."

Fuller backed off, saying, "You can be sure we'll do something the day we get control of the government benches."

"Yeah," she said loudly and disbelievingly. "Half of them'll be dead by then."

Harry Lindsay was squirming in his chair. "Jesus, Dell, what're you doing?—what're you carrying on about?"

"They make me sick."

She realised that she'd been mouthing a few of the things she'd heard with Kim and the others at meetings she'd been dragged along to and those parties where they'd talked about it for hours while she stood drinking and wanting to dance, or trying to talk to those crummy rich bitches from the university in their St Vincent de Paul clothes. And the demonstrations where she'd walked around and around in circles.

They made her sick. It made her sick too that she'd been using Kim's words. Falling back on him.

"Well, it's nice to be back anyway, Harry," she said. "Get another beer," finishing off her first.

"Sure, Dell," he said, with his voice showing how unsure he was of her now and how uneasy.

What did she care?

He'd drop an oxy torch on his prick if she told him some of the things she'd done since leaving this hole. Some of the things that had been done *to her*, more like it. Once she'd gone with three boys in a park—each had done her twice.

After a few mouthfuls of her second drink, Harry said, "You're not a commo, are you?—I mean, it doesn't matter a damn to me—I couldn't give a stuff about it all."

"I'm a Trotskyist," she said, for the hell of it, marvelling at the sound of it.

"A what?" Harry said, as though he were getting into a bog.

She studied his wrinkled eyes, and wondered if she could explain. Did she in fact know what a Trotskyist was? She didn't.

"Not a communist," she said. "A Trotskyist supports the real revolution—the real revolution of the people." She remembered something. "All power to the Soviets," she added.

Harry glanced to see if they were being listened to and looked back at her with a bewildered face.

Then she gestured at Fuller. "The Labor Party are all bloody right-wing social democrats." She spat the words the way she'd heard them in the city, carried away, wondering if that was what the Labor Party was, and why they were dirty words or did she have it all wrong? Of one thing she was sure: Harry wouldn't have the faintest.

"You've changed," was all he could say.

She sighed. "Not really," dropping into a little girl's voice, giving away playing the game, "not really at all—I'm all mixed up, Harry," she said, meaning it, patting his hand. Why didn't she just marry him?

"You sort of sound it," he said.

They ate their tea—Kim would probably have called it dinner but you don't eat spaghetti on toast for dinner—with the noise of the kids and her mother's constant reprimands and calls for a little quiet, and the silence of the father who took no notice of anything.

She watched him push away his plate having eaten the spaghetti in what she thought was a minute flat. "What's this bloody politics nonsense I hear you were on about in the pub this morning, which is no place for you to be anyhow?"

"I'm a big girl now," she said.

He muttered and laughed to himself.

Her mother took on her puzzled look again. "What do you mean, politics business," again terrified by what she didn't know. Her father turned his chair away noisily from the table, stretching out his legs and picking up the Sunday paper for some sort of shield—looking for something he hadn't already read.

"Oh, she was blowing her mouth off in the pub at Fuller—I heard it was a right bloody scene."

"It was no scene," she said. "He ran like a startled rat—or a cockroach."

Her father almost grinned. "You should shut up—there's only one way to get along in this world—shut up."

"What you know about politics?" her mother said, suspicious, as though she'd suspected she might also know about sex.

"More jam, Mum," Terry shouted.

"Wait, there's pudding," her mother said, going about getting the pudding.

"Nothing," she said, realising she loved spaghetti on toast, not having had it for a year, "but more than bloody Fuller."

"That wouldn't be hard," her father said, "but it's no reason for you to be a knowall."

"I don't like you going to the pub on Sundays—and in the morning too," her mother said.

"It was a joke on Harry, really," she said, laughing at his screwed up eyes. "He nearly ran out of the pub."

Her father snorted.

"He's doing very well," her mother said defensively. "He was keen on you before you went away."

"He's not any more—that's for sure."

"So you fancy yourself as a bit of a politician," her father said, trying not to show any interest beyond the Sunday paper, she sensing that he was sort of fascinated. Realising that they were talking to each other instead of shouting, would you believe.

"Oh—I went out with a boy who knew a lot."

"Not the schoolteacher?" her mother said, trying to keep up with the conversation and pass around the pudding. Saying it as though there was something nasty about a schoolteacher being interested in it, putting it together with the word "odd".

"Yes."

"Schoolteacher," her father said scornfully. "Straight from school to school—what the bloody hell would they know about anything?"

"He had a degree from university," she said, as much a defence of herself as Kim, "but he was a bit much." She laughed at what she couldn't tell them, saw herself lying face down naked on the bed with him putting his prick up her arse, screaming, "No, it hurts." And all the rest of it.

"What's university?" Terry asked.

"Shut up and eat your pudding," her mother said.

"They're a pack of bastards, politicians," her father said, dealing with the question in one blow. "They know how to look after themselves."

"I think I'll go into politics," she said, quite without thought, just for the fun of saying it.

"You'll what!" her father said, looking at her. "Don't give me the..."

"She's only being funny," her mother said, uncertainly, "aren't you, Dell?"

"I'm in the Labor Party," she said, Kim having joined her once to get her vote at something or other. She hadn't turned up anyhow.

"They're bloody well paid but you'll never get your hands on any of it," her father said, going back to his paper. She could see him turning over the whole strange idea in his boozed head.

"It's no place for a girl," her mother said. "They don't let women into Parliament, anyhow."

"First I'll get elected to the union," she said, remembering Kim going on about that.

"You'll stay well out of it," her mother said, with the same horrified voice.

"Elected to clean the lavatories," her father said.

"She's only having us on," her mother said, pouring the tea.

Which she was, she guessed, and herself too. What else was there to do in this stinking world? And another thing, she may as well admit, she hadn't had her periods for two months and she was putting on weight.

Becker and the boys from the band

THE ANTIQUE poster on the wall of Sam's office read "Coca-Cola at soda fountains five cents delicious detach card at dotted line and present at fountain refreshing this card entitles you to one glass of Coca-Cola free at the fountain of any dispenser of genuine Coca-Cola."

"Well, Becker—come on—reaction!"

"Sure, Sam, it'll work—I just don't know the groups. I'm just not familiar with the groups—sure it worked in the States, local groups would be fine."

What worried Becker was D-E-S-T-I-N-Y, not pop groups. His destiny.

"The Hi-lighters? Know the Hi-lighters?"

"For Christsakes, Sam, I've been in the country four months."

He wanted to be back in Atlanta for one. Now. Instantly. Hotels, Motels, Blowtels. Blowing himself nightly was no life for a young man. Taking tranquillisers so he could simply eat; for Godsake, would you believe it? Just to eat a meal he needed to quiet down his jumping nerves. Everyone mistaking him for an American serviceman on R and R. Dancing with hostess girls in the dim joints, terrified to take them into the light where all the lumps and deformities showed. Perhaps he should go back to college. Now Sam talks about pop groups singing commercials. Capow.

"You OK?"

"Sure Sam, just pooped."

"Too much action?"

"In this city!"

Sam walked over to the water cooler and pulled them both an iced water.

Sam smiled and said, "Cocktail parties at the Cockburns' not sufficient?" Sam even smiled, whatdoyouknow.

"Cockburn and the bloody Civil War."

"Rotary?" Sam said. "I take you to Rotary."

Sam was really amusing today.

"They always stick that name tag into my living flesh."

Sam laughed!

"They do, Sam, I swear they do."

The dinner parties of the married couples.

He stared at his trouser leg. At least his clothes were in shape. That was something, wasn't it?—some achievement that—having his clothes in shape. That was really something.

Play a piano in a cafe. That's what he should do.

"They have an agent." Sam wrote on a pad and tore off the page and handed it to him. "See them, check them out. My kids like them."

Play a piano. Go back to college.

"How long you been here, Sam?"

"Five, going on six."

"How do you take it?"

"Love the country. Love the people. They work their hearts out for you."

He stood up, crushed the paper cup and missed Sam's waste paper basket. He moved to pick it up.

Sam picked it up.

Sam came around and squeezed his shoulder. "You'll be seeing some of the countryside soon."

Oh no. The city was bad enough for Christsakes, at least there were ten dollar screws—which made him as guilty as all hell.

"Sign them up," Sam said, leading to the door, "if you like them." Then Sam pointed at him, "That's right, you play piano—just the right man."

"Yeah—the Music Man," he looked at the paper with the telephone number and heaved himself together. "Leave it to me, Sam."

"Great—get more sleep."

"Which of you is the leader?" They sat around the coffee shop table.

"Him," one of them said.

"I am," the one said, from out of his small goatee beard, waistcoat, paisley shirt, wide fancy tie.

What to be said?

"You sing folk, then?"

"Folk, some rock, some soul, mostly folk," the Leader said.

"Blues," one said.

To break the quiz he told them, "I play jazz piano."

"You play the piano?" the Leader said, with strained interest.

Let it pass.

"I see here you sang in Vietnam," he said, looking at his background material from the agency. Vietnam hell, if someone else asked him if he was R and R there'd be murder.

"How was it?"

"Oh, fine."

"Really lets you see how things are up there," one came in.

"How are things up there?" Not that he had any burning interest. His sister's husband, was he there?

"Morale's great, simply great."

"They cry when you sing—great audience."

"I'm forever being mistaken for an R and R serviceman," he told them.

They laughed a big group laugh.

"What part of the States you from?" the Leader asked.

"I suppose Atlanta," he mused, "or Motel Travelodge."

They all smiled.

He leafed through the background.

"This Labor Party deal—you sang for the Labor Party?"

"Well," one of them said, looking at the Leader.

"It was just a gig," the Leader said. He tried to explain it away. "It was a washout but well paid—we did it just as a gig."

They were hungry for a dollar.

"We're not a political group," the Leader hastened to say.

He just stared at the notation Sam had made—"check", Sam had written. Well, he'd checked.

They bubbled and squawked something else—each one of them—like hungry birds—trying to explain. He was unnerving them, he could tell, by not speaking.

"No matter," he said. "Politics, Coca-Cola, Vietnam, who gives a five cent damn?—it's all show business."

They laughed, relieved.

"What is it—this Labor Party?"

"Oh, they'd never win elections," the Leader said. "We just did it for the money."

"They've got too many nuts and crackpots and old men."

"Crazy old men."

"They hired us to go around country halls."

"No one turned up."

"They paid us OK."

Oh God, he was tired. He motioned to the girl for service. "More coffee?" he asked, glancing at them. They nodded obediently.

"Politics is show business is politics," he said.

"Politics here is a dead scene."

"It's nowhere," said another.

He looked down at his information: "The show was cleanly produced. The four young singers appeared as four clean young men. It was all very unobjectionable and unexciting." Some of the other reviews were enthusiastic.

Anyhow, they wanted clean young people. We all want clean young people.

"You're clean young people," he said. "It says so here."

They chuckled as a group.

So he needed political and legal organisation, financing and accountancy, mathematics and statistics, industrial relations, decision-making theory, and a semester of group dynamics to hire a clean, hungry, little pop group to sing a commercial. He should be back in Atlanta. Everyone was going up the ladder but him.

"Like you're not all crazy demonstrators," he said, feeling he'd better ask. Sam said check. Who'd care if they were—Atlanta? Hell, they wouldn't. Chop chop chop.

He should have gone into the factors business. Now there was a business. He could have gotten into the Heller corporation. But that was just a swap of one big corporation's slippery rope ladder for another. Which people always tried to untie at the top.

There had been that deal about a fifty-five-pound motor scooter you could put in a carrying bag. People want to ride scooters not carry them. Let's face it, Becker, you haven't been meteoric. He'd end up like Sam.

"Will you contact Morrison?" the Leader asked him.

He'd forgotten the silence.

"Morrison?"

"Our agent."

"Sure—contact by end of week through Hansen Rubensohn—McCann Erickson." Brisk and businesslike was Becker. He pulled himself back to the situation. "Sorry politics got mixed up with the coffee. We really don't give a damn," he told them.

"We did it for money."

"That's all right—I had to check it out—see here," he leaned across the table holding up the folder of material with Sam's margin note. "When Sam says check, I check."

They all dutifully looked.

"Got to protect the Coca-Cola image," the fourth one said with a hesitant laugh.

"We're all a bit sorry we got mixed up in that thing at all," the Leader said.

After the recording session they went to have drinks and after drinks they went to the Apple Disco.

He entered into the coloured lights growing brighter now dimmer as the roar of the band changed from loud to louder.

"This where you always come?" he shouted.

"It's new," one shouted back.

Well, that answered his question. Sighting the girls—all attached, he guessed—no regular hostesses—he'd stay for one drink—what was he doing with the Hi-lighters?—what was he doing here? He couldn't hear what they were saying. He didn't want to hear what they were saying. They weren't talking anyhow. He didn't want to talk either.

He was left with the young one. The others danced with girls they knew.

He intended leaving after one more little drink.

He saw the young man staring at a group of girls sitting unaccompanied except for one young man in jeans. Attractively brassy girls.

"Question: What do monsters eat?

"Answer: Things.

"Question: What do they drink?

"Answer: Coca-Cola. Things go better with Coke."

The young man wasn't listening. The young man named, was it...Phillip?...wasn't listening.

Things go better with Coca-Cola.

He looked around. Freedom in the Golden Age of Athens.

The pianist couldn't play.
Another drink.
The pianist couldn't play ludo.
The young man couldn't take his eyes off the brassy girls. The young man... named Phillip?
"Let's go over and talk to them," Phillip said, nodding towards the girls.
"Lead the way—it's your country."
"They're TV."
He picked up the scotch.
They sat down with the girls.
"May we join you?" he asked.
It was unnecessary. The young man named Phillip knew them. Their voices.
They sounded like men. Dogs?
"These regular women?" he whispered to Phillip, uneasy.
"TV," whispered Phillip, "transvestites."
The word zotted through to him. Not for old Becker. "Not my scene, man," he said, working himself back on to his feet, staring at them.
He leaned over and said to Phillip, "You're supposed to be clean."
The young man Phillip laughed, embarrassed. "For laughs, man."
"On me," he said, and sat down. Too tired to move.
The Phillip was holding hands with one, for Godsakes. What was he doing here with one of them? And one of them was now beside him saying, "Do you come here often?"
"It's now," he said, "now I'm really going," he said, pouring a quick last drink.
"Oh, you're R and R," heshe said.
"Oh no, I'm not," he said, "I'm not R and R. Look, this isn't my scene."
"It's simply dreary, simply dreary, I agree," the man's voice came out of the make-believe woman's face, the golden wig, flowing gown, stockings, high heels.
Heshe said, "I simply adore talking to Americans. Could listen to them for hours."
His clean young folksinger was kissing, was kissing, one of them.
They were attractive OK, but they were men. Not his sort of

thing at all. Becker the executive.

He knew he had to get out. This was not his scene.

Heshe had taken his hand and put it on her stockinged leg. He could feel the web of the nylon.

He left it there. Why?

A groin stirring. Oh no.

"The light effect is marvellous. Fabulous," husky, deep, male voice.

"Yes," he said.

"I wish we had it at the Bird Cage."

"The where?"

"Oh you must be very new to town—our little place."

What was he doing with half an erection?

Oh Sam, if you could see me now. Oh mother and father. Out, he must get out.

"Come back for a party, darlings."

Phillip was saying something about yes, come back for a party.

"Bring the young R and R man," one said.

"He's coming, darling," heshe said, "with me," and gave the other a pointed look.

The bloody music the bloody pianist.

He grabbed the scotch and they grabbed him and wheeled him across the floor. And the young man in jeans.

In their car he was kissed lightly by—Kaye—all right Kaye, call her Kaye. He wanted out. He kept her at a distance with his hand.

Kaye said, "What are you then?—shouldn't ask, no names no packdrill, what does it matter, forever gay. I'll call you Jed. Marjorie . . ." Marjorie kept on talking. "Marjorie," Kaye screamed, "Marjorie, remember the R and R guy at the Cage, remember? You do remember."

"Shut up, Kaye, your stories aren't funny."

Giggling giggling.

His ears were blunt from the music.

He looked out at the streaming shop fronts, houses, poles, signs, bus stops, and wondered what was happening to him. And about Sam. What sort of guy was Sam?

"Look, I really must get out."

"You can't—remember, Marjorie, you remember? The Negro."

Phillip was kissing Marjorie.

Miss X was glumly driving.

"Why you sad?" Kaye said to him. "You Americans are all

the same and you get sad after midnight. All thinking and thoughtful; what you got to worry about?"

"Oh no. Look I must go, out, get out, I really must. Not feeling at all well."

"Have a drink at my place darling, and then off you go—have to be sociable, remember, Marjorie? You remember the Negro and the R and R, you remember, Marjorie?"

"Shut up."

The flat was screamingly feminine. He said he wanted to go to the john. They showed him where. As he went in the door he heard music leap scratching at his tired ears.

Knocking on the lavatory door, "Hurry up, darling, we are all rather desperate."

Love's dribbling dart. He tucked it back in.

Miss X pushed past him.

"Look, I really must go," he said to Kaye.

"You can't go," she shoved a drink into his hand.

Phillip and Marjorie were dancing.

"I must go—I have really had it—Sam says I have to get early nights. Look, I'm basically very square."

She was swaying to the music in front of him.

"Look, please."

He drank his drink. "Please, I must go."

He was sticky with discomfort.

"Please."

She took his hand and was trying to dance with him.

"Please."

He shouldn't be pleading. He should just go.

"Doesn't your R and R man dance, darling?" Marjorie said to Kaye; and then to him, "Dance, let yourself go, darling, really you must."

He was sweating too. "I'm sorry, I really shouldn't be here."

Miss X and her young man in jeans were shouting at each other.

What about the police?

He started for the door.

She tried to pull him back.

"Please." His coat came half off.

He pulled it back on.

"Come on, you don't have to go yet." She was becoming aggressive.

"Look, really, I'm pooped—please let go."

He detached her hand from his coat.

Marjorie and Phillip came over. Marjorie said, "Having trouble keeping your man, Kaye?"

"Bitch."

Then Kaye took Marjorie's hand and together they barricaded him—he couldn't reach the door. "Ladies—please," he heard himself say, "I must go."

"Don't go," Phillip said.

He ignored Phillip and tried to break through the two barricading his way. Kaye got him in a grabbing embrace.

Hot-faced with anger he pushed her away and she fell against the door jamb. "Good night," he said with finality and anger, making it to the door.

"Get stuffed," Kaye yelled at him and spat on him.

The spittle hit his arm like a drop of lava. He recoiled out the door, slamming it behind him, holding his arm bent away from him, staring at the spittle. He moved down the stairs, using his handkerchief in frantic swipes to wipe it away, keeping on with the wiping until he was well down the street. He threw the handkerchief away but still held his arm bent away from him to avoid contaminating the rest of his body.

It had begun to rain. It was always beginning to rain in his life. The dreadful smell of hair fixer from Kaye's wig smelling now from his shoulder where she'd had her head. The spit. He took off the coat and hung it on a fence picket. Cleansed by both the shedding of the coat and the rain drops. His sister came to mind whose husband was in Vietnam or based somewhere, perhaps just at Fort Benning. This Godforsaken country. He was being persecuted. What was happening Atlanta? To Rotary with Sam tomorrow. Exile. He waited in the drizzle for a cab, praying, "Our kind Lord and heavenly Father, we turn to you knowing we pray to one who hears and answers. We ask that you take us by the hand and lead us to the path of righteousness. Give others strength of heart. Strengthen those of us who are weary. Accept us as your radiant servants..."

The machine gun

"HERE are the magazines from Cuba."

He handed Turvey the magazines.

Turvey tossed them on the table which was obliterated by other papers, magazines, and books—all of it looked like postponed reading. "How long you down?" Turvey asked.

"The weekend—just till Sunday."

Turvey's dim bachelor house. He looked around. A bachelor poet's house. Che Guevara. A dirty cup and a dirty glass. A sketch of Adrian Mitchell. A poster poem of Christopher Logue's.

"You need a woman, Turvey."

"Haven't the time—travel light."

Turvey could almost have meant it.

"Can't pull yourself off all your life."

"I get the stray fuck," he said, unsmiling.

He sat down while Turvey leaned on his hands against a bookcase as if he was doing a physical exercise.

Turvey hadn't bothered to open the magazines from Cuba. He was a bit like that.

"What's happening, then?"

Turvey wriggled his shoulders—a shudder, a twitch—kicked the bookcase lightly. "Conferences, Left Action, demonstrations run by the cops," he gestured, "you know it all."

Turvey walked to the other side of the room and leaned against the window, not looking out.

"Where's your revolutionary zeal?"

Turvey shrugged, pulled out a book from the nearest case, as if at random, didn't open it, put it back, and with a wild turn, broke out, "I want to show you something."

He went to the drawer of the obliterated table and took out a key.

"Come on."

He got up and followed Turvey.

Turvey led to the garage. He shuffled away some newspapers and hauled out a long box by its rope handles, and opened it.

The box contained a Bren light machine gun.

"Jesus," he said to Turvey, "Jesus, where did you get that?"

"From a crim."

"Holy Jesus."

Straddling the box, Turvey lifted the gun by its carrying handle and, opening out the bipod, stood the gun on the concrete garage floor.

"But why for Godsake?"

Turvey lay behind the gun, pulled it into his shoulder, cocked it, and shot the bolt.

"What about ammunition?"

"Two thousand rounds," Turvey said.

"But why—why did you get it?"

He knelt down beside Turvey and took the gun, sighting along the barrel. He cocked the gun and shot the bolt.

"Things could get hot."

He looked up disbelievingly at Turvey, "You've got to be joking."

He didn't know what answer he expected. What answer would make sense? Turvey was one of those people who didn't feel obliged to make sense.

"The student-worker alliance—job power—people being screwed—Chinese infiltration."

"Chinese infiltration!—you're crazy."

It was hard to say to Turvey that you thought he was crazy because sometimes he really did seem...crazy. He lay there looking up at Turvey, the gun against his shoulder, hurt. He expected Turvey to be breathtaking but it hurt him when he was foolish. He was in awe of Turvey—Turvey's political intensity—the fact that he was a revolutionary poet. But he knew more than Turvey about theory and so on. "What do you mean, Turvey—Chinese infiltration?"

"The Chinese are sending in guerrillas—landing them in twos or threes off the coast."

"Bullshit." He pictured it like a movie. "That's all bullshit, Turvey." He saw them jumping from rocking boats up to their waists in water and scrambling on to the beaches. The submarines barely visible in the fog. "Who told you this bullshit?"

"Party sources."

"The CP?"

"The Maoists."

"You in with them?"

Turvey didn't reply.

"Come on, tell me more," pressing his disbelief hard against Turvey's sureness.

He didn't want there to be a distance between Turvey and him. He was more hurt by the distance than by the nutty theory or Turvey's private certainty.

Turvey kept staring away, as if wondering whether to say more.

"Where's the support," he said, "if they come?"

"People are becoming molten—it's beginning to flow—the Americans are sucking the country, the average guy is being sucked by everyone."

He couldn't get himself to believe it. About the Chinese, that was. He believed Turvey about the economic thing, the resentment. He looked back to the gun. It was easier to imagine himself back with the school cadets than guerrilla fighting in the streets.

The smell of the wet greatcoat. The abundant Q-store, arms, accoutrement for playing with. Kettle drums.

It seemed that everything was going well and five men had been sent to replace the ones stationed in ambush on the road, when shots were heard. We went there rapidly on horseback and came across a strange sight: in the midst of silence, four dead soldiers were lying in the sun on the sands of the river.

"It's a good gun," he said to Turvey, letting his hands move over the parts, searching out what he remembered from cadet instruction. The cool metal. Smell of gun oil. "Fired it yet?"

"You're the first person I've shown."

Turvey saying that was comradely and he felt back close to him again. Turvey was one of the few people he thought of as a comrade. He found it a hard word to use. He wanted Turvey as a comrade.

Turvey was bad with committees but in street fighting he would want to be with Turvey.

As normally as he could, he asked, "Have you met any...any infiltrators?"

"No," Turvey said, again with a sureness lying behind it.

Turvey didn't add.

He decided to let it drop. "Say, why don't we go to National Park and shoot? I've got the car."

They stood up, dusting their clothes. Turvey took some boxes of bright brass .303 bullets and two magazines. They loaded the magazines. The realness of the bullets almost convinced him of the rest, as though the existence of the *material* of revolution was evidence of its reality. They loaded them very quickly.

Turvey put the magazines down his shirt and together they carried the Bren gun in its box, draped with a blanket, out to the Citroen.

"It was stolen from army stores," Turvey said.

They drove to the park. Each suburban family in each suburban washed and polished car made him conscious of the machine gun but pushed him away from the belief in the nearness of revolution. Turvey tapped his fingers and jigged his foot throughout the drive.

They found a sandy track and drove low-gear along it as far as possible to cliffs overlooking the sea.

No lighting of fires except in authorised fire places.

They carried the gun to the cliffs overlooking the empty Tasman sea.

They fitted a magazine to the gun. Turvey lay behind it and fired, and a single shot whined out to sea. The gun stopped firing.

Their cadet training came back to them and they said, almost together, "Number one stoppage—gun stops firing—recock gun." They grinned.

The gun fired a single shot again and stopped.

"I've been taken," Turvey said, flaring, thumping the gun with his fist. "The bloody thing's no good."

"Replace the magazine—that's number two stoppage, isn't it?" he said to Turvey. "Check the magazine."

They changed the magazine and fired a single shot whining out to sea but could not get the gun to fire repeat or automatic.

"Shit and damn," Turvey yelled.

"I'll change the gas chamber to a larger port." He did so.

"Try now."

Turvey recocked the gun savagely and fired. This time the gun fired and kept on firing.

"Beauty," Turvey said, instantly jubilant, trembling.

"Number four stoppage—give only rank and serial number." They both laughed again.

Turvey put the gun to automatic and fired a burst. "Get some beer cans or something to shoot at."

He went to the scrub and found some cans and bottles—bones of a picnic.

Here's a nice spot, Kim. Find some firewood. I hope somebody remembered the salt.

"Point that bloody thing somewhere else," he yelled at Turvey, propping up the bottles and cans along the cliff edge, and coming back behind the gun.

Turvey fired a burst and blasted the asparagus, beer, beetroot, camp-pie, and baked beans tins into the sea.

We are surrounded by 2000 men within a radius of 120 kilometres, and the encirclement is closing in; this is combined with napalm bombings. We have ten or fifteen losses. We went to the place where the rotting corpses were but couldn't carry them all and so would go back tomorrow to burn them.

He propped up some more. "Let me fire this time."

He took the warm gun. He sighted and blasted the cans and bottles into the sea, feeling the gun throb like an animal, ejecting its hot shells in a flood around his elbows. Some of the shells rolled into the tracks of ants.

He stopped firing. A ringing silence. Cordite.

"You don't honestly think you're going to use it, in fighting, I mean?" he said, rolling over and giving the gun back to Turvey.

"Yes," Turvey said, "unquestionably."

He decided again to leave the matter alone but something clever occurred to him which he thought might be correct and which would intellectually satisfy him and put him back on the same band as Turvey. "Isn't the gun more a metaphor—a sort of political metaphor?"

"No, it's not a metaphor," Turvey said sharply.

Turvey then began firing and didn't stop until the magazines were spent. Not at any target, just into the sea.

"You bastard, Turvey—I wanted another shot."

They kicked the spent shells over the cliff. He didn't talk to Turvey for a few minutes because of disappointment.

In the hotel they talked about how things were politically in the city and the groups, but Turvey pushed aside the talk: "We could buy up old weapons—create a cache—begin weapons drill."

He tried to stop himself saying anything but couldn't. "Look, Turvey—attractive as I think the idea is—I simply don't believe the Chinese are here—or coming here. And I'm not convinced there's a revolutionary situation—yet."

Turvey said with a quiet iciness, "They are here, I tell you—being harboured by the local Chinese."

"Crap."

"Have it your own way."

They drank half a beer in silence. Of course he wanted a revolution—all his reading since school, all his serious talking, all his political work, and all his teaching were directed towards it. He wanted to own a machine gun too—say as a political symbol—but it was the rationale—the feasibility of it all—of Turvey's political fantasy that he couldn't accept. He was for violent assault on the system as much as anyone.

Perhaps it was true. Perhaps he should talk to some of the others.

Perhaps he'd got out of touch, teaching in the country.

Take out your books for dictation. Someone to clean the board. Turn to page 73.

"They're going to engage in military sabotage of the bases," Turvey said.

"I'll get some beer nuts," he said.

The soldiers advanced with little caution, exploring the edges of the river while looking for tracks and penetrated the wooded area before reaching the ambush. The firing lasted only a few seconds with one dead, and three wounded lying on the ground, plus six prisoners. My Garand jammed.

He half listened to Turvey but most of all he wanted to be behind the machine gun again. He wanted to be blasting away. He recaptured the release, the destructiveness, and the invulnerability he'd felt lying in the sun behind the gun firing into the sea. The living gun.

He wondered if Sylvia would like to fire the gun.

Sylvia making a toasted cheese sandwich in the electric frying pan.

Sylvia reaching for a can from a high cupboard.

Sylvia tucking the candy-striped sheets of their bed.

Sylvia pushing back the moons of her fingernails.

They decided to go to a party.

"It's at Angela's—the American girl."

"What about the gun—?" he worried. "We can't go screaming around the city with it in the back of the car."

"What if we were in an accident," Turvey laughed, "and the bloody thing fell out." Turvey seemed to like the idea.

"Very funny." He grinned. "Remember in that film *The Big Risk* they had a machine gun in a compartment behind the front seat?"

He didn't like it one bit, realistically, but they couldn't be bothered going to Turvey's place across the city and back.

They stopped in a lane and unpacked the gun, hiding it under the back seat.

The party burned with dancing, political talk, drinking, pot smoking, sexual hunting. But he was alive only to the gun.

It was the gun he was thinking about as the Canned Heat and Bob Dylan tried to engage him and he drank beer from a paper cup and talked about his country high school and conditions in Cuba.

"Where's Sylvia?"

"Didn't come," he replied, "I'm free."

"A bourgeois illusion."

He wanted to say to people that he'd been shooting a machine gun in National Park.

"No, I'm staying with Mum and Dad—pressure—you know..." he replied to someone.

A Rugby Union pennant. A stuffed rabbit from childhood. *The White Company*. A travelling clock from his twenty first.

He went to the back of the house and looked across the dark repetition of the two-up-two-down, back-to-back houses. Distant Saturday night laughter.

A third army truck stopped to see what was happening, then the road became obstructed. We forced the sergeant to give the watchword and took the post with ten men in a lightning action, after a good skirmish of cross-fire with a soldier who resisted. We captured five Mausers and one Z-B-30.

"Oh no, oh no, I don't believe it." He heard Angela. He turned towards the screams. Angela was standing just off from the front door, her hands to her face. Her long hair wrapped around her face, her "Oh no" rising to screaming pitch. He saw people nearby stop talking and turn around. Except some, some kept on—those too involved, or drunk. Two men kept shouting at each other despite the silence falling around them.

He looked through the hall of the house through the standing people and to the front steps and saw Turvey coming up with the Bren gun under his arm, a hand on the barrel, as if in combat.

Angela had cringed into the doorway-hall corner.

He moved, pushing through the people in the hallway. "Turvey," he shouted, "Turvey, put that damn gun back in the car."

"Jesus, it's a gun."

"Turvey, for Godsake—you'll have the cops here," he said, reaching Turvey.

He couldn't quite take in the incongruity of it—the suburban house—the party at a standstill, except for the record player, two shouting drunks, and noises from the other room.

The gun fired.

The firing deafened him in one ear.

The gun had fired. The reverberations skeltered down the hall and out of the house into the dark yard and further.

He didn't understand at first, nor did those nearby. No one seemed to understand at first, that the gun had fired.

It must have sounded more like a gun firing to those in the other room because the room fell absolutely silent and then the people appeared at the door of the room.

"That was a shot."

"Turvey's got a gun."

The gun had fired. The .303 bullet had gouged a long scar about seven feet along the plaster of the wall and then passed out through a shattered brick. There was a ragged trail of wallpaper.

"Holy fucking Jesus," he shouted. "Turvey, put the bloody gun down, put it down." He tried to force the gun down but Turvey stood there holding it rigid and staring at the gouged wall.

Angela was giving off moans.

"He's out of his mind."

"The bloody thing's loaded."

Angela was moaning and two girls were trying to help her. She had pissed herself. Urine had streamed down her legs to the floor.

He took the gun from Turvey.

"You could have bloody killed someone, Turvey," someone said, real terror riding in the words.

No one had anything else to say.

Turvey looked around. "I'm not scared of killing."

"He's mad."

The message of the firing had passed through the whole house and brought back a wash of cackling questions. The whole party crowded into the hallway. "Turvey's got a machine gun."

Someone had started to laugh about it.

Angela had begun screaming, "Get it out of here, get it out of here, get it out."

Get it out of here, get it out.

He and a couple of the others took the gun out to the car. He locked the car.

"It's a beaut weapon—the Bren," one said.

"There must have still been one round in the breech," he said obviously, in way of explanation to those with him.

They went back to the party.

The talk was all of the firing. They were looking at the path of the bullet along the wall, poking their fingers in the gouge.

There was no music. He couldn't see Angela. Some people were going.

He found Turvey alone, crouched, drunk, in the yard.

Turvey said, "Someone has to prepare them."

"Our revolutionary legend's a bit weak," he said, wondering why he should be trying to excuse them and himself.

Turvey went to sleep then, head on his drawn-up knees.

His liver was crushed and he had abdominal perforations; he died during the operation. He had been an inseparable comrade of mine throughout the preceding years. When he fell in combat, he asked that I be given his watch. We carried his body and took it to be buried far from there.

Becker on the moon

BECKER already had dirt, gravel, pebble or what-have-you in his shoes. He did not like this country—despite what he told everyone. There was one place and one place only he wanted to be—old Atlanta, hoisting himself up that old ladder of success. The way he reasoned it was that even if he was going to be ill-destined, that is, if his interior life was going to be stickily uncomfortable, it didn't preclude wealth. He was not a loser. What he meant was that one could be in a hell of an interior state without being a loser. But another thing was also true: the wealth, piled high in bags, was in Atlanta, not in this Godforsaken country.

He untied his shoe and, hopping on one foot, unbalanced, emptied out the gravel.

"Having trouble?" his hostess asked through her sunglasses. He struggled to grin back from behind his sunglasses.

"I'm no country boy," he said.

"The club president, Bob, is checking over the glider now."

These situations were always identical, he observed. You liked the proposition, the invitation sounded fine, just fine, but then you found that the promised climactic pleasure was wedged, if not sunken, between or under two fat slices of boring make-ready and tedious waiting. And the getting there and the getting back. Oh brother, the time he'd spent waiting for *it* to happen—it was the same with water-skiing. Now why couldn't they get everything ready and *then* bring him out here. Instead, he stood, stood interminably in the neck-burning sun. And at the end of the sun's rays were flies. He didn't like walking over paddocks. The growth, alfalfa or whatever, was so damn spiky, seemed to fight him every inch.

And yes, a rash of spear seeds up his trouser leg.

"The club hardly owes any money on the glider now," his hostess said. "We pay it off by charging the guests."

Oh boy.

"You need a Coke machine," he said, always the aggressive sales executive.

His hostess blushed, "We do sell soft drinks but not Coke," she apologised.

"Oh hell, it doesn't matter to me—I'm off duty," he said, touching her arm.

He could push the local distributor into placing a slot machine out here. The far reach of the Coca-Cola empire.

"You must be hot in that suit," she said.

"No, it's not absolutely appropriate," he said. "But I have this associate to see mid-afternoon."

They stood watching the almost imperceptible action surrounding the preparation of the glider.

"We attach it to the pie cart, and the pie cart to the winch truck and the boy rides the bicycle beside it, guiding the wing—out to the field," she informed him.

She told him about the fatality. Compared with the sun and the raw ruralism death didn't seem such a distressing alternative.

As they sat in the cockpit she told him, "We need a thermal," searching the sky, shading her eyes with her hand.

The wire towing rope tightened and they were trundled to a fast speed along the strip.

She described the updraft of hot air, the thermal, as they soared up into the sky, unhitched the wire rope and began to wheel.

You just keep your hands on those controls, lady.

He thought he saw himself back down there on the strip, which almost fused his nerve circuit. He took what he thought was probably a grip of himself. Easy boy.

Perhaps Atlanta had a contract out on him. Maybe this gliding lady had the job.

Keep your eyes on that altimeter, miss.

"I feel I'm above myself," he shouted, sociably, philosophically.

No need to shout, no engine roar, just the wind stream.

"Doesn't look as if we're going to get the thermal," she said, despondently.

He found himself braced for a fall.

He wanted, of all things, a Coke.

They began to spiral back to the strip.

He looked away to the banks of clouds, the streets of clouds, he looked beyond them to Atlanta and glimpsed, piled high, the bags of wealth.

At his hostess's small town house where she lived in business-like spinsterhood, Becker relaxed with three stiff shots of scotch. "Help yourself," she'd said.

"I find it funny—you working for Coca-Cola," she said, "not meaning to sound rude."

He moved his head and neck, no-offence-taken.

"What is it that amuses you?" Wait for it.

"Oh—I don't know—perhaps the fact you travel right across the world to this town—just to sell Coca-Cola."

That's funny? It didn't amuse him.

"I'm here to rationalise distribution," he said, recalling that apprehensive briefing those many months ago, "to advise the franchise men."

"Do you like it—Coke, I mean?"

"Oh yes, yes I do," he said, he really did, he really did. "You have to swear to like it and drink it when you join the outfit."

"I don't believe you."

"It's God's truth."

"Music?" she asked him, laughing. She went to the record player.

"What do you like—music from the shows?"

"Jazz," he said, "but please—no folk."

"No jazz, I'm sorry, I haven't any jazz."

"Oh, music from the shows would be great. I like show music, I like the music from *Hair*."

"No, I don't have *Hair* yet—hasn't reached here yet. *The Music Man?*"

"Sure—wonderful—yes, *The Music Man*." Sam called him the Music Man. Here's to you, Sam.

He felt like putting his head on his knees. What would be the time in Atlanta—he looked surreptitiously at his Omega moon watch. It would be morning. Those old railway lines would be jumping. The newspapers thumping on the dewy lawns in Peach Street, Ponce de Leon Avenue, Pace's Ferry Road. Coffee percolators burbling. Those old Blue Ridge mountains. Old Atlanta, Georgia.

She was still talking and he realised something. He was being preliminarily seduced—or courted, was it?—by this spinster gliding woman.

He looked at her anew.

She served white wine with the dinner and port with the coffee. He told her the funny story of how in New Orleans he'd learned that dessert wines were not served with dessert, "And damn me—they cleared away everything off the table," he told her, laughing like a Rotarian.

He told her about Atlanta, about the Stone Mountain, "sheer naked granite," he told her.

In the lounge-room after dinner he noticed the lights were subdued and half way through *Oklahoma!* he took her hand lightly and she almost jumped on him with a kiss.

They went after a while to her bedroom with her saying something like, "We're old enough to know our own minds."

He worried whether he'd picked up anything from a whore he'd gone with in the city.

She had a dressing-room off the bedroom and came back in a nylon nightdress.

He sat waiting in his shirt and undershorts morosely interested in her. His drink clutched.

Into bed.

As she moaned, simulated or not he didn't know, he thought of her searching, soaring, wheeling for that thermal.

I'm not a great lover, he thought, but hell I try.

He had no idea whether she was through or not but he figured he'd given her a reasonable length of time and he couldn't keep going for ever and it could become a little tiring for both of them. He made some noises to let her know he was going to give it to her and then, his mind picturing the whore, he gave it to her.

They're not going to remember me as a great lover but I'm considerate to a limited degree which is all we can ask of one of God's less radiant servants.

"Don't take this as prying," he said, "but do you usually invite travelling strangers to your bed?"

"No," she said, somewhat guiltily, "I liked you but I do have a boy-friend—he runs the Tourist Bureau—we escort each other, have for a couple of years."

They both smoked.

To kill the bed silence he thought he'd tell her a story apropos of nothing.

"I made a decision for Christ once," he said, "when I was an adolescent teenager—in the Billy Graham Crusade."

She was staring at him.

Well, OK, he was somewhat of a sensationalist.

"I went down when they called, I went down through the thousands there at the Bowl with their peanuts and Cokes and Bibles and I went forward to the counsellors and I was about to kneel when I realised something. I realised what I wanted was not grace but a slice of God's business. I didn't want my soul cleansed—the five minute soul wash. I was really attracted by the way Billy and God had packed in all these customers. And there I'd been an innocent kid turning over in my secret mind how I could get a piece. Once you've come down through all those thousands, you can't change your mind and go back. So down I knelt, made a decision for Christ, and filled out a card."

"Are you a practising Christian?" she said, missing whatever the point was, puzzlement stammering her words.

"Oh no," he said, "I just like religion—there's a bit of the evangelist in all of us. Here I am—pushing Coca-Cola."

"You're a strange man."

"I sure don't think of myself that way," he said. "I think of myself as everybody's plain man."

There was another smoking silence, and then she said, "I can't ask you to stay the night—country town and everything."

Termination.

"That's all right."

They didn't kiss again or touch and they parted.

He felt OK. Sex sometimes did that for him, that at least.

On the way to his motel he counted the street-facing Coke signs in cafes and milk bars. He thought hungrily of the jar of hot mix in his suite.

I'm a very religious man, he thought, in my own way. That's part of my trouble. I'm soul conscious, too soul conscious. That's why I had to tell that gliding girl that parable about the Rev. Billy.

The wide country street made him stride it out and he thought, there's a bit of the cowboy in all of us, but not too much in him. He was just about all evangelist. If at all cowboy he was strictly a town cowboy. Not one of God's range riders. He was strictly a motel cowboy.

He went to the milkbar for cigarettes as they were closing.

"Closing up for the night." he said cordially, full of good will. Counting the Coke signs.

The Greek in the fawn apron-jacket with green trim said, "You American?"

We're both on the ball tonight, Becker thought.

He nodded.

A younger Greek was sweeping up at a great pace.

"That one," the older Greek nodded, "he like the donkey—going to work in the morning he don't remember the way and you have to drag him along. In the night when the work finished he remember the way home all right and he go like mad."

Folklore was not exactly to Becker's taste, but he chuckled.

Hearing his chuckle Becker became uneasy about his feeling of well-being. This was not him. Not the queasy radiant servant he knew.

How it happened he was not positively sure. He would have liked to get his feeling of well-being back to the motel. Just once.

Perhaps the old drunk said, "Hey you, you American." But from his uneasy sense of well-being he was hauled and launched up into a wild, buffeting thermal of truculent exchange—about, of all things, the moon landing.

"*Does grass grow on Mars,*
Are there minerals on the moon,
They think the radar telescope
Will tell them very soon
But they cannot find a person
Or an aeroplane that's lost
Or a ship in distress at sea
But they'll see a thousand miles," the old drunk recited, then demanded of Becker, "Do you know how much it costs to put those two galahs for a stroll on the moon?" belching from a stall where he was eating a meal, the last remaining customer.

"Really, it's not my line of business, sir," Becker cried out, dealing with the cellophane wrap of his cigarette packet.

Becker had been turned around by the exchange, but the drunk did not look up from his steak, onions, and chips.

"The moon doesn't heed the barking of dogs," the old man said, "but the leaders are going to get away in a space ship."

Becker said, "That could well be—I could well believe that."

Mouth stuffed with food the drunk said, "We pay for it so you Americans can get out in time."

"Not all Americans," Becker laughed, with strain. "I don't think I'll get a seat."

How true.

"Hydrogen only appears to defy gravity—but it shows there might be some unknown law which would enable speed above the speed of light."

"I wouldn't know that, sir."

"We pay for it."

"I could use some of that budget myself," Becker laughed, wondering what to do with the crushed ball of cellophane in the swept cafe. "I pay," Becker said, "you should see my Federal tax—oh man," rushing to prove his share of the cost.

"Tell me this," the old man said. "How fast would you be walking up the carriage of a train which was travelling at sixty miles an hour in the direction of the earth's rotation..."

"Sixty miles an hour?" Becker checked, preparing himself for mental arithmetic.

"Sixty miles an hour in the direction of the earth's rotation and further consider the speed at which the earth orbits the sun, the sun moves in our galaxy and our galaxy moves in the universe."

Too many unknowns. Becker shrugged his head.

"What's your name, son?"

"Becker."

"What's your line of business?"

Becker felt like resisting the interrogation, but the man had the clinging insistency of drunkenness and cranky age.

"Beverages, sir."

"What?" Beverages seemed not to be one of the man's words. Becker spoke out: "Coca-Cola."

"That's your line of business?"

"Yes, sir."

Becker didn't know whether the man lost interest or whether his mind had wandered or what, but that was the end of the conversation. The man went on fully occupied with mopping his plate with bread. He didn't speak a further word, leaving Becker's soul deep deep in a conversation crater.

A person of accomplishment

THE invitation to go home with him to his place was absolutely unexpected. There they were writing up test analyses in his office, her mind running a fantasy about going to MIT for a Ph.D. and finding a big buck Negro in a white lab coat, when she'd felt a hand on her knee and heard him say, "Why don't we stop at this point and go back to my place for a drink?" The pressure of his hand on her knee said drinks and sex.

Her second thoughts were whether she'd stay overnight with him. Whether she'd need a change of clothes for tomorrow and other things. She was also faintly blushing.

She felt like saying, "But we hardly know each other," but that was not a particularly liberated thing to say, and checked it. Nor particularly honest because she'd never made this a real requirement with other men. Unexpected, that was what it was, unexpected. Over the months there hadn't been a sexual breath to stir the clinical atmosphere between them.

"I guess you must have sensed I was going to invite you home one of these fine nights," he said.

She looked at his smile. "Well, not exactly..."

"You will come, though?"

"Well, yes," she said. There was the slight obligation of an invitation which comes from an associate professor to a humble research assistant—and then the difference in their ages—twenty-eight and forty, gave him some sort of command. She also felt gently encircled by his clean, serious, American gregariousness. His American geniality.

At his place he took her in his arms in the clean kitchen and with her backside against the stainless steel sink, kissed her very seriously.

"I've been wanting to do that for some days," he said, with some satisfaction, and having got that out of the way, went about getting her a drink and putting out black bread and cheese—two types—on a cheese board.

He showed her around. Showed her his study with its carved pipe rack, Steel-bilt filing cabinets and Tensor reading lamp.

Besides his doctorate from MIT and his pharmacy degree from the University of Nebraska, Lincoln, framed on the wall, she saw a cup for canoeing and a silver chess piece from some American competition.

"Spacious," she commented.

"I prefer it to my office at the university," he said. She mentally corrected it to "room at the university".

Back in the living room she ran her fingers along the keyboard of his piano.

"Do you play?" she asked.

"Yes. A little." Sitting down, he played.

"Schoenberg—discordant? You find it discordant? Twelve-tone system—a rigid intellectual exercise—say, like a sonnet."

"You seem to have a wide range of interests—chess, canoeing, piano..."

"There's a reason," he said quietly, stopping playing. "I had a marriage break up on me—years ago—when I was young." He shrugged, looked at her, and then seemed to decide not to go on.

She felt unable to inquire further.

He swivelled on the piano stool, looking fit and spruce.

She was frightened then for a second that the conversation had lapsed and the situation would become physical. She wasn't ready.

"Do you cook?" she said, looking through at the shadow board and the shelves holding the kitchen utensils—the natural colourings of the handmade wood and pottery and the machined brightness of the duralumin and stainless steel. She could see a cutlet bat, a red casserole dish, brownware dishes, wooden cutting board with inset blades, a crescent-shaped double-handed chopping knife, and a mortar and pestle.

"A playboy cook." He chuckled. "Get the woman to do the vegetables and set the table." He chuckled some more. "Yes, I cook, I cook a passable *coq au vin*—provincial style—actually I'm a peasant cook—love the primitive. You must let me cook dinner for you one night."

Whatever sort of cook you are, she thought, you're not a playboy.

"Oh," she said, "here I am at twenty-eight and have never cooked *coq au vin* in my life."

They sat there, he talked about cooking. She heard Bearnaise, Bordelaise, and vaguely listened while thinking about him, trying to get a feel for him. She was brought back to the conversation by him showing her a hand-written recipe book which she riffled through but could not concentrate on. A book, he told her, begun by his pioneer grandmother, which he had continued. It was in his handwriting, with great clarity—like one of his experiment reports. She saw the headings, Corn Fritter, Rye Bread, Wheat Cake.

"Another drink?"

"Oh yes," she said, looking at her glass, wanting another drink all right, "yes please."

Coming back from the kitchen, smiling, the host, "Would you like to hear a record or tape?"

He opened a large cabinet containing records and tapes.

"I'm a hi-fi fanatic," he said. "Constructed this set-up myself." And burbled on about sound reproduction as though switched on by the opening of the cabinet.

She went over and knelt beside him in front of the cabinet. "About five hundred records and as many tapes." He handed her a catalogue.

"Done by your last research assistant?" she said playfully—it was indexed under title, composer, and musician.

"Oh no," he said, "myself—all my own work."

"How impressive."

"Not really—clerical, simply clerical."

She couldn't think of a record—the choice was too great. "I can't think," she said. "You select something."

"A tape?" he said. "Let's see—Aboriginal music—actual field recording, how's that?"

"Field recording?"

"I was cook on a dig once."

"Dig? Cook?"

Her queries seemed imbecilic.

"Cook—sound recordist—pharmacist." He smiled at her. "I went with some of the Anthrop people—up North—fascinating—

actually managed to get a superb collection."

He put on a tape.

They settled back in their chairs. She didn't know whether one talked during the field recordings. "May I talk?" she whispered, childlike, above the scrape and clack of the music.

Although there seemed plenty to talk about she had nothing to say.

"When's your book coming out?" she said after a longish pause.

"Which one?" he asked.

"I thought there was only one—*Drugs and Body Chemistry*."

"Oh, August," he said, "but I have another book—poems—a slim volume."

"You write poems?" she said, almost disbelieving.

"Yes, I'm no Holub, but I have two slim volumes."

He went to the bookcase and pulled out a couple of books. He handed them to her, *Neutrons and Neurones—Poetic Explorations I—XII*, and *In Praise of the Epigamic—Collected Poems*. She opened them but her mind was still preoccupied with him and his atmosphere and she found she couldn't read. "I can't concentrate now," she said. "May I borrow them?"

"By all means," he said. "Better still," he jumped up, "let me present you with a copy of *Praise of Epigamic*."

"I love the title," she said, as he left the room.

He came back with a copy, autographed. He must have a stock of autographed copies for his lady visitors.

"But this one is different," she said, comparing it with the other, "it's a thicker and richer kind of paper."

"Yes, if you look closely you'll see the binding's different too."

She examined it.

"I hand-printed it, hand-cut the paper, and hand-bound it."

"You did it yourself?"

"Yes," he said without boast, "I have a friend who has a printery—he taught me the rudiments."

"But it's beautifully done," she said.

"Thank you," he said.

"Fancy writing your own poems and then setting about printing and binding the book!"

He laughed. "This will amuse you too," he said. "I mix my own inks."

"No!" she said, marvelling. She looked again at the ink and saw that it was a delicate strange brown. "Well," she said, "too much," and then felt that not enough and added, "I'm impressed once again."

"You shouldn't be," he said. "It's simply a matter of following a recipe—as it happens a fifteenth-century recipe."

"Fifteenth century!"

"Little more than lampblack, iron, manganese oxides, linseed oil—the early inks are fairly stable—although modern inks probably have greater longevity—we don't know of course," he grinned, "superior compounding. I had most of the copies done with modern inks."

"Oh."

"Want another little surprise?" he said, boyishly.

"I don't know whether I can stand it."

"The paper—I made it—even pulped my own wood—sulphite —although it's mainly macerated old rags."

"I'm flabbergasted."

They sat there for a few seconds in silence. She could think of a hundred banal questions about how and why but stubbornly resisted asking them, perversely—she didn't want to be an interviewer. To further compliment him would be embarrassing for both of them. For one thing she was running out of natural compliments.

He mended the conversation by saying, "Have some cheese." She took a piece.

"I suppose you made the cheese too," she said, chomping hard as she caught the sound of it—worried that it carried the implication he was a tiresome boaster or that she resented his accomplishments. She willed that it didn't sound that way. He didn't show any offence.

"I don't," he said; hesitated and smiled and said, "I do make cheese—it just so happens that it isn't mine."

Under her breath she said, oh no. She thought he might be joking and looked again at his face. He wasn't joking. He went to a board in his study containing carefully labelled keys and took down a key. "Come with me—I have some cheeses ripening."

He opened a three-quarter door under the stairway, switched on a light and, taking her hand, led her down the stone steps to the cellar.

"I hope I didn't sound offensive just then," she said, "about the cheese."

"About the cheese?" he said, puzzled.

"It doesn't matter," she said.

She loved the cellar. "This is a really authentic cellar—just how a cellar should be—stone steps, stone walls, cheeses ripening—oh, and racks of wine."

She didn't have to ask about the wine because she could see the bottling equipment and the wine press and stainless steel vats in a section at the far end.

"They're not cheeses," she said hesitantly, pointing at cylindrical moulds hanging from a frame.

"No, they're candles," he said. "I turn out my own—God knows why—both paraffin—stearic acid and tallow—I suppose it makes dinner party conversation.

"Here are my cheeses," he said, taking her to another part of the cellar, "still fairly green—that's Brick, sweetish type of cheese—and the rest are dull cheddars."

She didn't hear his description of the manufacture of cheese—she kept looking around and thinking, my God, he's buried his wife down here.

"I worry about tyrotoxicon—aptomaine—so far I'm still alive."

"It's rather cool down here," she said, moving towards the stairs. "Could we go up?" She didn't want to hear about the candles or the tyrotoxicon—she didn't want to be buried with his wife either. But she wasn't really scared; it was simply a game of nerves.

They went up the steps. He closed the cellar door, locked it, and switched off the light.

He still held her hand. How sweet, he liked it.

"I'd love a drink."

"Of course."

"Any other hobbies?" She wondered if "hobbies" was the correct word.

"Oh, I do a few other things to fill in the time," he said humorously.

Like strangling women. She laughed at herself.

He didn't offer to tell her what they were. But she knew she was obliged to ask although she felt she didn't really want to know. She might even enjoy saying something about herself—but there didn't seem anything to say—he was a hard act to follow. What else could she do?

She asked.

"For instance," he said, "I make my own furniture." She looked around and could see now that it was not factory furniture.

"How unobservant of me. Do you design it?"

"I design it—and also make the glues and the nails—I take the fact you didn't notice it as a compliment."

She looked at him.

"Did you say 'nails'?"

"The nails I made from iron ore—at a small foundry not far from here—a very low grade steel—but my own."

She must have had a why-for-Godsake look on her face.

He seemed to rush to tell her, "You see I like to follow a process right the way through—if it's a thing I eat, I want to grow it, harvest it, cure it or whatever. Usually it's not possible," he said disappointedly. "I have actually cut the timber for furniture—not this furniture—other pieces I've made..." He was scrutinising her and his voice was trailing as though he needed to be reassured that he didn't sound nutty.

"You don't think I'm..." he tapped his head.

She shook her head. "You made the mat then," she said, looking down at the coarse weave.

"Yes—that's a good case in point." He gathered new impetus. "I actually sheared the sheep, spun the wool, dyed the wool, made the dyes."

"What about the machines—the tools—and so on that you use to make things—do you make those too?" It sounded as though she were trying to catch him out.

"Ha! now you've got me—but I have made some simple tools—and I made a spinning wheel—but lathes, no, electric drills, no, saws, no."

"You didn't build the house," she said looking around, laughing, almost out of control, almost rudely.

"No, I didn't build the house, but..."

She interrupted him, "Let me guess—you could if you wanted to—you know how."

Modestly, quietly, as though he'd gone too far, he said, "Back in the States I built a four-room sod cabin using the techniques of the pioneers—up in the Pine Cat Range. It leaked."

His first joke. She laughed and let herself fall back on the settee. "Another drink, please," she said, holding out her glass—noting that she was drinking quickly.

"I didn't make the whisky," he said, grinning.

"But you did back in the States—in the sod cabin."

"No," he chuckled, obviously pleased with his humour, "it's illegal—all the same I do have a corn mash still under construction—out the back in the workshop."

She giggled and giggled, shaking her head. "No—please—excuse me," she said, choking, "I can't help laughing—with admiration."

He knelt in front of her in quick unexpected movement. She stopped laughing instantly. Holding their empty glasses still in his hands he put his head on her lap. She had stiffened. "You're a very attractive woman," he said. "I want very much to impress you."

"You have," she said, embarrassed, wanting him to get up, unsettled by his sudden seriousness, "you have impressed me—and you're a very attractive man," she said, wondering if in fact he was, and sorry she couldn't do better than directly return his compliment, "a very attractive man."

She sensed he felt it time to make advances and to move towards sex.

"Will we take our drinks into the bedroom?" she said softly, trying to make it smooth—and in a way, to get it over with. She was as ready as she'd ever be.

He looked into her eyes, "I want to make a request."

She readied herself.

"I hope you have no objections," he said, perhaps fearfully but certainly determined to ask it, "and I hope you don't find it insulting."

"What is it?" she almost shouted.

Still staring into her eyes he said, "Would you take a bath with me?"

The request wasn't as odd as she'd feared. It was his possible motive which perturbed her—he was going to drown her and bury her with his wife.

"I don't mind," she answered, a little unsteadily. "Why?"

"I'm glad you will," he said, relieved. "I know it sounds a queer deal—but—I like to begin from the beginning."

"Oh."

"Are you with me?"

"More or less." Less than more.

He began to talk very quickly, trying to convince. "A bath is a symbolic beginning—a rebirth, so as to speak—we remove all connection with the everyday world—our clothes—and we wash away the traces."

He looked intently at her. "Odd?"

"I can follow you," she said, noncommittally.

He coloured. "I know it sounds odd."

"Oh no," she said, lying, but emotionally spellbound by the gregarious pipe-smoking associate professor from MIT on his knees struggling to gain her approval, captured briefly by his mesh of theories and practices. "It's just different," she added, for honesty.

"Good," he said, rising to his feet and guiding her up. "First, a taste of my wine—light red."

"Yes, I saw the equipment down in the cellar."

"I don't grow my own grapes—I buy them." They went to the kitchen. "I like to finish the evening with something of my own. Simple vanity."

In the kitchen he took down two wine glasses and took a bottle of red wine from a rack.

"The glasses!" she exclaimed, "of course—the glasses—they're home made—you made them."

"Yes, I blew them," he said.

He led her then into the bathroom. It was large with a large almost square, almost Roman, bath—which could hold at least two people. "Why, this bathroom is fantastic," she said.

"I didn't make the tiles but I did design it," he said. "I very much wanted to build it—but really the only thing of mine is the towels."

He turned on the taps.

He coughed. "Could I take your clothes?"

"Oh yes," she said, swallowing the unnaturalness. She stripped. He stripped along with her.

He took her clothes and his and went out. He was going to burn them and keep her prisoner, she thought—or more likely he was going to fumigate them. Or do something kinky with her underwear.

He came back. "I use the tallow for both candles and soap," he said, handing her a cake of yellow-brown soap, almost larger than her hand, "coconut oil—resin—the usual phosphates—and the rest—common household formula. I faintly odourised it with lavender and cassia."

She smelt it. "It smells positively caustic," she said, the cavernous bathroom making her sound like a small girl.

She felt bizarre standing beside the nude forty-year-old American professor, his hand on her arse, holding a cake of handmade soap. It made her think of Nazi prison camps.

"Shall we bathe?" He tried the water. "It's OK." They both went into the bath. He began to scrub her with the soap, quite hard. She simply sat there in a half slump. She did as she was told. He washed her as though she were a little girl—between the legs and under the armpits.

"Your hair, too," he said.

"My hair?"

"Just put it under the water, the soap makes an excellent shampoo." She wasn't so sure. She wasn't so sure about putting her head under the water with his hand on her neck.

She braced herself for a life or death struggle.

But he was gentle—and practised.

He complimented her on her body.

"Thank you," she said, aroused in a way by his scrubbing touch and his strong intention—aware that he knew precisely what he wanted to do with her and intended doing it.

After drying her with a coarse handwoven towel he took her upstairs to the bedroom where they lay down on the wide bed which she could see was hewn from logs. He lit a small oil lamp beside the bed. Her damp hair made her slightly uncomfortable.

She was relieved to see her clothes in the room—carefully folded and hung.

"Do you have trouble with orgasm?" he asked, softly.

God. She lay there irritated, without answering, disliking the question.

"I suppose not," she said, thinking that she'd never had to worry much about it.

"I mean do you take long? Should I wait for you?"

Not only was she embarrassed, she was affronted—did he have a questionnaire?—"I really don't know," she said. "I haven't timed myself." A little nastily.

"I don't mean to be embarrassing," he said, apologetically, "but I always think it's best to get these things out—out of the way."

He was stroking her legs with his hand and feeling her breast.

"You tell me when you're ready to climax," he said. "I'll wait for you."

She didn't speak. His strong sense of intention had frayed into a desperate effort to please. She was turned off.

"All right?" he asked.

"Yes," she said, closing her eyes, resigned to enduring it.

"Do you like breast stimulation?"

She didn't answer.

They fucked, she didn't relax and faked climax, telling him by sounds, she hoped, that she'd finished, although he kept saying, "You right? you right? you finished?" and to stop him she nodded and then he whispered, "That was great—was it great for you?"

She again nodded, keeping her eyes shut, and reaching blindly for cigarettes she'd put beside the bed.

He chattered for a while about the nature of orgasm; sexual difficulty; being candid about sex; and how few men and women knew women had orgasms. She didn't comment. She wondered how many women had lied to him about himself and about their reaction to him. What could you do?

She stubbed out her cigarette, feeling bad, and feigned sleep.

She was awoken in the morning by him doing his exercises on parallel bars at the far end of the room. He didn't say a word or smile or wink but kept solidly on. She watched him from the bed, dying for a cup of coffee.

When he finished he came over panting and sat on the edge of the bed. "Started," he panted, "on the 5BX—Canadian Air Force—have developed—my own—programme—a hybrid of yoga and Scandinavian gymnastics."

From a drawer beside the bed he took a book containing hand drawings of various exercise positions and tables—all lettered in his handwriting. "That's my programme," he said.

She could think only of coffee. "I don't even exercise—let alone have my own programme," she said. "I'm basically unhealthy," she said with barely concealed hostility.

He went to the kitchen and returned with herbal tea and meal porridge, hand ground—"See if you like these," he said.

She left half of both.

And as she smoked her second cigarette he said, "Well, how do you feel," anxiously, and she saw that the question was directed at her psyche, health, and mood all at once. As though he was saying, "How was I?"

"Oh, great," she said, not wanting to give any sort of analysis of the evening, not wanting to deceive him any more than she had to.

She washed with the home-made soap she now found repugnant, and dressed. They walked through the garden of the house.

"Would you have time to look at my observatory?" He pointed to a dome structure at the back.

"No, must rush, really, some other time," she said.

"Then there will be another time?" he said.

She'd trapped herself. "I do have a regular sort of thing with a boy," she said, as a way out, smiling.

"Then there won't be another time," he said, logically.

"Let's leave it to chance."

They walked for a distance without speaking.

"Do you find me a bore?" he asked.

She went on guard. She did. But what could you say?

"But you're a very interesting man," she said, "a very accomplished man."

"My wife—just after we separated—said to me, 'The trouble with you, Hugo—you're a damned bore!'"

"That was a fairly destructive thing to say."

"It gave me a devastating insight—I was a damned bore."

She went to her bag for a cigarette.

"Her words are forever inscribed on my mind as a warning—and it permitted me to correct the fault—in your words I made myself, 'an interesting man'."

They reached the gate.

The first personal statement made during the whole overnight visit or the months, in fact, that she'd worked with him. She had to get out before she felt she had to be honest with him. She had her own problems.

She kissed him on the cheek and said, "You are—you are a very interesting man—you must be a very fulfilled man." It sounded so formal. Too bad.

"But one needs more than that, one needs more, one needs a woman—about the place," he said, hopelessly, pleadingly, not only to her, perhaps not to her at all, but to all damn womanhood.

She nodded sympathetically. "I really must rush," she said. "I must be off. I must rush."

The Coca-Cola kid

"I DON'T know why we're here," she said.

They slammed the Citroen doors in unison.

"You know why we're here," he said.

They walked across the lawn to the door of the Yacht Club. She didn't answer so he answered for her " . . . to meet the enemy," he said, as they went from the chirping country darkness into the rattle.

The Young Liberals were not yet drunk. A few couples had begun to dance but were not yet loose. All the poker machines were in use. The band was playing—staring out, in a trance, to the private world of dance musicians. The stewards swayed with trays of drinks, rushing with a professional slowness. The dance music and intermittent slugging of the poker machines filled the crevices between conversations.

They left their coats at the door.

"Perhaps I should've worn a dinner suit," he said, not meaning it. Trying to fill the dull emptiness between him and his wife.

"Only a few're in dinner suits," she said.

He knew why they were there. They were there because they were bored and lonely in a town where they hardly knew anyone—let alone enough people to pick and choose politically. The town didn't even have a Communist Party.

He looked for a drink, to ease himself into the ill-fitting situation. A shoehorn drink.

He stopped a steward with one hand and turning to his wife

said, "What'll you have?"

"Beer," she said.

He wanted to throw a few down fast.

"There's Kevin and Gwen," she said, pointing her beer across the dance floor.

"The revolutionaries made it," Kevin said, greeting them.

"We're waiting to be thrown out," he said.

"Please—no politics tonight," Kevin said laughing. "Remember I arranged the invitation."

Kevin introduced them to another couple. They talked. Then he danced with Sylvia. "Now you've brought us here, at least be agreeable," she said to him. He felt as soon as she said it that the party was a mistake.

After the dance he drifted off and lost four dollars on the poker machines and resented it.

"I warned you to limit yourself to two dollars," his wife said when he drifted back to where Kevin, Gwen and she were seated around a jug of beer.

He wasn't looking for chastisement. He glanced at her but didn't retort.

He began an aggressive talk with Percival who was on the executive of the group—one of the political ones.

"I agree," said Percival. "Take the farms away from those who mismanage them."

His aggression was seeped away by the agreement.

"I'm pleased you agree," he said, not meaning it, with it sounding so agreeable that it disgusted him. He was caught in polite conversation. He wanted to be disagreeable. He wanted to demonstrate where he stood, who he was. He wasn't one of them.

He caught his wife's expression which said, "Must you talk politics?" and looked away.

He stood up and left the table. He was alone again. He resisted the temptation to go back to the poker machines. But he didn't want the small talk of the table. He didn't want the bitchiness of his wife. He stood alone, a hand in his pocket, drinking too fast.

He went to the balcony of the club. It was then that he met the American.

He was standing alone leaning against a wall, drink in his hand, bow-tied, looking across the water. He turned and acknowledged him with his eyes and raised his glass in salute, saying in a slightly slurred American accent.

"*I must go down to the seas again to the lonely sea and the sky.
All I ask is a tall ship and a star to steer her by.*"

A smile squeezed out of him involuntarily as he heard the American's recitation—it disarmed him.

"And furthermore, buddy, I know the last stanza too," the American said,

"*Must go down to the seas again to the vagrant gypsy*...da da dah da dah...*and all I ask is a merry yarn from a laughing fellow rover.*" The American seemed to falter, paused, and then continued, "*and a quiet sleep and a sweet dream when the long trick's over.*"

The American's face then sagged, sadly. He drank from his glass, his hand wrapped around it in a tight grip.

He said to the American, "I thought only Australian and British kids learned Masefield."

"I learned Masefield, buddy, I learned Masefield." His face tightened up again for performance,

"*I'm going to be a pirate with a bright brass pivot gun,
And an island in the Spanish Main beyond the setting sun.*"

"I don't know that one."

"The Tarry Buccaneer," he said, "The Tarry Buccaneer."

He lapsed again.

"Do you sail?" he asked the American, again writhing against the compulsion to be "sociable".

"I fly," the American said, and then in a formal voice, "So you'd like to be a pirate with a big brass pivot gun—come in, sit down—do you smoke?—no, have one of mine—I think we can find you a suitable position—provided of course that you have the requisite qualifications—have you a brass pivot gun?" It was a meandering performance for the American's private amusement.

Then the American turned to him as though he had remembered his presence and became genial. "My name's Becker—Atlanta—the Coca-Cola kid from Coca-Cola City."

They shook hands heavily and overlong like two drunks. "How do you mean Coca-Cola kid?"

"I'm the Coca-Cola kid—Coca-Cola—work for Coca-Cola—here from the parent company."

His resistance to Becker grouped instantly, his sociability

strong-armed out of the way. An enemy.

"Out here to rot some teeth," he said, softening it only mildly with a quarter smile, glad at last to be critical, although aware of the effort it took to be unpleasant against the mood.

Becker smiled, puzzled, and seemed to fumble to make out the true nature of the remark, as though only hazily aware that it was not just facetious.

He wished he'd been able to say something that let Becker know he'd met the unexpected—that he was face to face with a radical.

"Hey, hey, hey," Becker said, coming to a realisation, almost singing, "what have we here—an enemy of Coca-Cola?"

"I guess I am," he said, trying to be firm—it wasn't exactly how he'd seen himself—"among other things."

Becker shook his head with disbelief. "Could not be—could not be—the enemies of Coca-Cola have all been liquidated—Atlanta had them all liquidated."

He didn't smile at the humour.

"How could you talk about the Holy Water like that?" Becker said. "Why, we made a profit of eighty-nine million dollars last year—why, baby, the whole world drinks Coca-Cola."

"A few million people can't be wrong," he said, coldly.

"A few million? Baby, ninety-five million people drink Coke every single day—you saying people don't know what they like?"

Becker saw a steward. "Steward, my good man—" he turned to him and asked what he was drinking and then ordered.

"Why, Coca-Cola," Becker went on, "is an everyday word in every language—it's in the dictionaries."

"Truck drivers wash their engine parts in it to eat away the grease," he said, "and stomach linings and teeth..." He wanted to say something about economic priorities.

"Their parts?—I wash my parts in it too. Don't tell me the one about the tooth dissolving overnight in a glass of Coke—I don't want to hear that one." He shook his head. The steward came back with the drinks.

"What do you do for the good of the world, Kim boy?" Becker drank deeply.

"I'm a teacher," he said, feeling a certain virtue.

"Yes," Becker said, looking out to sea, "you teach good habits, I teach the bad."

"If that's the way you feel," he said, seizing the point, "why don't you get out?"

Becker turned back with a grin. "Hell, I'm not serious—I like Coke—hell!"

He blushed at having failed to see Becker's flippancy.

"Now look—" Becker said, with a loud selling voice, "you might give kids a lot of good ideas but you give them a lot of God-almighty crap too—I just push a good soft drink—the best as it so happens—nothing more, nothing less."

"But the waste of it all." He moved on to the line he wanted to argue. "The waste of resources when they could be used for food. Socially desirable ends."

"I notice you spending a few damn dollars on social undesirables," Becker said, clinking their glasses to make his point.

"Personal charity is no answer."

"Stop." Becker held up his hand in a halt sign. "Stop—the game's over. I'm here to get drunk, not to sell Coca-Cola or debate the world."

He wondered if he'd scored against Becker. It was typical of people like Becker that they could switch off matters of conscience.

Becker had gone for more drinks.

He came back. "I'm going to be a pirate with a bright brass pivot gun." Gracefully Becker presented the drink. "I want to tell you a secret." Becker sounded drunk. "I don't want to be the Coca-Cola kid," he shook his head, "I want to be a jazz pirate."

"Jazz pirate?"

"Jazz pianist—jazz penis," Becker said.

"Why don't you?" he asked without interest. Becker was obviously not going to talk seriously.

"They don't have jazz penises any more—not any more." He waved his drink around. "I practised every day—I wrote for lessons—filled in a coupon back of a comic book."

At first he thought Becker was rambling on with nonsense but realised he wasn't altogether joking. He looked at him with slightly more sympathy, although jazz pianists weren't actually in the vanguard of social reform. Decadent white jazz.

He stood there to finish the drink with Becker, who didn't say any more. He seemed to be conversing with his own thoughts.

He found himself with nothing to say either and stood for a second rebelliously uncomfortable—stymied—unable to engage

127

Becker. Then he wandered off, with a glance at Becker, who wasn't looking and appeared not to notice.

He saw his wife dancing with Kevin. They weren't aware he was watching. He felt as if he were spying. He was spying—but his wife was innocently serious and there was a quite proper distance between them. They were talking more than dancing. He joined them when the dance finished.

"Where've you been?" his wife queried.

"Talking to an American—the Coca-Cola Kid."

"What's he doing here?"

"Reciting Masefield."

Her face expressed irritation and she turned to Kevin, obviously with no intention of forcing her way through his enigmatic answers. He didn't care to help.

Most people were on the way to being drunk. The poker machines were rattling faster. The dancing was full of sex.

"Enjoying it?" he heard his wife say politely to him as though she felt it necessary to say something to link herself with him, perhaps as a conciliatory offer. He recognised it as a move to end the bad day they'd been having together.

"What can you expect from the sons and daughters of graziers and Coca-Cola executives?" he said, matching the effort of her wifely question with a husbandly tone. But it really didn't dissolve the bad feeling between them. Somehow he didn't care, somehow he preferred the bad feeling.

Later he went to the lavatory. In the lavatory standing side by side at the urinal he heard two young men talking about skiing. "She had the bottom part of her leg in plaster, you see," one said, and the other laughed.

He felt distaste and resentment. Because of their exclusiveness.

He decided to look at the other rooms of the club. Along a corridor he heard piano playing. Sloppy piano playing. He followed the sound into a small carpeted room with glass cases containing a few books fallen like dominoes. A few dusty trophies. Over in the far corner in the half light Becker was playing the piano, his drink on the piano seat beside him.

He felt obliged to say something now he'd entered the room.

"Practising for that job as jazz pianist?" he said.

Becker looked at him but didn't say anything. He kept on playing, slopping his head with the tune. His bow tie seemed to fit the part.

He stood and listened. He realised that Becker wasn't going to talk while he was playing. He drifted over to the books—yachting records. Joshua Slocum. Peter Heaton.

Becker stopped playing and drank from his glass.
"What do you know about jazz, Mr Teacher?"
"Very little—the Negro struggle..."
Becker didn't say anything in reply.
He felt dismissed. He felt he'd been assessed and dismissed.
Becker began to play again.

He stood there half listening to the playing, but Becker's eyes didn't return to him, didn't further acknowledge his presence. Becker sang in a deep imitation of a negroid voice, snatches of song, but not for him, not for any audience. Occasionally Becker would look in his direction but not at him.

He became aware of his own body, his feet, legs, torso, hands, arms, neck and head, standing there in an upright position on a floor, in a club, in a town, on an orbiting planet—standing in stark isolation as the world orbited the sun. He didn't belong with Becker's playing. He didn't belong with the trophies. Or with the crowd outside. Even his wife—he was not in contact with his wife.

He listened to the playing but always thoughts about himself pushed in between him and the music. Not that the music was easy to listen to. It broke and fumbled with Becker doggedly retracing his fumbling.

He stood there, not having the urge to do anything else but stand. Realising himself unacknowledged by anyone.

His thoughts were not anything more than pings of discomfort and a rasping uneasiness. He desperately wanted to be pleased with himself. Standing at the Yacht Club with Young Liberals dancing around him, out of place, argumentatively drunk and no one to argue with. He felt distinctly displeased with himself.

He wanted to assert himself with Becker. With Becker especially. Because he was American. For some reason he felt free to say anything to Becker, no holds barred. But Becker had eluded him. He could not snare Becker.

Becker's and his eyes met. Becker held the stare and sang at him and then looked back to the keys. Becker had sung the song against him.

He felt he had to go. Again he didn't know whether to try to indicate goodbye to Becker. He watched for an opportunity but it didn't come and the playing stopped him from saying anything.

He gave a slight shrug and left the room.

Just outside the door he heard Becker say, "I didn't want to be a jazz pianist. Or a brass pivot gun. Because I'm the Coca-Cola Kid."

He stopped. So Becker had been aware of him. But nothing came to his mind to say to Becker. Despite an aggressiveness the statement was full of some sort of appeal. It deflected attack. But he couldn't respond because its special appeal was too subtle, and he was too blurred with drink. He was opposed to Becker, but he wasn't game enough to risk being wrong or embarrassed with Becker. So he walked on. Becker would think he hadn't heard.

Out in the bright noise he was able to merge with the crowd and did not feel as intensely isolated.

He played another dollar in the poker machines and won sixty cents.

He wasn't socially acceptable or socially adroit and he didn't claim to be or try to be. So what? There was something phony about a "good mixer"—a good mixer had to smother his real reactions. He didn't have time for niceties or phoniness. Other things were more important.

After a while he moved back to his wife and the others. They chatted.

His wife said, "You've been great company tonight." The wound opened again.

Then the band played the anthem. He hadn't realised it was so late.

"Have a drink for the road," Kevin said, "if you're in our party." Friendly sarcasm.

"Where have you been all this time?" his wife said, annoyed.

"Looking over the club—listening to the American playing the piano."

"The mythical American—was he reciting Kipling again?"

"Masefield."

"Why didn't you bring him over if he was so captivating?"

"He was drunk."

"You're *not?*"

The crowd was a criss-cross of unravelling knots. The band was shaking spittle from their instruments, unscrewing mouthpieces.

A sudden movement attracted his eyes. A young man in a dinner suit with thick blond hair had changed from a party-goer into an official. He was walking urgently through the crowd with a steward. They went through the doorway to the men's lavatory. Outside in the hall, on the edge of the unravelling crowd, a couple of stewards had taken off their bow ties and they were stacking chairs.

Kevin came over with the drinks and as he handed them around he said, "A fellow tried to hang himself in the men's—they cut him down in time."

He sensed it was the American and tightened.

His wife said, "He's still alive?"

"Yes—just—an American—" Kevin turned to him. "Must be your American."

"The Coca-Cola Kid—Becker." He was galvanised. For the first time that night he felt lifted out of his isolated preoccupation.

"The one you were talking to?" his wife said, her voice loud with the shock of it.

"He was playing the piano about half an hour ago—I was listening to him."

The crowd had smelt the event and were looking towards the lavatory. Murmuring questions.

"He was blue in the face," Kevin said. "They're rushing him to hospital. A steward told me he was quite a mess when they cut him down."

They drank their last drinks watching the lavatory but the American was not carried out.

"Must have taken him out the back way," Kevin said.

"He told me Coca-Cola was a common noun," he told them, and being English teachers they smiled.

They moved towards the door. "He didn't seem suicidal—just drunk," he told them.

Outside they separated from Kevin and Gwen. He said to his wife, "Seemed just another genial American," and then added, "the man who presses the bomb release, lynches the Negro, drops the napalm is just another genial American—good fun at cocktail parties."

His wife didn't comment.

As he started the car he said, "I suppose working for Coca-Cola would be enough to make you want to kill yourself."

"Come off it," his wife said, irritably.

"A victim of a personality destroying system," he said, niggling her.

131

"Must you always be so doctrinaire?"

"I hope he dies," he said, goaded further, driving hard over the cattle grid at the gate.

"Kim!" she turned towards him, "don't be so heartless."

"You're getting soft," he said. "How many Asians starve to death so the Americans can drink Coca-Cola?"

He swung hard but hit a bad bump.

An empty bottle on the floor of the car rolled wildly under their feet.

"Do you want me to drive?" she said, slightingly.

He ignored it.

"Things aren't as simple as you sometimes see them," she said. Then, lighting a cigarette, she laughed derisively. "You'd have fainted if they'd carried the body out."

"Lenin never watched executions," he said, accelerating on the straight road towards the scattered light of the town.

He saw her snort and look out her window across the corn fields, turning completely away from him.

Soft drink and the distribution of soft drink

"BECKER?
 "Becker?
 "Becker?
 "Becker!
 "Becker!"
Becker heard his name, heard the voice of Terri, heard the coin tapping like a blindman on the window of his motel room, felt his sleep decamping. He opened his eyes, and yes, saw Terri peering through the window into the darkened room. Sweating, he was left, high, wide and awake by his fleeing afternoon sleep.
 "Becker, it's me, Terri."
 "Now what the hell!" he cried, irritably. Becker, in his undershorts, lumbered up and went to the window.
 "Let me in."
 "Terri, now listen, what is this?"
 They faced each other through the glass. Terri tapped at it with the coin. Becker opened the window. Terri swung a leg over the sill and entered, jeans, Women's Liberation tee shirt, barefoot.
 "Didn't you hear me knocking on the door?"
 "No, I was asleep." He had heard the knocking but had chosen to sleep.
 "Knocked for ages."
 "Yes, all right, I did hear but I chose not to answer."
 "American directness. Why are you sleeping at this time of the day?"
 "Terri, what are you doing here?"

She went to the dressing table and examined his toiletries, his aftershave. She tossed them one by one into the wastepaper bin.

"Why are you sleeping in the afternoon?"

As if he didn't have sufficient headache and ulcer with the seminar itself.

"Terri, what are you doing here?" he demanded, picking up the toiletries from the waste paper bin.

"I came down to listen to the pollution."

Becker sat down tiredly, reaching for his Old Crow under the bed and took a swig, rinsed his mouth, and spat into the garden.

"I really came to see you."

Why him? He took another swig and swallowed.

"Do you usually drink so heavily?" she said, condemnatorily. "John Barleycorn must die."

"I'm not drinking heavily, I am simply bringing myself around. Care for a drink?" he proffered the bottle without overmuch grace.

"No—I'm off alcohol."

He poured himself a slug and added ice from the polyurethane cooler.

"I really came to see you because you haven't been in the office and things were so hung up between us when you came to my place. And that telephone call! I want to know you!"

"Look at my personnel record, and furthermore I'm working —not socialising."

Terri sat on the bed, rolled on to her back and reclined.

"Be my guest," Becker said grumpily, head hanging towards his knees.

"I'm attracted to you—madly—isn't that typical? You're madly attracted to someone and everything fouls up every time you try to express it." She was cheerfully resigned.

"Now looky—you have lately come from a psychiatric clinic— you have this drug thing—you're all screwed up—you admit that yourself—you could hardly, really, seriously say you're ready for a...ah...straight...normal...association—and furthermore Coca-Cola don't like their executives fraternising with female staff and furthermore you scare me—you scare the very hell out of me, and furthermore I want no complications. No complications."

"I think you're fighting yourself. Furthermore I'm just a casual typist not permanently working for Coca-Cola—and furthermore you find me physically attractive but you're resisting it."

He had to admit it.

"Well, take me."

"Now, Terri..."

He closed his eyes, "Terri, please go away."

"Is that what you really want? I'll forget I'm in Women's Liberation—just go ahead and use me, take me."

Becker gave his thirsty soul a drink of Old Crow.

"Go on—fuck me. Then I'll go away if you want."

She scored highly on audacity.

He wavered. He was not a man over strongly disciplined by moral restraint. He was not Baptist. He was, he considered, inclined to lust. *Inclined*—it was more a capsize than an inclination. It would be his downfall. It would rob him of his slice of the cake. Sam wouldn't suffer from lust. Sam had will. Sam was married, though he'd heard it said that lust couldn't be contained, that it always overflowed its container. There was something generous about lust. Lord Rochester. The rot had started with his reading Rochester. That weirdo English teacher back in Atlanta had done it. The inclination and capsize had started there. That had been the end of the Baptist.

She was unzipping her jeans.

"I knew you were attracted to me—I could tell. Usually, I'm all shy, twitching with it, but with you I knew."

He looked at her. She arched her backside and pulled her jeans and pants down—he pulled them from the ankles. She sat up and bending forward pulled off the Women's Liberation tee shirt. Naked, she was of excellent figure.

He took off his undershorts—"let's get this job done"—and rolled on to the bed.

For simplicity, directness, and lust, Becker thought, it was hard to beat.

Becker had once, and only once, read an obscene New York newspaper called the *National Expose*. There was something from that paper which described a girl and a dog. It had stayed in his mind. It went something like this: "He was very sensitive like a human being (Becker liked that). We talked to each other. He understood me with his eyes. He'd lick my breasts and then look at me to see if I liked it. Then down on my belly and look up again to see if it was all right. Just like he was human. Then he was at my side licking it. I just reached over... it was already out of its sheath and I began to play with him...just like I would a man and then he started to mount me."

Out the front of the lecture room the man from the Department of Agriculture who looked like a dog was licking down the belly of the audience, pausing for signs of delight, and then continuing his passionate talk about pollution and its effect on animals.

Becker was thinking what a crazy way to promote soft drink—here Coca-Cola was putting up good money for a bunch of earnest people to feel better because they sat through five talks on pollution. I feel better myself, thought Becker, but not that much better.

Terri was sitting beside him reeking of lust, having bluntly refused to shower. She'd accused him of taking "American showers". She'd mocked him for over-showering, especially after sex.

He'd yelled at her, "If you won't do it for personal hygiene—do it for the cause of air pollution." She'd laughed.

If everyone in the village kept their stoop clean, the whole village would be clean, thought Becker, recalling his grandmother.

He didn't see this seminar as the way he wanted to go about selling Coca-Cola. He liked the direct approach of good, old, honest selling.

Display.

Availability.

A strong single product.

Pollution, it occurred to him, was probably all to do with self-destruction. We're all in that business. We pollute ourselves, Goddam. That semester of existentialism had done him no good. People wanted health but all the time they did unhealthy things. The unhealthy was always a better proposition. Why was that? Terri was unhealthy and uncontrollable. He liked a little control. He liked a lot of control. Terri was, to be precise, a kook. She was a persistent kook. She was, like unhealthy things, a desirable package. She was a plastic bomb.

He preferred control yet so often he was flung into the oily whirlpool. There was a question. Why did he consort with pollution? Why did he skirt the odorous abyss so perilously?

At the conclusion of the session the chairman said, "And we'd like to thank Coca-Cola for making this seminar possible."

It sounded as if had Coca-Cola not existed there would have been no pollution.

And then the chairman invited Becker to come forward on behalf of Coca-Cola.

They expected dollars, not words, to come from his big American mouth. That was all right by him. That was what it was all about.

"All over the world," Becker began, "the Coca-Cola company has been pointed at as meaning...ah...nasty American...bad teeth of the children..." Some laughter. Laughter is the best medicine "...up in Asia you get students even burning down the plant...and they cry 'American Imperialism'...and so on...all that...I want you just to think for a second what Coca-Cola is...it's a beverage...a simple Goddam soft drink...it's not a Sherman...a napalm bomb...it's not a damn political system... Goddam, it's a soft drink."

Becker pulled himself up. "To conclude, my grandmother used to say if everyone in the village kept their stoop clean, the whole village would be clean."

Clapping.

He was about to return to his seat, having turned smiling to the chairman, when the guy shouted—not shouted, said with oratorial boom—"Coca-Cola, sir, pollutes the blood."

People screwed around in the seats to look at the speaker.

"Our vegetarian friend," the chairman whispered, smiling, and then said to the audience, "Well, that closes our seminar and I'd like to thank you for your attendance."

"Pollution of the blood."

Becker tried to pretend it wasn't happening, not the troublemaker, not the audience buzz, not their expectant looks, not anything.

"Well, that closes this seminar. If there are no further questions, we hope that it has given you food for thought."

"I said, sir, pollution of the blood."

Becker looked at the man.

"Perhaps the gentleman from Coca-Cola would be so kind as to answer me this...."

"I'm sorry," the chairman said, smiling, placating, "the seminar is closed."

"Pollution of the blood stream, sir."

"I'm afraid that closes the seminar," the chairman said, trying to give finality to the situation by gathering his papers.

"Eat only the foods of the earth," the vegetarian said.

"Oh shut up," Terri cried from the body of the hall, "shut up, you stupid man."

Becker was surprised and warmed by her support. He was not accustomed to support.

"Pollution of the blood."

Unnecessarily the chairman said, "Thank you" again, coloured, and left the rostrum.

Before Becker could move from the rostrum the chairman had scurried away, and the people, deciding there was to be no clash, emptied out.

Becker, in his crumpled white suit, was left standing before the empty lecture hall. They sure knew how to empty a hall.

A great note. A great note to end on. Wait till Sam heard.

Terri came to his side.

"I was going to punch him," she said.

Becker, thumbs in his braces like a country sheriff, hummed "Sweet Georgia Brown", to calm himself.

A great note, all right, to end on.

"Can I come to the party with you?"

"I can't guarantee you'll be at ease," Becker told Terri.

"Coca-Cola people?"

"No—people I've met through business."

"Business people?"

"Business people."

She sat quietly as they drove back from the seminar.

"Will they mind me without shoes and in jeans?"

"No—couldn't imagine any objection—it's a casual poolside party."

"They'll be expensively dressed."

"Uh uh."

More quiet.

Becker also remarked to himself that they would also not be heavy with the odour of lust and spent sex.

"Do you want me to come?"

Becker hesitated. "I can state quite straightly that I don't see you fitting in very well—that doesn't worry me if it doesn't worry you." In truth it worried all hell out of him.

"Well, I'll come then."

"As you wish."

They drove.

"What's a soda?"

"How do you mean—what's a soda?"

"You hear Americans in films ordering sodas."

Becker spoke sadly, softly, "Good sodas are a rare and dying commodity—not many around who can throw together a good soda."

"What are they?" she repeated.

"Firstly, the glass must be chilled—some guys just use the glass direct from the wash and it's hot—the syrup must be chilled, the water must be chilled...a soda is a very cold drink...it's designed as a very cold, cold drink...one scoop of cream...just one...not fluid milk or whipped cream...just cream...the ice cream and the syrup are mixed in with a jet of soda and then you fill the glass with soda and mix it with a few sharp squirts, so." Becker imitated and gave squirting noises, "That's a soda. Aren't many guys around who can mix a good soda."

Talking about sodas made Becker aware that he was a long way from old Atlanta, Georgia, and the action.

Terri considered it for a while and then said, "Why do you know so much about sodas?"

"It's my business—it's my business to know about drinks."

"Do you know what a 'red' is?"

Becker thought, "You've got me."

"It's the drink the kids are mad about in hotels—when their parents take them to pubs—it's lemonade and grenadine—and a straw. It looks grownup."

Becker chuckled. "I like that," he said. "Do you know what grenadine is?"

Terri shook her head.

"French cordial—made from pomegranate fruit."

At the party Terri and Becker took their drinks and smiled.

Becker thought, Terri, to her credit, was trying. Barefoot, jeans, and Women's Liberation tee shirt and stinking of sex, she needed to try. However, she didn't appear as dishabille as he had privately worried she might.

The house bared itself to the sea and cradled a swimming pool.

A white-coated chef cooked silently at a barbecue surrounded by drunken noise.

Becker was then approached by the one overdressed woman at

the party who by her overdressed presence threw Terri into relaxed and appropriate contrast.

"Oh, you're the American," the woman said, a matronly marcasite brooch tied in a knot on her breast. "Oh, you're *the* American."

She sat down beside them. "I adore American fashions."

"Are you in the fashion business?" Becker guessed, finding it difficult to believe from her appearance.

"I'm about to make a triumphant return from ten years buried in the graveyard of suburban martyrdom."

She'd said that before, Becker could tell. He observed, on the other side of his brain, a comfort from the pressure of Terri's nonconformist denim leg against his.

"I feel that the fashions have turned the full circle and caught me up—it's back to me—I'm a fashion commentator by profession —these maxis are so feminine, definitely me," she said, overloudly for confidence, drinking her brandy crusta.

"I suppose you're delightfully uncaring about dress," the ex-fashion commentator pelted at Terri, glancing up and down the jeans.

"I'm turned on by Indian styles," Terri said, ever-so-politely.

"Oh really, how fascinating," the woman said, with the emphasis which Becker observed began with unfelt enthusiasm and died immediately to intentional uninterest.

"And what burning cause does the tee shirt represent?" the ex-fashion commentator asked, as they were joined by another lady.

Becker knew that Terri would break. Becker knew he had goofed in bringing her. This was no place for kooks. His mistake.

"Women's Lib," she said. "Women's Liberation."

Becker wasn't sure what Women's Liberation were on about. He remembered something from *Time*. But he knew this—it was giving the two ladies an instant pain in the gut. He sensed that for a discussion topic it had a dangerous wail about it.

"Oh, the men haters," the second lady said. "Why, darling? Why do you hate men?"

"You were just complaining about housewives in suburbia," Terri pointed out to the ex-fashion commentator, "and I only hate some men," she said to the other with bare politeness, "and a lot of women," she added, "especially those who do dirt on their sex."

Oh oh, here we go. Inside himself. Becker whistled a hymn of deliverance, as he watched the personalities take a collision course.

"Oh, you resent ladies who love their husbands and their families?" the ex-fashion commentator said.

"Yes," Terri said loudly as they met in collision, "I'm a man-hating, bra-burning, lesbian member of the castration brigade. My mind's between my legs because it suits men to keep me in underpaid mentally unfulfilling jobs, make women have backyard abortions, fuck them without caring if they like it. You women stink and your men stink—from their mother-fucking socks to their short back and sides, from their piss-stained jockstraps to their Apex badges. All power to every woman who's been put down and fucked over and I'm going to tell every man who does—to go suck his own cock and to every woman who submits—go lie in their own shit."

It was a speedy speech, similar, Becker imagined, to being thrown through a plate-glass window. He stared deeply down into his empty glass wanting to be huddled there at the bottom. He looked up and thought the two women had lost their face muscles. Then one laughed, a squeezed-out little laugh, and said, "Really? Oh there's Jenny—I must go over."

The other said, "I must go to the little girl's room," and then hearing her expression and guessing that it was probably a liberation crime, laughed neurotically and left Becker standing with Terri and their empty glasses.

Becker knew one thing. The party was, for them, over.

Close to tears, Terri said, "I'm sorry—well, they asked for it. Women's Liberation is not a big thing for me at all—they asked for it, that's all. I got it all from Kate Jennings."

"It's been quite a day, quite a day," Becker said, more to God than to Terri.

"I want to go."

"Sure."

"Hold on." Terri went to the lavatory, not, Becker prayed, to continue the encounter. He rocked there for a minute on his own, managing one uncertain chuckle. A bad day for PR. A bad day.

Cockburn came over. "Nice to see you Becker. Those outlines are finished. I'll drop them in on Monday. The figures too."

"Fine, fine."

Terri came back and after pleasantries with Cockburn they left.

"I wrote, 'Women Demand the Right to Control Your Own Bodies' on the wall of their bathroom in texta colour," she said. "They'll never get it off."

Becker reeled as her confession smacked into him.

His social life was already, to say the least, thin. Oh, this country.

"But Terri, why?" he groaned.

"Propaganda."

They were driving when Terri said with a giggle, "I also wrote 'Becker Sucks Cocks'."

Bang. His palms wept sweat. "Now, come on..." He turned to her, disbelieving, horror-struck. "No?"

She giggled.

He dabbed his sweating brow, wiped his palms.

"I wrote it on a mirror," she said. "They'll be able to rub that off easily."

"Oh good," Becker said, absolutely horror-struck, "oh good, that's just fine, that's good, very good, it'll rub off easily, will it? Oh good, very good."

"You didn't really?" he pleaded.

"I didn't think you cared—it was a joke—those people are so crummy."

As they drove, Becker to escape his horror told Terri, in a low homesick voice, about the Dogwood Festival in Atlanta where he dearly wanted to be.

"We have the usual thing," he told her, "you can go to the sculpture—they pile in all the First National Bank lobby and they have all the gems and such at the Fulton Bank. Square dancing with the Greater Atlanta Federation of Square Dancers—in Lenox Square —the Bottle Club have a show."

She butted in, "I'm sorry about writing that if it's upset you—you sound so...crestfallen." She touched him. "They'll take it as a joke."

"Please, let's not mention it again. And no, they will not take it as a joke." Cockburn might, he thought, but the others...Jeez-us!

Becker persevered with the programme of the Dogwood Festival.

"There's the jazz—the jazz down in Ruby Red's warehouse— Dixieland jazz—lovely, oh boy, lovely."

He mused, he recollected, "The Atlanta Dixieland Jazz Society, I was a member, albeit not a very active one."

She was crying now. She should be crying.

"Why the crying?" He placed an awkward arm around her.

"Why do you do it—why do you mix with those shits, those

business shits, and their frightful women?" she cried.

"Oh, they're not so bad," he said, "just react badly," and then he lied, "They don't matter over much to me—just acquaintances."

"But you don't belong there."

"Yes I do," Becker said, "yes I do, I'm their sort," or at least he had been.

"You're not," she shouted, stopping her crying, "you're not, you're not—you're different."

"No, Terri," Becker said, this time surely, or at least trying for certainty, "I'm a man of business, a merchant, a pedlar, and I work for Coca-Cola and I like it. I'm in soft drink—soft drink and the distribution of soft drink."

"I don't understand you."

Terri sat in total silence, crying a sob now and then. Becker gave her his awkward comfort.

A few miles further on she turned to Becker and said, putting her hands on him, "Jesus, I like you."

Becker was touched. It almost compensated for his social destruction back at the party.

"You kook," he said, "I like you," and gave her his awkward affection.

"You're not a business man," she said, trying another tone, "not really."

"I am," he said. "I'll prove it—now, take investment—now, accepting losses is the most important single investment device to ensure safety of capital. It is also the action people know the least about. Too often the investor is prone to say that losses are only paper. He looks at the dividend and capital gains and forgets that some capital losses are inevitable and must always be deducted from gains. Whenever an owner gets a small profit he takes it and when the stocks sustain a paper loss the stock is held in the hope it will come back and eventually of course, the account is frozen..."

"Stop it," Terri said.

"Convinced?"

"Yes, I'm convinced."

At Terri's flat they made love and Becker felt a very tender affection for her and her kookiness. At other times he thought of other such things as Carolina and Georgia in the springtime. The cherry blossoms of Charlotte in April, the tall Charlotte banks, higher than any blossoms. The jazz at Ruby Red's. He also thought of these things: grenadine, chilled sodas, lime fruit, Justerini and Brooks, Denominazione di Origine Controllata, Wolfschmidts, Lowenbrau, and other things which afterwards he could not recall for listing. He also racked his brain for a way of explaining to his friends and associates the scrawled message, "Becker Sucks Cocks", but was unable to find one.

The St Louis Rotary Convention 1923, recalled

Becker meets the kook

BECKER was thinking this: how rarely in this foul country did the milk carton spout open as the printed directions promised, "to open push up here"—push up where, for Goddam. It had to do with the spread of talent across the land. For a country with a population so small they should, in terms of technology, still be peasants. That was his feeling, harsh as it may be. The way he figured it, the high-performance five-percenters were spread over too diversified an economy. By accident of history. The accident of history, as Becker saw it, was that they were English speakers. They attempted the higher technology of the main English nations. That was it. Result: milk cartons which wouldn't spout.

Some theory Becker, you could go back to the alma mater in Atlanta and package that into a Ph.D.

Of course, it explained his presence in the foul country. "To the foul country," he toasted with the milk carton, drinking through a jagged spout torn with his envelope-opening dagger. He was there to reinforce the top echelon of the country's paltry beverage technology—"to advise and counsel the franchise men on marketing".

"Here's to you, technological missionary, evangelist, old dog." He was, and he often thought it, he was an evangelist of sorts. The Peace Corps sort: he really sometimes feared that he had the Peace Corps mentality. But somehow the Corps never had seemed to him to be the classic bourbon-drinking type of organisation. And he was the classic bourbon-drinking type.

The felt-penned drawing on a large sheet of pasteboard came down before him on the desk from behind, covering his hands and milk—as though he'd lost his hands to mid-forearm in some disappearing act.

The relief secretary was standing there. He was unnerved. She herself had an uncertainty in her smile, her stance. She was waiting for him to put *her* at ease. Who would ease him?

"That me?" he asked.

"Yes—do you like it?"

Becker often felt that not a day went past when someone didn't inflict some extraordinary demand upon him way beyond what he felt should be expected of him in his job with Coca-Cola or of his guarded, programmed, elementary motel life. More in fact than he thought life itself had any right to throw up. He had not begun life visualising, encompassing, such things. Nor was he equipped or adequately trained. They are tests, Becker, tests. Yes, but tests for what, where was the diploma, where was the payout?

"Well, do you like it?"

He'd been staring at the drawing—the drawing obviously of himself.

"What am I doing with my hand shading my eyes like that?"

"You're searching."

"Searching for what?"

"New horizons."

OK, he would pursue her meaning. He didn't want any. He wanted to reduce the enigmas. Back to the drawing. What he feared was that she was going to "reveal" him.

"New horizons?"

"New horizons for Coca-Cola."

Well, that was damn true. "What's the Coke bottle doing on my head like some William Tell apple?"

"You have it on the brain—you're a coke-head," she giggled. "What's your star? Let me tell you—you're..." she hummed and ha'd staring into his eyes until not blinking hurt him, "you're Pisces—sensitive, unlucky, and melancholy."

"You're damn right—about the star, that is." Further unnerved—"Say, how did you know that?"

"I knew it." She gave off noises of self-delight.

"You looked at my personnel card," he said, "and anyhow," changing the subject swiftly, "is Coca-Cola subsidising art now—don't we give you enough to do?" Becker, wielder of the corporation inflation axe, pruner of manpower wastage.

"I did it in my lunch hour. Don't be mean."

"I like it—it's kookie but I like it."

Becker worried that Sam would come out and see the drawing. Sam would show it to the others and they'd all have a great hee-haw. He didn't care for that.

Her name? "You're—?" he snapped his fingers. But she left him hanging there, pinned there, endeavouring to remember, just too long, for politeness, for social ease, and he knew it, she liked, he bet, she liked to see men sweat. A Western Union thought arrived also: the drawing was a pass. There was a rule he recalled, about fraternising with female office staff. Perhaps that applied in Atlanta but not here.

"I'm Terri."

"Becker."

"I know—we met before."

Sunburst symbols, high signs, hash bag

Her flat asked too much for Becker's liking. Not that he objected to art. Or fad art. But he found that he was most at ease in an electronic and technically servile five-star motel room. Nothing talking back at you. In Terri's place it was all talking at you. Everything she'd done to the place was a message. From the time he stepped in he was warding them off. The pottery, the artifacts, the prints, the posters, the sketches, the photographs, the pinned-up clippings, the dyed drapes, the books, were all like yelping dogs or crying children. Sunburst symbols, assorted carved statuettes from the East, high signs, and a hash bag hung on a small hookah.

"What's that burning?"

"Ethiopian sandalwood—incense."

"Uh uh."

She went about doing things in another room.

Motels. Now a motel was five-star living. Bourbon, a jar of hot mix, of which he was inordinately fond, a prewar movie or perhaps a Dashiell Hammett, cleanliness, air-conditioning, and refrigeration. Motels kept him a today-man because there was no yesterday around to hold him back.

"Say, you must be an artist," he said, catching her signature on some of the paintings.

"I did a course," she said. "I'm really only a passable sketcher, that's all—nothing more."

"Impresses a cowboy like me."

"Are you really a cowboy—I mean from Texas or somewhere?" she said, her words muffled by the sweater she was pulling over her head. He could see her through in the bedroom.

"I sometimes see myself as a motel cowboy," he said, "but no, I'm strictly a city boy."

"How disappointing, that you're not a real cowboy—not that I mean to be rude," she said, with a laugh, "it's just that I haven't met a cowboy."

"No offence taken."

"You're going to my home town next week," she said, back in the living room, handing him a drink, apologising because she had no pot.

"Is that a prediction of the stars?"

"No," she laughed. "I was typing your itinerary."

Sam, please, not the rural. Becker, the motel cowboy, painfully rides his itinerary into the setting sun.

"Oh, where's your home town?"

"It's really a city."

She rattled on about it. Her father was a big shot.

King of Jasmine, speed freak

As he was taking off his trousers, he said, "I shouldn't be doing this—I think it's against company rules."

"You don't really allow them to tell you who you go to bed with?"

"I try to keep the contract." Of which Becker had his own interpretations.

"You're a victim."

"I keep the contract—I contracted in."

"But it's a matter of personal freedom—and control of your own work scene. I only work when I want to."

Becker didn't know precisely what she was on about.

He kissed her. "I'm here, aren't I?"

In the bedroom she had King of Jasmine burning.

"I've never seen a man, a young man, wearing suspenders with his socks. Only my dad."

They lay on the bed.

"Some socks need suspenders."

"Aren't you going to take off your underpants and socks?"

"I thought we'd lie here for a while, kind of talk, finish our drinks."

He held his drink to his lips with both hands. He studied the black and white print of the Archfiend in Goat Form with the Satanic curse, "Palas aron Azinomas".

A voice, which he took to be Godly, called to him, "Becker, what are you doing?" He shook his head.

"Why are you shaking your head?"

"I was shaking my head?"

"You clown," she kissed him, and sat back, cross-legged on the bed, naked, staring at him. "I like you."

He attempted a lying down shrug. "I'm grey flannel commerce."

"I know—that's why I shouldn't like you—and American—but I do—you're my sort of person."

Jesus!

"I want an opinion," she said impulsively, rolling sideways off the bed, saying, "What do you think of a father who writes this sort of letter?" She went to the dresser.

Why me? Why Becker?

He put a hand to his face, two comforting fingers on his eyelids. Why?

"It's supposed to be personal but he dictates it to his secretary and it has a file number. I'll read the best parts."

She read: "'Our dear Terri, your mother and I were dreadfully disturbed to learn of your "illness"' (quotation marks for illness) 'but are relieved to know that it's now behind you and you have sought medical assistance. Many of these troubles are purely physical. I have enclosed an article on the subject from the *Reader's Digest* concerning this.'"

Why me?

"'In my own life I have always placed the greatest value on fellowship and ethics and security'—he means money," she interpolated. "'I hope this upbringing will eventually pay dividends'—for whom?" she asked.

Why?

"'The incident you so painfully bring up had all but been forgotten by me and I see no purpose in your raising it again or telling it to the psychiatrists. I feel those childish acts are best kept within the family. Our thoughts are with you, Father!' " She threw the letter back on to the dressing table. "Keep it within the family," she screamed, laughing, "isn't that too much—he wants me to conceal things from the psychiatrist."

"You go to an analyst?" Becker asked.

"I did, I stopped."

Why me?

"Can you guess what the 'illness' was?"

Becker didn't want to try. People always asked you to guess the unguessable. He had a personal policy of not trying to guess. Why did people want him to guess?

"You tell me."

"No, guess."

"I couldn't guess in a million years."

The guessing challenge side-stepped, Terri was all too damn eager to tell.

"I had a crack-up—really freaked out on speed—an incredibly bad scene—raving, and they put me in security with bars on the windows—where they put the real maddies and the 'bad patients' —they didn't treat me—just locked me away—and I looked out on a courtyard where all the maddies and morons walked about tearing off their clothes and eating their own shit—and when they undressed me I bit two male nurses on the legs—is that significant? Then they gave me a canvas night shirt and put me in this cell. It was a real cell and I pulled the bed apart to make a key—I don't know why I thought I could make a key from the bed—and they took the bed away and made me sleep on the cement floor on strips of canvas."

"Hey now—wait on—you don't expect me to believe this happened in these times—why, that's positively medieval."

Before his very eyes, the kookie, swinging relief secretary from the agency had become a neurotic problem. Sexually, he began packing up.

"I'm not lying," she said, begging belief, "and my parents knew what was happening to me—and they let them do it—as punishment for me being sick."

"How long did they keep you in this...hospital?"

"Fifteen days."

"No." Becker was truly shocked. Wondering whether to believe all.

"I was locked in the cell for fifteen days. After, I was put in an ordinary ward where I got off with a fifty-year-old alcoholic under the hospital on some old bags, in the foundations, you could hear the people walking on the floor above..."

"Spare me the details," Becker said.

"...we took librium to get high—ten milligramme capsules. I took a handful one day and they put me in the cell again for punishment—for another two days and shaved my head."

"No, they didn't shave your head—Terri, that's not credible."

Becker found he'd sat up and was staring at the girl—she was speaking in a torrent.

She gulped her drink.

"Well, not shaved—but they cropped it—they said there was a lice infestation."

Lice was one of the things Becker had not had to face in life. He was not going to face lice now.

"They discharged me to my parents and as soon as I arrived home I took a bottle of chloral-hydrate and a packet of those tranquillisers you get from the chemists without a prescription—and they put me back in hospital."

Becker wondered how to get out without hurting her and whether there was anything Coca-Cola could do to help her. Whether there was the remotest possibility she had lice. Now.

"The reason people are down on drugs is they resent people escaping and having a good time—like fantastically good sex—I was just having a bad scene. That letter from my father was his full-bit response—that was all he could say—do you know what the 'painful incident' was? The one my father would rather I didn't mention?"

"No," Becker said, not wanting to know—not wanting to know a further item.

"It was during my 'active phase' as the shrink calls it—when I was younger, I stripped naked and got into bed with my father while he was asleep and slashed him with a razor blade—not badly—just superficial cuts—is that castration?"

"...just superficial cuts," Becker said, nodding. Becker knew nothing of castration but he was having none of it. None.

Protesting a backache he proceeded to remove himself from the situation.

"You mean you've been kissing me and we're undressed and now you're going without making love to me?"

She seemed not to believe that he could. He was sure he could.

"You think I'm mad, don't you?" she cried, complaining, wanting, he could tell, for him to say no. Which he couldn't.

"I'm concerned, Terri—maybe, I thought—maybe the office might be able to...a lot of people don't realise how good Coca-Cola is...about these things."

He, too, had his doubts.

"You're too much," she said nastily, and began to laugh in a way which was like sobbing, which caused Becker to look again. Indeed she was laughing at him, and she continued to laugh at him, saying now and then, "Oh my God," and "Too much," shaking her head while he dressed. When he looked again she was masturbating with her two hands between her legs as he tied his laces.

No prayer

Becker had a stiff Old Crow straight from the bottle in the motel and sang to himself, "Becker the brave, Becker the free."

He realised it had been a dumb thing for him to have suggested help from Coca-Cola.

Anyhow, he didn't think Sam would come at it. Sam believed in will and pep, and grit.

No prayer came to mind.

Coincidence: non-negotiable experience

"We have with us tonight, as my guest, a visitor all the way from Atlantic City, Georgia, from the Coca-Cola company."

"Atlanta, Georgia," Becker corrected, with a good-big smile.

"As you were, 'Atlanta, Georgia'."

The Rotarians clapped.

Becker was again introduced to yet another country Rotary club. He rather saw Rotarians as those who had the treasure that he was after. It worried him that they had the treasure but didn't know how to eat well.

Where is Rotary going?

Rotary is going to lunch—to a bad lunch.

The other thing he objected to was that in every damn town he visited and fell in with Rotarians—the local distributor in this case—

they took him to the meeting...never invited him...never gave him an out...they *took* him.

"My daughter, Terri, is at present working in your city office," Rotarian T. George McDowell, classification: catering, said, introducing himself across the table, half-standing, napkin under chin, arm outstretched. Becker didn't like coincidences because they were an imposition, an infringement of the straightforward. They had the bad odour of mysticism about them. Coincidence led nowhere. Where do you go, what do you do with a coincidence? It was what Becker called non-negotiable experience.

But strictly this was no coincidence. It was no surprise. "Pleased to meet you, sir, Terri mentioned you were in business hereabouts. I meant to get around to calling."

Becker had hoped to ride his itinerary in and out of the fibro town without so much as a glance towards T. George McDowell.

"She shouldn't be working in an office," McDowell said. "We put her through art school—has just thrown that aside—wasted it."

McDowell showed instant concern, injury, and then, placing a hand on Becker's arm, changed to smiling. "I love Americans—both my wife and I love Americans."

"That sounds too generous a statement," Becker said. "You must have to make many allowances for some of us."

"Not at all—I and my wife love you all—how many times would you say I'd been to the States—as a guess?"

No guessing.

"You travel a good ideal?" he rejoined.

"I've been to the States now seventeen times." McDowell sat there, travel-proud.

"You must have a fascination for our country."

"You know what I admire about Americans?"

Becker looked at him, resisting a no, and resisting a guess.

"I admire your mental tidiness."

McDowell invited Becker back for a drink after the meeting. "Can't have you going back to some miserable motel room—not that I'm saying the accommodation in this city is bad—how could I? I'm in catering myself."

The St Louis Rotary Convention 1923, recalled

Becker wondered how he could fit himself into the McDowell

house, so much carpet, so much bric-a-brac, so many pieces of furniture, so many clocks, so many standard lamps, so many souvenirs, so many barometers, pianos, and palms.

"The house is too large for the wife and me now that the children have grown up and flown the nest."

His wife was in bed with backache.

"What will it be?"

They sat and drank.

"My first trip to the States was to the St Louis Rotary Convention of 1923—with my father—I wasn't a Rotarian myself then but joined Rotary the following year."

"That's a fine record."

"Oh that was some Convention—the pageant at the Coliseum —corner of Jefferson and Washington Streets."

"You remember the streets!"

"Not bad for an old fellow—how is it that I can remember the address of the St Louis Coliseum from 1923 but I forget the name of someone I meet ten minutes ago? Why is that?"

"It's an often remarked characteristic of later years, sir."

"I remember the flowers—the Rotary Garden of Nations— and they had young girls and boy scouts—and the Rotary Band and the singing of a choir—the Italian Choir of St Louis—don't know why an Italian choir—do you know St Louis at all?"

"No, sir, I'm afraid I don't." Becker shook his head, readying himself to be out-knowledged on America throughout the conversation.

"There it was in this vast auditorium, massed humanity—you know how many delegates and observers attended that Convention?"

"No, sir."

"...that's with wives, guess?"

"No, I really have little idea."

"Six thousand—nearly seven thousand—and this was 1923."

Becker moved his head, impressed, liking a good crowd.

"It was almost pitch black when we went in. The light gradually brightened for each part of the opening ceremony until the whole spectacle ended in a display of electric light. Now at the beginning there was the sound of a trumpet."

McDowell made a trumpeting action—imitating the sound of a trumpet.

"A spotlight then revealed a single figure up there on this long flight of stairs—I think if I remember it was meant to be Columbia —standing on top of these stairs. The stairs were covered with green carpet leading to a terrace filled with potplants. We had the chorus of welcome sung by the choir—that Italian choir—then a shrill whistle brought the boy scouts into the hall through the audience, each bearing a flag of the nations represented in Rotary."

"It must have been truly impressive," said Becker from behind an empty glass, thinking, especially, of the spaghetti choir.

"Oh, that was just the beginning—another fanfare."

McDowell again made the trumpeting action and the sound.

"Another fanfare and from the top of the terrace in sets of four trooped twenty-eight girls—twenty-eight nations in Rotary then—all dressed in those classical robes and each wearing a band of flowers around their head—they represented the national flowers of the nations of Rotary."

"Twenty-eight."

"Twenty-eight—each girl being one of those nations—they carried on their shoulders a huge garland—like a rope—which they carried down to the main stage and presented a dance which was a salute to the visiting nations and an expression of their joy and exhilaration at being present at such a gathering. At the end of the dance the maidens—the girls—went back up the stairs to the terrace and their garland was twined among the flags—the flags that the boy scouts had carried up—can you picture that?"

"Yes, sir, you certainly remember it—more trumpets?"

"No, no more trumpets—the strains of the triumphal march of Aida—the rope of flowers was drawn up to the top of a gold flagpole now—with your flag, the Stars and Stripes—this was the main feature of the spectacle—and at the same time a huge Rotary wheel in gold and blue—Rotary colours—glittering, was lit up, twenty feet above our heads—can you imagine it?"

"You are describing it vividly, sir."

"John Henry Lyons—I think if I remember he was from Tacoma, Washington—led the singing—do you know Tacoma?"

"No, sir, I'm afraid not."

"I've been there—have been to the States now seventeen times, but I've told you that. John Henry Lyons led the singing— we sang the 'Star Spangled Banner', 'God Save the King', 'America', and 'Old Black Joe'—we had song books of course—but I have never heard men sing out like that since."

"It must have been some occasion."

With a mustering of fervour, McDowell said, "I have never seen anything like it in my life—it has never been equalled in my experience."

McDowell sat there, back among the fanfares and the dancing maidens and the boy scouts.

Then he returned, the host, to fix the drinks—but again paused, mid-flight, both empty glasses in his hands, before the ice bucket, finding the return from 1923 difficult.

"Rotary," McDowell held on to the word, "Rotary is my religion," he said, re-engaging—putting down the glasses and going on with the getting of drinks. "I hope you don't find that sacrilegious, me saying that, but Rotary has guided my every adult act," McDowell said.

"Oh no—no, sir."

"I'm not the church-going type—but I'm an ethical man and I believe there is a Great Chairman in that Other Country which is the destination of us all."

Mortality was always not far from Becker. Becker, replenished by his drink, wanting to ask about the poor food of Rotary and about the treasure, said instead, "I have never been in one place long enough."

"I often say that there is no need to be in a club to live by the principles of Rotary—what we need is not more men in Rotary but more Rotary in men," McDowell hammered out.

Then McDowell mused, "It has guided my family life. Now take my family—there is high authority, you'd probably know—for the proposition that a child owes no natural affection to the parents —that such affection will, however, result from kind treatment, companionship, and studied care. The sacredness of the whole family, I argue, is largely due to the environment of fellowship that is made around it. That's what Rotary and life are about. Complexes cannot live in the Rotary house of fellowship—do you agree?"

Becker scratched around in the remnants of Course 231 Social Psychology. "Complexes, sir? I don't fully follow."

"A complex means that people aggravate their differences, while fellowship is generally interpreted as a development of the principles on which there can be agreement—one is destruction: the other, harmony."

"I follow."

Again McDowell slipped down into reverie.

Becker slugged down his drink.

McDowell came up out of the reverie saying, "What is your honest opinion of my daughter Terri?", a darkness of trouble about his face.

"I really don't know her that well—I spend so little time at Head Office.

Two hands masturbating between her legs.

"We haven't seen her for a year," the darkness blackened and without comment McDowell rose and left the room, returning with a letter.

"I want you to read this—tell me what you think of a daughter who'd write this to her father."

"Really, sir, I don't think it's my place..."

"Go on—I'd like your opinion—I like the American approach." McDowell shook the letter at him in the agitated way of the elderly.

He knew the contents of the letter. He knew no response to the contents. He was thinking of the wording of a response, not reading the letter—he saw it all there in key words from the night in the bedroom under the Archfiend in Goat Form. A loud, blurred letter written with a felt pen. He saw the words, shave head, castration, lice, methedrine, a pit of snakes, your cursed daughter. You didn't need Soc. Psy. 231 to know it was the letter of a speed freak screaming to her father.

"Really, sir, I don't think it's my place to comment..."

"Please, I'd be grateful—for any comment—it's so difficult to seek advice... in this town... about this sort of thing."

Becker returned to the letter, pretending to read, and then said, "I guess, sir, it's part of her search."

McDowell didn't acknowledge but said, "Do you read the *Reader's Digest?*"

"Yes, sir, I do."

"I like the positive American approach of the *Digest*—it's the only thing I've got to go by—this drug thing comes stealing into the home—remember also that this is not the behaviour of a teenager—Terri's no mixed-up child—she is nearly thirty—nearly thirty." McDowell was grim with bewilderment. "She is nurtured in good fellowship and the ethics of this home—I can only put it down to the city life and the company of artistic types."

Becker had not realised Terri was thirty. Some search. Some of us, he guessed, were looking for more than others. Take himself.

Becker handed back the letter. The apple, he observed, probably didn't fall far from the tree.

"Her search, you say?" McDowell seemed to be having trouble with that. "You must stay the night."

"Thank you, sir, but I have luggage at the motel, and I'd like to return there."

"Why, Mother would be very hurt indeed if you didn't stay."

"Really, sir, I'd prefer. . . ."

Becker stood up.

McDowell stressed the invitation, the insistent host. "After you've been of such good counsel."

"Please, sir, I wish to return to my motel, if you would excuse me."

In the car, McDowell laughed again heartily, and said, "I put a strong case—but always remember this, there are three sides to every question—your side, the other fellow's side, the right side," and laughed.

Becker was not clear in his own mind, to what, if anything, this related.

The telephone as bolas

All right, then, it was a transactional world. Becker had learned that early enough—one good turn deserved another, a little kindness will be returned a thousandfold, smile and the world smiles with you. Sam was fond of saying, "Every conversation is a transaction." Well, Sam, what was the trade tonight, what did I give, what did I get?

The motel room was a comfort to be sure. Not that he was retreating from L-I-F-E, no sir, not by a dandy long shot. He was still ready to get out there and dig for treasure. But he couldn't see why he should have been selected tonight in this fibro town to receive the ass-pains of Rotarian T. George McDowell and his errant daughter.

A bourbon with ice. Fire and ice. "I think I know enough of hate/to say that for destruction ice/is also great/and would suffice."

Becker was not averse to poetry or to jazz music. He sometimes wondered if this didn't soft-edge him, business-wise.

Motels. A clean safe passage-way around the world. He could be in Manitoba or good old Atlanta. The security of standardisation. All he asked of his little old hunk of life, for that year, was the standard four-star motel. Five-star tomorrow. And for the next day, treasure and a castle.

The telephone rang, causing Becker to drop his bourbon.

Ah shit.

Who in damnation!

He heard the plug of connection—the telephonist said long distance person-to-person, "Mr Becker?"

"Yes, this is he."

He heard the wires—saw them stretching along the coast of this fibro nation—he saw the wires stringing him together with someone—a bolas—against his preference. He watched the mute whites and greys of the television from the telephone, awaiting the intrusion of the call to bring him stumbling down.

"Hello, hello, hello," he said impatiently.

"Hello," a woman's voice, "it's me, Terri."

Terri.

"Jesus! What is this—I've just this moment come from your father's house and now you're busting in down the line."

Becker checked the anger in his voice.

"I want to talk to you and apologise for my uncouth conduct the other night—the seduction hassle—it wasn't cool, me unloading all that on you."

"Oh hell—forget it."

"What did Father say?"

"We talked some—we talked about you—say how did you know how to get me here—and why this time of night?"

"I made the bookings, remember?"

He remembered now all right. From the mit of the father to the mit of the daughter.

"Tell me what my father said."

"Now look—it's very late."

"Did he tell you his daughter was a head? I bet he didn't."

"He showed me your letter yes."

"He showed you my letter!" Outrage. "He shouldn't have done that—that's not fair."

"Look, if you don't mind me saying, I seem to know more about you and your damn family than I want to damn well know."

"He shouldn't have shown you that letter."

Becker began to wonder again. Why? She went on complaining.

"You can see he doesn't love me, can't you?" Becker took the question, stretched the telephone cable to its limit, and using one hand poured a drink, adding ice.

Becker was in need of a prayer as well as a drink.

Here we go, "No, I don't think he loves you. Not in the way you mean. No."

Rotary love, maybe? He didn't bother to mention it.

Terri shut up. The line was empty of voice.

"How can you say that?" she came back, almost anguished.

Again the silence. He could hear a drumming on the line. Wind?

"No one has ever said that before—everyone has always said he does love me and I wasn't being fair to him."

"Well, you asked me, that's the way I see it." Becker watched television.

Further silence, and then. "Well, at least you're straightforward."

"I'm going now, I have to get some sleep—hit the sack, I have a big day."

"Selling Coca-Cola," her voice, returning to normal, was good-natured, but had a derisive edge.

Becker had met derision before. Becker knew about derision.

"Yes, goddam it—doing my simple self-appointed task of selling the best damn soft drink in the world—the best damn way I know how."

Becker believed, among other things, in prowess and the pursuit of excellence.

Jesus said to watch for twenty-eight signs

BECKER could explain why he continued to see Terri—lust. But lust alone couldn't explain why he ended up with her in the lavatory at Coca-Cola. That had to do with environmental stress.

He knew he was dying. He knew that being an ocean away from Atlanta and the sparkle, in an alien distribution zone, was killing him. He'd read of cases. People died from being isolated from their intimates and people lost control that way.

Environmental isolation and stress put him in the lavatory with Terri that frosty Friday.

In the lavatory, Terri went down on him, he ducking his head below the three-quarter cubicle door so that anyone coming into the men's wouldn't see him—one foot braced against the marble wall, trousers around his knees. He feared that they'd see Terri and his feet—to do that someone would have to lie on the floor. That wouldn't have surprised him. To him anything could happen.

She'd talked him into it.

She'd made horny gestures and typed a hot note.

He'd protested. God be his witness, he'd said, "No Terri, please, Terri, no—leave me alone—not in the office, please. Discretion."

But it hadn't been there. The words had been spoken but were nothing more than a platoon of trembling cadets. His sense of discretion, a vague memory trace.

She'd gotten him to the lavatory by seduction, but that his will was shot to pieces was not lust but environmental stress.

He grunted from the stimulation of her mouth.

She rested.

"Jesus, don't stop now—go on—Jesus, go on."

When the panting was all over Terri said, "Now are you glad you let yourself be seduced?"

Life had him in its undertow.

"Let's get out of here."

In addition to the Southern Baptist Convention there are 29 other Baptist bodies in the U.S. They range from the tiny Independent Baptist Church of America, which has only 25 members, to the National Baptist Convention of the U.S.A. Inc. which has five point five million members and is the largest Negro church in the country. All told there are some 25 million Baptists in the U.S.

And now, Becker thought groaningly, the Baptists of the Lavatory Inc.

Back at his desk he looked at his crumpled suit and stains.

Becker, you're a-dying.

Then Sam called for him.

"Becker, a member of staff—you won't believe this—has come to me and stated that he saw you in the gents with a girl—one of the relief typists." Sam tried to put the question humorously.

Oh, Sam.

"Sam, you must be joking."

"I'm trying, Becker, I'm trying."

Aw hell.

"Aw hell, it's God's truth, Sam, it's right—don't ask me how." Becker raised both hands. "It happened I don't know how—that's the living truth."

Pain, weariness, despair, disappointment, doom and gloom, packing in around Sam like crushed ice. "Becker, I've been with Coca-Cola thirty-one years. I've been in this country nearly six. I have never..."

Becker could list the twenty-eight steps which led him to his first trip and his first mixing with drugs of any kind—Old Crow bourbon excluded.

The first had been during High School when he'd learned to play piano from a coupon course mailed from the back of a comic book.

The second had been reading the poems of the Earl of Rochester at college.

The third had been carrying the poems of the Earl of Rochester in his head, after college.

The fourth had been a semester of Existentialism which led him to ponder destiny and life.

The fifth had been Course 231, Social Psychology, which had given him a soft-edged business approach.

The sixth had been seven hundred miserable Rotary lunches.

The seventh had been avarice—seeing the riches of the earth and over-seeking them. Cupidity.

The eighth had been his ever-present willingness to succumb to the harlot itch—to leap the fence of restraint.

The ninth had been turning his back on God's Prophetic Clock which was ticking away.

The tenth had been his willingness to even consider coming to this forsaken country to advise the franchise men—too far from the action. He'd lost altitude.

The eleventh had been the heat of the forsaken summer of the forsaken country which overactivated his thirst and lust.

The twelfth had been the fibro towns and the cities that looked like they should be metropolises but underneath were towns. The Coca-Cola signs were a disguise.

The thirteenth had been dancing with a transvestite who had put a hex on him. It had been a mistake, he'd mistaken the transvestite for a girl.

The fourteenth had been lying to himself about mistaking the transvestite for a girl. He'd known all along.

The fifteenth had been weakening the stockade of his existence —the motel—by opening the window that day to allow Terri to swing her leg over it and climb in.

The sixteenth had been life's gradual smudging of his sartorial standards.

The seventeenth had been taking off the sunglasses of his soul to anyone, least of all Terri.

The eighteenth had been listening to Terri's personal story with lust in his heart.

The nineteenth had been taking Terri, reeking of sex, barefoot to a business party.

The twentieth had been letting Terri out of his sight long enough for her to write "Becker Sucks Cocks" on the wall of the bathroom.

The twenty-first had been forgiving her.

The twenty-second had been letting Terri get him into the lavatory at the office for a blow job.

The twenty-third had been the foolhardy incaution of being seen pushing Terri through the louvre window of the lavatory.

The twenty-fourth had been someone telling Sam. Firstly telling Sam about the message "Becker Sucks Cocks" which he'd denied any knowledge of, and secondly, about the lavatory incident which he had not denied.

The twenty-fifth had been Sam's abiding despair.

The twenty-sixth had been him leaving the office for ever with a glazed Sam gently stabbing the desk with a paper knife.

The twenty-seventh had been going to Terri's flat that same afternoon full of bourbon and the release of absolute defeat—freed from the battle.

The twenty-eighth had been Terri saying, "Come on, Becker, honey, come away with me, come away with me on a trip, on a trip, to an acid wonderland where we'll find what sexuality is all about, and what God intended."

As far as Becker could remember there were twenty-eight signs which Jesus said to watch for.

Jesus, he should have watched for those signs. Oh boy—the distance he'd travelled, the many signs he'd passed, unheeded, to this.

On his trip he became a little boy at Terri's munificent maternal breast.

He tasted once again the sweet sustaining milk, hitting his lips like electric glucose.

The flesh of her breasts and the all-yielding rubbery nipple gave a milk odour so reassuring that all fears and woes subsided.

Terri's maternalism lifted him high and embraced and held him.

Her enveloping legs and the immense soft hairiness of her crutch swallowed him.

He was swallowed and locked in her groin.

He was washed by her pungent flooding.

His stomach and lower thighs were enveloped by the moist warm suction of her womb.

She drew his sperm from him in a long steady unpulsating stream, like a child peeing.

For a micro-second he rested.

After resting he grew, his penis a sapling, and he saw, for the first time, his muscles rippling.

Sap came through his body, in a rapid hurry.

His penis filled her to the point of pain, she opened and closed in moaning reception.

The fluid of her vagina was hot, lubricious.

He burst into her, pulsation after pulsation which lasted until he fell, drained, exhausted, crying on her hair, feeling that he had almost totally expelled himself into her, to the edge of disappearance.

He wept for his lies.

He wept for his knowledge.

He saw the fires of hell but they weren't for him.

Not today, anyhow.

Later in a great silence and tiredness Terri and he lay in a bath.

Apart, points of their bodies touching.

Now and then his mind trembled through his body.

She said she'd had other private feelings at some times, away from him. But she'd been his mother at the time of the suckling and his woman at the end.

Well, Jesus, what now?

In a deck chair, Becker read the interview.

An American jazz pianist, Mr Beckar from Atlanta, Georgia, has been hired to play for a season of twelve weeks at the Silver Spade, Surfer's Paradise.

(The manager had said, "If they like you, you stay—if they don't, you're out. We ain't never had jazz before.")

Mr Beckar, aged 35, was formerly a member of a group in Atlanta known as the Bourbon Hot Mother Blues and a member of Atlanta Dixieland Jazz Society.

(The Bourbon Hot Mother Blues had consisted of him, his piano, and a bottle of Old Crow.)

He also played at Ruby Red's Warehouse, well-known as a jazz centre in Atlanta.

(You may not remember me, Ruby—but I did break down your piano one night after the band packed it in. So had most of the audience.)

He told our reporter that he had retired from business to become a professional musician.

("Retired" was their word—he'd left it vaguer than that.)

"I learned to play the piano by mail order," he said. "I wrote for lessons by filling out a comic book coupon."

(The *Lone Ranger*, to be precise.)

"Piano jazz until recent years has had a doubtful reputation among some jazz people—but you have many great jazz pianists."

He said that in his opinion the masters were Fats Waller, Pine Top Smith, Jimmy Yancey, and Cripple Clarence Lofton.

"I play a lot of very traditional works," he told our reporter, "the usual twelve bar blues—using the left hand as walking bass—the right for rhythm—a lot of cross rhythm—very traditional."

(No funky-hard bop for old Becker.)

Mr Beckar said he would like to pay homage to the music of Fats Waller.

"He's often criticised for being too commercial by people who don't like popular music.

"Fats managed to give an unaffected, bantering style, even poetry, to otherwise sentimental songs."

(Well, he guessed he'd said something like that.)

"And anyhow what's wrong with making money?"

Mr Beckar said that this own style owed much to the celebrated Fats Waller.

(Forgive me, Fats.)

Becker wears maroon bow tie, fancy arm bands, floral braces and drinks Old Crow while he plays.

His average weekly earnings are about eighty dollars with a free suite at the motel.

Becker often thinks that he would like to rest his head in the lap of authority—say, the lap of Billy Graham—but cannot surrender.

He finds that he still admires the organisation of the Southern Baptist Convention as a way for the world—no church congregation is bound by the Convention. Each goes its own way.

Apart from wanting nothing of it, he has no strong feelings

about Vietnam. He is, however, part of a pipeline which looks after deserters from Vietnam. Thanks to Terri.

His mother and sister write. "What went wrong?" "When are you coming home?" "What about your position?"

He lies around a lot. He doesn't exercise. He surfs reluctantly, unenthusiastically.

Terri waitresses at the motel. She has begun painting again. She is as unstable as jazz.

Terri says he is free now.

That is a joke. But Terri speaks like that. He has an inkling that stress and pollution are what the world is all about.

He sometimes misses stress and pollution. He sometimes misses Sam, Coca-Cola.

He has a scheme for manufacturing cassette programmes of unusual material which would be delivered with the milk on Sundays.

He is fond of saying, "If we are the last of the bourbon generation, let's be good at it."

He also likes to say that he is the best jazz pianist from Atlanta who has ever worked for Coca-Cola.

Becker wears maroon bow tie, fancy arm bands, floral braces and drinks Old Crow while he plays at the Silver Spade.

George McDowell does the job

HE assessed himself as "up to the date". Perhaps in his thinking he was already one calendar ahead—perhaps already into 1939. Anyhow, quite a modern man. He was fortunate too in having a wife who shared his Life Plan—a situation which, in his case, meant that his capacity was doubled rather than halved as in sharing, say, a cake.

He often said that if it wasn't for Thelma he would not be where he was today, although he was a self-made man (but not one who worshipped his maker). She had, though, worked for him in the business without wages during the early times and more recently during the economic depression. She was far more diligent at bottle inspection than the average bottle-washer. Like all cordial-makers he lived in a nightmare that one day a bottle would slip through inspection and poison a customer.

So therefore, although he and she did not go about the town propounding it in conversation, as up to the date people they believed and practised family planning through birth "control". His wife was also a practising Anglican. He was, well, put him down as one who served his fellow man, a business man, and a Rotarian.

To have a family plan went with having a life plan. Nothing could be accomplished without a Blueprint.

Together, of course, with initiative and capital.

They had two well-spaced children and intended having one more to bring the number to "three". "Three" seemed to him to be a manageable and modern number, although they had both themselves come from large families. His wife had been fitted with a diaphragm by a city physician, but she asked that he also wear a condom "just in case", and he did. He himself was a precautionary man, although it was true that all business did involve risk-taking. He had never said this to Thelma, but he felt that somehow the time when they were trying for a child, as it were, was made somehow tingling for them, because on these occasions they did not use, of course, any—precaution. He supposed it was because then, as it were, his "skin" touched her flesh, the flesh, that is, inside her. George McDowell cleared a tickle from his mental throat.

They were, certainly, the times most vividly recalled. Intercourse, he realised in maturity, was not everything it was cracked up to be. They had not let it become a "complex". His wife, he sometimes thought, was herself not a highly sexed woman, and although he became quite aroused at times, he was not overly preoccupied, he hoped. He had exercised self-control, as harsh as it was on her, in regard to the policeman's widow. He observed that the limitations and restrictions on the matter of sexual indulgence, placed by Thelma in their marriage, sometimes aroused him, her unwillingness, he had perhaps that sort of personality which was, which savoured, well, the restraint she imposed, the limitations on when, and her refusals. And now and then, though rarely, he imposed himself on her, and the silent, wordless, impositions he enjoyed too. It had to do, he speculated, with the basic economic principle of scarcity. Though really, this aspect of their lives he did not truly understand and did not ponder over much and which was not to say, either, that they did not conduct their married life *correctly*.

She insisted that the condom be flushed down the lavatory immediately after, and that he wash.

She did not, quite properly, want the girls finding them around the place or to step out in the morning to be confronted by it.

He badly wanted a son.

"I think we should have, that it is really time for us to consider having, another child if you still want for us to have a third."

She said it as they prepared for bed. He was brushing his teeth with Kolynos dental cream and going over in his mind a Masonic catechism he needed to know for Tuesday's Lodge. He did not know why he kept it up. He continued brushing, knowing what she meant and feeling in his pubic region that instant stirring. He smiled boyishly at her but she did not smile. Perhaps the toothpaste around his mouth, and he removed the smile, changed his voice to a proper tone, and said, yes, he would like another child to bring it up to "three", spitting into the white porcelain basin.

He went to bed without his pyjama trousers and without precaution.

After, because of germ life, they usually washed, she first, and he second, but because they were trying for a child she did not douche. When he returned from washing, she said to him, "People will think I'm awfully old to be having another child."

"You're older than customary, I suppose."

"Forty is really quite old. To be having a child."

"We've always said we'd have three," he said firmly, referring to their plan.

"After this birth I think I should perhaps have an operation."

"*Shusssh*—don't talk that way," he said, holding her Hercosmelling hand, squeezing it, not liking the clamminess of the idea of a surgical operation on that area of the body. He himself had had no sickness in his adult life to talk of.

But thinking also that at the same time it would mean an end to birth-control devices, although, on the other hand, a feeling that she would then be simply, well, a hollow body—and maybe of no interest at all.

He thought then about the Group Scout Meeting that would be held later that week. The plans for the camp up at Mt Keira and the log cabin they were building. Some were in favour of a rustic way of doing the window frames, while he himself preferred a tradesman-like job all round. He would argue that. No one preferred rusticity when it leaked.

Head on pillow looking up at the new plaster egg-and-dart cornice there in the dark of their new bedroom of their new house, the curtain lace lapping against the window and the breeze slightly bumping the blind cord, lying there he concluded that as far as he could see, everything in his life was being correctly done.

He was being recognised. He was becoming a person-about-the-town.

The new house was finished in detail right down to the built-in holder for toilet-paper rolls, and furnished with a number of electrically operated appliances and a new Stromberg Carlson which gave static only during storms.

He had been elected District Scout Master. In his speech he had said that the supreme challenge of each generation was "holding" the next generation. Keeping control of the young. That it was possible for a generation to be "lost", for control to slip and for civilisation to be without a generation to take over. He referred to the twenties in America, where a whole generation had been "lost". Maybe the law of oak inheres in oak, he'd said; nevertheless, while membership of a family can ensure that the values of that family inhere in the children of that family, Community Organisations had to police this and to ensure that "replacement parts" were available for those families lacking values. Community Organisations had to give these children replacement values.

He was outspoken in the Chamber of Commerce but was keeping an open mind on tourism. On one hand the tourist spent in the town—on his soft drinks, he was pleased to say—yet he could concede that they depreciated local facilities and roads without paying rates. He was able, he hoped, to place his own personal advantage aside when considering community issues.

He had reluctantly joined the Sesquicentenary Committee, reluctantly, because he felt the country areas had not received the sort of subsidy needed. He suspected it was someone in the city with a big idea for getting themselves knighted, and that the country towns were expected to obey. The city was beginning to look upon the towns as retinue.

He had refused a donation to the Roman Catholic School Fund because he did not believe in such schools separate from the public schools. Schools should, he thought, mirror the community in all its diversity—the rich, the poor, the bright, the dull, the protestant, the Roman Catholic. This way the child was prepared for the sort of community which lay ahead for him. Education occurred in the playground. One day this division between Roman Catholic and the rest would lead to bloodshed in this country. They had made the division themselves. He hoped, of course, it could be avoided.

They owed allegiance to an authority outside this country.

He had moved a motion at the A and H Society to refuse gypsies admission to the showground.

Gypsies.

He had a morbid feeling about the gypsies. He stopped once when they flagged him down, parked on the roadside in their American Buicks. A rather pretty gypsy girl just out of childhood, her hair half covering her dark face, and close up he could not judge her age—thirteen?—had flagged him down. Gypsy girl. Had smiled at him in a certain way. He rather thought, self-control slipping, that...maybe...the gypsy girl...would...he had lost his self-control for that instant, she called her mother, his hand on her arm, she had called her mother, groin against her, she called her mother, and the mother was morbidly attractive too, aroused in his trousers, he wanted to offer money to lie down in the bushes with the gypsy girl... maybe an arrangement, but he could go no further than £1. They wanted, instead, to tell his fortune.

Really, he thought, pulling himself together, he had thought really they were broken-down, needing assistance. The mother asked him to take everything from his pocket to tell his fortune, his handkerchief, his keys, his penknife, his loose change, his wallet, of course, yes, of course, to tell his fortune. She asked for the silver and he gave it to her. Instructed him to do it, and he felt rather hot and helpless. She asked for his hand, of course, he held out his hand. For the telling of his fortune. He tried to look for the young gypsy girl. For the telling of the fortune. The coming of a female figure, a child, a female dark and of a troubled nature. Thoughts of suicide. He looked for the young dark gypsy girl. Other girls in the back of the black Buicks. He had a hand which held money, through which the light did not shine.

He became uncertain, it seemed to be getting dark, where were his possessions, who was at the car? He could not see the young, alluring gypsy girl. The older gypsy had the things from his pocket. He was prepared for her to have the silver. He wanted his things back.

"I'm sorry, I would like my things back, please return my things."

She asked for a £1 note for the telling of the fortune. He grabbed and took back his things, backing towards his car, she held things to him withdrawing them when he went to snatch.

"Take the change, the silver."

He had his wallet, she took £1, she was putting it in her bosom.

"I thought you needed help or something. Take the silver."

She kept mumbling and coming towards him and being close to him, and it seemed to be growing quickly dark.

Sweating cold, he clambered into his Ford. He drove fast but stopped a mile or so along to check his things and found £2 missing from his wallet. How she'd taken it, he did not know. He saw no way of returning to them and getting his money back. He'd been a damn fool. Then he noticed that his new horn, which barked like a dog for moving cattle off the road, was also gone.

He ran out of petrol at Jaspers Brush. They had milked his tank.

He did not mention the stopping for the gypsies, the loss of the money, the horn, or the milking of the tank, to Thelma. Or anyone else.

The little dark-eyed gypsy girl.

"Again?" his wife queried, as he rubbed himself against her.

"I feel like it again," he whispered.

"All right," she said, moving apart her legs. "It's not like you."

He had moved that the gypsies not be permitted to enter the showground at showtime, for the purposes of fortune-telling.

He had never been bitten by a snake. He had always taken the snake-bite as a mark of carelessness in a man.

Fred Watts had been bitten by a snake only last week and in delirium saw all his old friends, some dead for forty years, and some he'd seen only the day before up at the Adelong Races, saw them all marching in file past his eyes, down into a black cavern. They had turned their eyes neither to the right nor to the left, and gave no sign of having seen him. They were dressed in the suits and hats of their times, some in the dress of forty years ago and some in the dress of today. Every person he had known in his life passed before his eyes.

Fred had treated himself with nicotine, which was useless. Fred was, and always would be, slapdash.

George McDowell, without conceit, concluded that his personal book-keeping was in order.

Yes.

He had heard the arguments against planning of the family. That it did not build the nation. That the yellow and black peoples of the world would soon outnumber the whites. He believed that birth control should not be used for avoiding family responsibility. He believed each parent should have one child and that a third should be for the building of the nation. That seemed to be a scientific and modern number.

"You haven't been to the bathroom," his wife murmured.

She meant after the second time.

Tiredly he got up, feet swinging into his slippers, and went to the bathroom to wash himself.

Love of luxury and not birth control he blamed for the decline of the British stock. The line between comfort and luxury had to be drawn. Comfort was the justified basic wage for hard effort. Luxury was excessive self-reward—over-paying. Hot water, refrigeration and electrically operated applicances, were the New Servants and he did not consider these luxury. They were necessary for the recharging of the body's energies.

He believed in Modernisation. What did the job best. Birth "control" seemed to him to be a good example of the modernisation of married life. Good business kept the community up to the date in its commodities. Good tradesmen kept up to the date with new materials and methods and cleaned up after the job.

George McDowell smiled, there in the bathroom: smiled at himself in the mirror on the cabinet door; a tentative, uncharacteristic smile of a distantly related, unofficial self: not the sort of humour he cared for, because, although one should be capable of laughing at oneself, one should not laugh at one's values and ideals: but, nevertheless, he smiled as these words formed in his head, "You are a good tradesman, George, and you clean up after the job."

The words and the smile were then expunged from his mind, leaving behind no trace or residue of self-mockery.

George McDowell changes names

ON 9th July 1938, when George McDowell strode home from business that evening to eat his tea before going to a meeting, his wife, leaning back from the rise of steam while straining the beans, told him that she was expecting their third child.

He kissed her on the cheek, she averting her eyes from the beans as a gesture of appreciation for the kiss and to separate the announcement from her task of straining the beans.

"In or about February," she said.

"It will be hot in hospital," he said, frowning at the bad planning.

"Doctor says to expect a somewhat difficult birth because of my age."

"Forty isn't that old," he said, himself being thirty-five.

"For having children, the medical profession seem to think so. I told him that three was our plan."

He washed his hands in the bathroom with Solvol.

Of course it meant the training of another child. The training of a child had always been heart-racking. He did not relish the punishment of children, the beatings, the smackings, the sobbings, the locking of children in the broom closet. There was always, too, what seemed to him to be the unnecessary messiness and untidiness of untrained children which remained for him a puzzle of nature.

He was pondering also the coincidence that on the day his wife should be pronounced pregnant, he should change his name.

As they sat down at the dining-room table, the girls prim and quiet, serviettes under chin, "The Lord make us truly grateful", his wife asked, "At work today, dear, anything of interest?"

"Yes, as a matter of fact," he said, twinkling, glad at last to be asked, having waited for what seemed a correct and decorous length of time and distance from his wife's announcement of the coming of the child, "I changed my name today," he announced, light-heartedly.

"How do you mean?'" she said, moving fruit in the fruit basket, a way she had of making herself steady, by being busy.

The children looked towards him with wide, unsure eyes.

"How do you mean, Father?"

"I'll show you," he said, and, leaving the table, he went to the sideboard, failing to find paper, he went then to the telephone table.

He returned with a pad and indelible pencil.

With a flourish, determined but not yet habit, he wrote, "T. George McDowell." He licked the pencil and wrote in indelible purple, "T. George McDowell."

"It's longer," was the first thing his wife said, staring at the new signature, pushed across to her on the pad headed Messages.

The children peered across.

"Why, Daddy?"

"What does T stand for?" the older daughter, Gwen asked.

"T stands for Terence, Daddy's other Christian name," Thelma told the children.

He went on eating, looking not at the food but at the new signature.

"Why don't you use it if it comes first?" Gwen asked.

"A long story," T. George McDowell said, returning in a flash and a spin to a boy with a leather schoolbag monogrammed TMCD with a red-hot piece of wire, riding a pony to a one-room coastal school, a drawing illustrating all the people of the Empire by children in different colours and national dress, all smiling, toothily, the enterprising spirit of the Anglo-Saxon race. "At my school, you see, we had two Terence McDowells, and I being the younger had to use my second name. As so often happens, it stuck."

He never quite overcame that bewilderment and displacement of having met, so early in his life, among such a small group, some-one of the same name.

"Why have you changed your signature now? And what about the bank and so on?" Thelma asked unsurely.

"For emphasis," he said. "It has more oomph."

He had wanted to change his name to T. George since 1923,

when he attended the St Louis Rotary Convention, an event which charged his life with zeal and which had begun him on his realisation of his System for Success. But only now, some many years later, did he feel established enough in the town to, well, "get away with it".

"T. George McDowell," his wife said in a low voice. "T. George McDowell."

"It will help, I think," T. George said, "especially in my dealings with the city and when we travel."

"Does it change our names too, Daddy?" asked the younger.

"I expect the locals will give you a bit of good-natured fun about it."

"I suppose so. I took it down to the printery today to have the new letterhead set up. Backhouse said it looked 'Americanised'."

Backhouse saying that pleased him, although one didn't know about Backhouse. Backhouse held himself off, was inclined to make remarks which meant more to himself than to the person addressed.

"Yes, it does," his wife said, saying T. George McDowell over in a low voice, as if trying to recognise the name.

"I've noticed in Rotary that many of the Rotarians from the city have adopted the use of their initial."

He masticated a mouthful of food. The family waited for him to go on.

As if they were waiting for yet further explanation.

"It makes you stand out from the herd. That is the theory of it. In business," he said, beginning what sounded like a speech, "it pays to have something which catches the eye—makes them remember you next time."

He patted his mouth with the white serviette, leaving a beetroot stain.

"A lot of the fun that is poked is at those who dare to be different. It is a way of getting people back into the common lot. There is nothing most like better than to pull a person back," he told the girls and Thelma.

"The lowest common denominator," his wife agreed.

"I see where Australia is producing its own tacks and wireless valves," he said, opening the newspaper, changing the subject modestly.

"Don't read at the table, dear. It's a bad example for the girls."

Pouring the tea from the traymobile, Thelma said, "I expect at

177

the long weekend we'll have quite an exodus from the city coming through."

"Boiled radiators and punctured tyres. Should sell plenty of drinks. We'll be working back to build up stocks."

"It's such a messy way of spending a weekend. Nowhere to wash properly."

"Can we go camping, Mummy?"

"When you become a girl guide and learn to camp properly," Thelma replied. "That is more than half the trouble. They come from the city and have not been trained to camp."

"Harry Fox is grumbling that the tourists camp in his paddocks. But some of the more tourist-minded in the Chamber want the farmers to let them camp."

He found he had picked up the newspaper again and Thelma took it away, putting it out of reach, and then said to the girls, "You must not talk to strangers."

"I gave a young fellow a lift today."

"Oh yes."

"He was dressed in black. I asked him about it and he told me it was a German-style uniform. It was a black uniform which he got while in Germany himself. Black shirt, black trousers, black leather knee-boots. You couldn't miss him. He stood out beside the road."

"Was he German?"

"No, Australian."

"I don't know what to think of that business over there."

"All you can say is that he's getting the place into shape. But he cannot last. Dictators do not last. No man who doesn't smile can last long in any public position. I never have seen a photograph of Adolf Hitler smiling."

He had once, at a sideshow in 1919, been tempted by a gypsy to be hypnotised but could not submerge himself. He wanted to go and be hypnotised but could not hand his will over to another. He stood fixed in the sawdust outside the sideshow tent as she coaxed him, staring straight into his eyes, there in the crowd, saying, "Come on, young man, venture into the dark beyond, you will become my slave."

He'd felt sickly weak, drawn, but wouldn't give his feet the instruction to go. His mind said no, but his whole physical yearning was to go and give himself over to her.

He was an individualist. A student of electricity and magnetism even then, a scientifically minded person and would not give himself over to hocus-pocus.

About the German thing, he saw the appeal of the torchlight and the singing and the wearing of national uniforms and leather knee-boots. It would be good for a country to march and sing together in a surge of unity. As opposed to all the political back-biting and squabbling. But no he was an individualist.

He had stared at the man in black uniform but found that he was not a Nazi but an adventurer, and his nervous curiosity about the Nazis was then deflated. One heard so much.

"Was he pleasant?"

"A little strange."

The man in the black uniform told him stories of midnight raids and the searching of Jewish women. Of the German secret police who made women strip, forced the women to be their whores, to clean and polish their boots with their mouths, lips and then to crouch naked and polish them with their pubic region.

"Hadn't you better leave for the meeting?" Thelma reminded him.

"Yes," he murmured and told the girls to help their mother.

He would try out the new name on those at the meeting, although he didn't feel in the mood to have his leg pulled.

He remembered that the child was expected and before he left, after putting on the armour of his best suit, he went to the kitchen and kissed his wife again on the cheek.

"I almost forgot—I'm glad about the planned child."

His wife smiled, pleasantly, and said, "It had gone completely out of my mind for the time being."

Business no picnic

IN 1929 George McDowell went to the Highlands for a weekend to examine his life and to try to get the cafes to start taking bottled soft drinks. Married one year, his cordial factory was making a profit, but other problems, however, hovered. He had not really mastered shyness, for instance, although his Powers of Concentration had improved, he thought.

Apart from questions of personality and philosophy of life, there was the world. The economic crisis looming, though few seemed to believe it, and the implications of electricity now that the town supply had been switched on, though most ignored that too, except to debate whether the street lights should stay on all night or be turned off at midnight.

His cordial factory was linked to the town electricity, one of the first. His trouble was not electricity but the town water. It needed triple filtration. Competition from Nowra or the city could hurt him especially if they extended the rail past Nowra. But he did not fear competition, he reminded himself. He believed that when it came to foodstuffs, people would buy only from someone they knew. His living presence on the coast was a guarantee.

His car boiled and while waiting for it to cool, he sat on the running-board, made a cup of tea from the boiling radiator, and ate Thelma's tomato sandwiches.

When he reached the town, the guest-house, Wychwoode, seemed oddly quiet.

At the sound of the car James Coffey, owner, in plus-fours, war-limp, came down to get the bags, his cigar plugged in his mouth. George always thought to himself that the cigar in Coffey's mouth always promised more than there was.

"Wonderful to see you, George. Bad news though—but, anyhow, how are you?—domestic staff, would you believe it, are on a strike. On a strike."

Coffey took both bags. "Here let me—that's what a guest-house is all about."

Strike?

George didn't feel right that the older man should carry his bags, but he took it as a tribute to his rising in the business world so young.

"Do?" said Coffey. "What can I do? Nothing." Coffey made it sound like action and decision.

George remained impassive towards his fellow business man as they climbed the stairs and said nothing suggesting endorsement of Coffey's inaction. He had learned only recently that an impassive appearance could be used to lead the other person to say more, to go further than they wanted, to reveal—usually their weakness. Coffey went on firmly about there being nothing that could be done. He did not like Coffey's confidence of defeat.

Cigar or not.

The guest-house had electricity, but although the main light in his room worked, the bed lamp did not. Typical. George carried his own globe because hotels used weak globes to save money.

George braked the Chev too severely and stalled it, so impatient was his movement, so determined was he to sustain his impulse. To get things moving.

People who rely on inertia, he believed, are easy prey to a man of action. A person who made a move stood a high chance of success. There were so few who did. Most people waited for things to happen *to* them.

Mrs K, the housekeeper at Wychwoode, sat in her tidy house with her hands crossed tidily on her lap.

"You can't strike against your own town. That's what you're doing. A place of work is like the family—pride and loyalty are owed," he told her, pacing about her living-room.

"We have," she said, shortly and hopelessly.

"To strike against your employer is to say that he is a dishonest man."

"That's not what we're saying, Mr McDowell. I don't like

going on a strike any more than the next person, and this is the very first and only time."

She was outwardly firm, but George sensed her desire to be back at work, her misgivings, her unease amid an unfamiliar situation.

He played on her desire to be back doing what she knew.

He went on, "...why, grown people each sitting at home sulking. Working for each other is our sacred interchange. A town is a co-operative reliance on each other to do his job."

His voice had strength and bluster which spurred him on as he heard himself. He did not know what he was saying at the time, but he knew when it was having effect.

He said things about goodness' sake, Mrs K, you have known James Coffey for how many years and the economic crisis and hard times.

After shaking her head during most of it, she did then get up resignedly and get her things.

"What about the others?" she said with some trepidation. "I'm letting them down."

"I'll worry about the others."

She said, no, she wasn't going, and sat down again, her things on the floor beside her.

George talked on, paced about. "We all live too close for us to be striking against each other. Striking is for those who don't know each other. The city."

She got up again, sat down again, but at last moved towards the door.

"Mind you," she said, "I'm only going back to talk. I'll not do a touch of work until this is settled properly."

Yes, yes.

Finally he got her into the car.

The cook said she'd put up with conditions long enough, and the cook at Bundanoon only worked forty-four hours and no broken shifts.

"Mrs K is out in the car and she's going back to work. She's willing to go back—to keep this in the family of employment. Not to make wounds which might not heal."

Agnes looked out the window to see for herself.

"For heaven's sake, Agnes, you're the last person I would

have thought needed looking after by people from the city. By some Union People you've never seen."

"I suppose if Mrs K is going back... but there'll have to be some immediate..."

Yes, yes, yes.

Two down.

The others were easy. Mrs K and Agnes in the car did the trick. He blustered them and held the curtain of their front window to show them. His two prisoners-of-war.

"Strike at Wychwoode! This is not the way country people settle things."

"But the Union Man over the telephone said to stay out until he got here."

They'd actually telephoned the city.

"Damn it, do we trust the voice on the telephone now more than the voice of those around us?"

The telephone made things happen too quickly.

Which one of them had the nerve to book a telephone trunk call to the city. That took some nerve.

"Some things," he told them, "are too important for the telephone."

People got things wrong over the telephone because they were too nervous. Many letters answered themselves in a fortnight, he always said.

So they'd actually telephoned the city. Fancy that.

"Who made the call?"

They didn't answer. He looked over his shoulder at them, huddled and glum. He looked at Agnes beside him. No reply. They weren't telling.

The boots, Old Simon, odd-jobman, cow-milker, wouldn't go back to work. He said he had made his decision and he didn't care what the others were doing and no young whipper-snapper was going to tell him what to do. He wouldn't rat on the union.

How had Coffey let things get so bad with his staff?

Whipper-snapper George gave up on Simon, shutting the weathered door of the weathered shack behind him, full of stuffed parrots and sea trunks. Beer bottles trimmed the edge of the dirt path.

183

He couldn't believe Simon would have made the trunk-line call to the city. He could not imagine Simon with a telephone in his hand.

He dragged the gate shut. Simon's tethered goat whinnied at him.

In the car the others were sitting low, probably fearing that old Simon would come out and berate them.

He told them the white lie that Simon wasn't feeling well.

This seemed to hearten them. He sensed that Simon was the backbone of their little nonsense.

He got the Chev into gear and turned around, when Simon came to the door and shouted, "You can all go to bloody hell—ratting on the union."

He revved the car up to block out Simon's voice, waved with mock cheeriness, as if they were great old mates, and shouted back, "Tomorrow—hope you're feeling better." Being on the side nearest Simon, he hoped the others didn't catch what he'd cried out. If they did, they perhaps chose not to show it.

At full throttle the Chev jerked off down the rutted road.

Agnes was even singing as she prepared the evening meal and the others were all seemingly, at least, relieved to be back at work.

They knew how to do their job: they didn't know how to have a strike. No one liked doing unfamiliar things. He'd banked on that.

The few guests who'd stayed, fending for themselves, were relaxing now in the lounge. Coffey was effusive, expansive.

What had Coffey done! Nothing.

He said to Coffey, "The only socialists I've ever known talk about work and the value of work but never do any."

Pleased with himself for having got things going, exhilarated too with having come through a private Shyness Test, he allowed himself a rare glass of stout with Coffey. He had to screw himself tight inside to approach people. To get out from inside took a lot of personal electricity.

"The working people have a puny spirit which is a direct result of lack of self-confidence. They always have to be bolstered up by some agitator. Our task as business men is to offer them superior leadership," he told Coffey.

"This Tea Rooms Award...."

"Every work-place has its own nature—an award never takes heed of that," he told Coffey. "One set of conditions cannot be imposed on all. No two enterprises are alike. They're trying to make everyone wear the same clothes.''

Coffey nodded, drinking down a whole whisky. George didn't quite know if his words were wasted.

Coffey was no thinker.

"There are two classes—those who are Self-movers and those who have to be coaxed, cajoled, and pushed.''

He stopped talking and looked into the empty stout glass. He had drunk that quickly! He refused another.

For heaven's sake, here he was, needing to cajole Coffey—a fellow business man.

Coffey was not quite up to the mark. The burned-out globe, that sort of thing. He played the big fellow about the town. Golfing and so on.

After tea they joined the guests around the pianola and a chap from Bega played the banjo. George excused himself early. Thank god, he thought, for wireless; it'll spare us the amateur musician.

He felt tired right out—a business man was up against it— one man against thousands. One man against the power of the Unions. It was lonely and hard being a small business man. A Problem-solver. A Self-mover against all the obstacles of the world.

Next day, after calling on the two cafes and giving them a sample range of his cordials and some sales talking—although he'd promised Thelma he would take a complete rest—he returned to the guest-house and saw Coffey talking with a stranger in the downstairs hall.

It turned out to be the Union Man from the city, arrived on the midday train.

George noticed he wore riding-boots—from the city and he wore riding-boots.

From the look and sound of it, Coffey was taking a brow-beating.

George joined them, standing hands on hips, eyes to the floor, listening to the Union Man with great impatience.

"And you'll pay them for their holidays,'' the Union Man said.

George had always found this outrageous. Why should he pay for another man's holiday?

George butted in, "Every business has to arrange its own affairs.''

"And who the hell are you?"

George decided not to answer. The Union Man turned to Coffey and said, "Who is this person?"

"This is George McDowell, a business friend."

"George McDowell—by God, I know about you—some sort of damn soft-drink factory down the coast—my God, yes, I've heard all about you. You keep your nose out of this McDowell."

George was rather pleased that he was known, but did not have a clue for what reason he might be known.

"I'm making this my business," George heard himself say.

"Look, McDowell, go back down the coast and back to your rot-gut lolly-water."

In a second of fury George was about to say, "I'll take you to court", but remembered he was opposed to using the courts in man-to-man situations, and so, instead, he seized the Union Man by the scruff of the neck and seat of the trousers and tried to frog-march him out of the guest-house. They stumbled together into the slow sunlight of the afternoon.

The Union Man freed himself with a twist, caught more by surprise than by George.

Shouting at George, he said something about the Factory Act and being empowered and not to lay a finger.

Coffey limped quickly down the steps, upset, restrained George, muttering, "Trouble enough."

George said, "You better not show yourself around my factory."

The Union Man said that was just what he intended doing and thanked him for the idea.

They stood there in the street, opposed, and out of breath.

"Please," Coffey said, holding George's arm.

Delighted to his heart that he'd thrown the Union Man off the premises but urged away by Coffey, George went off, leaving Coffey in his own mess. Coffey lacked stomach.

George slapped his thigh with exhilaration as he went along the streets in no particular direction, reliving the incident.

Finally he went to the California Cafe and had a soda with plenty of chipped ice.

He said to Margoulis that enterprise, freedom to run our own lives, would be finished if we let inspectors, city Union People and all the rest push us.

Margoulis appeared not quite comprehending, nevertheless agreed, and went on wiping the glasses left by the Saturday matinée interval.

He took the opportunity to point out to Margoulis that with bottled drinks and straws he wouldn't have to wash up the glasses.

But as a gesture of goodwill he admired Margoulis's new soda fountain, refrigerated wells, goose-neck taps.

Riding-boots.

He'd like to see him try.

The remark which hurt the most was the Union Man saying something about him living in the dark ages.

For a go-ahead man, that hurt.

Back in his room at Wychwoode, no sign of the Union Man, he lay on his bed in the late hot afternoon, hands behind his head, and drifted from exhilaration into miserableness.

He had a thought about himself which made him miserable. It was this: I am a man held in my interlocking restraints: I am not free to enjoy the fruits of pleasure.

Interlocking restraints.

Sometimes his spirit cried out, wept, he wanted sometimes to be, just for one day, indolent. To say, drink alcohol, like some of the others. To lay down the burden. He could see nothing in gambling. But yet there must be something in it for men to pursue it fanatically. That was just another pleasure he could not touch. He was locked in place. In the yoke. He feared the rules. He was frightened that relaxation was irreversible. That, once relaxed, the rules would not return to place. A slide would begin. Into what? What did he fear?

Into insignificance.

He did not want to be insignificant. That was his terror, his nightmare.

Sin wasn't a matter of hellfire for him. Sin was for him misdirected energy, if it was anything.

He really didn't know how to sin.

He was swept with tearfulness, like a rain squall across the sea.

He pulled himself together.

Up again, he washed his face, wetted his hair, parted it, and went downstairs.

The Union Man was definitely gone. Coffey was at golf. That

dejected him. He played no sport himself. After throwing a stick to the dog for a while, he decided to go back a night earlier than planned.

Packing the car, he jarred his thumb on the door. He could hardly bear it. He hopped about blowing warm air on his hand, damning and blasting and f-dashing. It hurt like the blazes. It was a bad sign, lack of inner co-ordination.

Driving along with his aching thumb, on his way out of town he pulled up at the railway station, idling there and looking about for the Union Man.

The Union Man was there. Riding-boots and all. George saw him from a distance. He was talking with the station-master. George switched off the ignition and went onto the platform. George then noticed something. He noticed that the Union Man was about his age. He'd really thought him older. And he noticed this also, he saw that the Union Man was clenching and unclenching his hand behind his back as he talked with the station-master.

Why, thought George, this Union Man is a nervous sort.

George watched from the platform entrance. No, I have nothing more to say, and went away without the Union Man seeing him.

We are all shy, observed George wondrously, we are all shy people.

Driving off, his thumb aching as he bumped along the bad mountain road. He admitted that he could not relax—too bad. Coffey at golf. He didn't care. Every existence its own rules. A long drive ahead on the rough, dusty road. He didn't mind that.

He had one vice which he could not explain or put a word to, which made him sick to bring to mind. It intruded in his dreams. But he was still a young man, although considered old for his years, and he could and would expunge it.

He had a flat at Fitzroy Falls and skinned his knuckle changing the wheel. He almost wept with the feeling of being so jangled, so rattled. It was the body turning on itself.

Back on the dusty road down the mountain.

A question kept coming to him. Who had, in all hell, made the telephone trunk call to the city? A trunk-line call.

Whoever made the call had something in them. But it was still unforgivable—the bringing-in of outside people to handle town problems.

That old buzzard Simon would never have talked on a telephone in his life, but he had a feeling it was him.

For George, the weekend had pulled apart like a bad soldering job.

Thelma expressed surprise at his early return and asked if he'd had a "nice time".

He said business was no picnic.

He went to the bathroom, locked himself in to bathe his jarred thumb and skinned knuckles.

Rules and practices for the overcoming of shyness

Rules and practices for the overcoming of shyness

1. Always walk up to a man as if he owes you money.
2. Train yourself to look at the bridge of the other man's nose, to give the impression that you are staring him straight in the eye.
3. Speak out with a loud voice and you will finish strongly: begin weakly and you will finish weakly.
4. Sometimes to be heard amid the shouting it is necessary to speak softly.
5. Learn when to remain silent, thus forcing the other fellow to speak.
6. Before meeting with a stranger, make a list of conversational items.
7. Learn the beginning and the end of a speech, so that you begin and end fluently.
8. Go out of your way to meet the Great. Keep the company of those older and superior to yourself. By doing so, you will gain knowledge and, at the same time, gain confidence through observing the weaknesses and foibles of your superiors.
9. Joust with your shyness by putting it constantly to the test.
10. Remember that these are but tricks and rules. Learn your trade well. Self-confidence grows from ability, as does your value as a person in the society of men.

Even so, in 1936, George McDowell was still dogged by shyness. The typed-out rules hung, pasted on cardboard, but he had to admit they'd become somewhat a fixture in the office. But also, he sincerely hoped, a fixture in his mind.

His experience with American Rotary during a visit to that country as a young man had convinced him of the need to overcome the unconfident reserve in the Australian character and the shyness so painfully hobbling his own character. Yet one had to avoid also the adolescent boisterousness and Sentimental Bloke cockiness which the working-class used to conceal their inferiority. In a talk only recently to his own Rotary Club he had recalled that visit and said, "We need to cultivate bonhomie and, to some extent, 'abandon' (there had been some winking, a rustle of chuckles at this). As business men we come to dinner bearing the impression of the day's work, but we need to throw this aside as far as is humanly possible and give ourselves up more to a free exhibition of fellowship."

The words expressed his own deep yearning and in some ways his deepest regret that at thirty-three he was known as a man difficult at times to approach and of formal manner.

Although this appealed to him as an image also of "strong character", he did try at times to relax it. He diligently learned jokes to tell so as to put people at ease, especially staff and such, but, no, he was a stiff man. He didn't drink, which was a drawback.

He'd even been embarrassed when, after giving his talk, "Bonhomie—the French Have a Word for It", he was approached by a visiting Rotarian from Nowra who congratulated him on the talk and asked for concrete suggestions on how to achieve this "bonhomie".

He could only repeat in a rather unhelpful way the idea of "stunts" at club meetings, which was an American idea.

What he thought, but could not get out with any clarity, was that "making a fool" of oneself, or at least "playing the fool", was a way of "getting outside oneself".

Yet one had to know how to play the fool without becoming a fool. And he opposed alcohol at club meetings on the grounds of standards. Meetings could become nothing more than smokos with blue jokes, which was not what Rotary was about nor what he had in mind. No, he wanted a sort of circumscribed and clean playing-up, but he had not made it at all clear and nothing came of his talk. He heard later that after he'd left, a few of the jokers at the club had chosen to take his talk the wrong way and to suggest that he had some pretty wild schemes for livening up the meetings. There was always someone who never missed an opportunity to take things the wrong way. Sometimes, he thought, joking was used to chase away an idea.

His life was a Shyness Test.

He was shy but not *timid*. He drove his spirit into combat with shyness, and although on each occasion he defeated shyness, it came back, shyness returned, refreshed.

He went out of his way to meet the great. He'd met Paul Harris, founder of Rotary, on his recent visit to Australia. He'd met the American writer, Zane Grey, down at Bermagui. But this year one event, more than all others in his life, had seemed to diminish his shyness, terrorise it even, so that it receded as a factor in his life.

The event was his burning-down of the Crowhurst house.

H. C. Crowhurst, retired accountant, old friend of George's father, had lived with his two aged sisters, who both predeceased him eighteen and twenty months respectively, and his will stated that, there being no surviving relatives, their house and its contents were to be destroyed by fire.

"I do not wish strangers to trespass on, or have the use of that which my dear sisters and I cherished, shared, and partook of, throughout our lifetimes together on this earth." The will named George as executor.

Crowhurst had declined in the last year, rarely coming down to the town, although he had, until a few years back, done George's books. George out of respect for his father's old friends had continued the weekly call, expecting as he walked up the path, on each visit to the house on the hill among the Norfolk pines, to find old Harry dead.

As it happened, the District Nurse had been the one to find old Harry dead.

George had at first made some remarks, along with the rest, about the seemingly wanton destruction but inwardly found the commission emotionally quickening, lured by its abnormality. Such an unnatural act for the town, striving as it was to shape itself, the homes and shops along the gravel streets, to make itself a normal town along with the rest in the State. But just this once he was quickened, and allowed himself to be. He went along with the unnatural act which had befallen him. He kept, however, a solemn face when confirming the legality of the will with Sime, a city lawyer.

For weeks he gave detailed and private consideration to the technique for burning the house and its contents. He even thought of explosives. He tried to talk confidentially and scientifically about it with Tutman, a scientifically minded friend from childhood.

Tutman in the old days would have entered into it with relish but now lacked the spark. Tutman had sunk personally through business and other difficulties, maintaining a false sense of superiority by mixing now with inferiors in the public bars.

So he ended up doing it alone and was glad.

Although he told only the local fire brigade and police sergeant, the word got around, and children and others drifted up to the house on the hill to see it burn.

He began by drenching the contents of the house with kerosene. One musty room after another. Sloshing the kerosene over the lace doilies, the crocheted tablecloths, the antimacassars, the rotted brown flowers in vases, the worn arm chairs, where Crowhurst and the sisters had sat each evening for fifty years or more, the potted ferns, the bamboo hall stands. The books of Keats, Kipling, and the complete novels of Sir Walter Scott. The oilskin on the kitchen table, the kitchen smelling of toast, preserves, lysol, and carbolic.

He drenched the concertina files of letters, the spiked receipts, dockets, years of petty transaction.

Backhouse, from the local newspaper, joined him and wanted to remove the books.

"A crime, George. Give them to the School of Arts."

He respected reading and agreed with Backhouse about the crime, thinking as he did that he had never committed a crime, and thinking then that this was not legally a crime, yet resembled criminality. However, he told Backhouse, one undertook a commission in every detail and to the detail, or not at all. "I'm that sort of person."

"I know you're that sort of person, George."

He went on drenching. Backhouse shook his head.

Backhouse's disapproval and the books in the bookcase soon to be aflame opened a throttle in him and he vibrated inwardly with the complete unnaturalness of it, the permitted unnaturalness of it. He drenched the rows of books with great vigour, seeing the kerosene spread and seek its way down the spines, running along the gutters of dust at the tops of the books. Literary genius about to burn. His spirit, far from quailing, was empowered.

Paintings hung on the wall—of English villages and rustic scenes—none, he'd been told, of high value. He drenched those too.

The Hoe Man. He stopped at the painting of the Hoe Man and remembered Hubbard's lines: "Let us all hoe a little and then the hoe man will not for ever be looking at the soil."

"What is it, George?" Backhouse's voice reached him distantly. "Second thoughts?"

"I was thinking of the Hoe Man."

"You know the poem?" Backhouse seemed surprised.

"No—an essay by Elbert Hubbard."

Backhouse smiled, knowingly. "I didn't think it would be the poem."

"I maybe read the poem, but I don't recall its wording."

"Not actually your sort of sentiments, George."

He didn't ask Backhouse what he meant.

He went on with the drenching, soaking the carpets. He found his breathing came out with irregularity because of excitation, but he made out, in front of Backhouse, that it was from exertion.

He wished damned Backhouse, with his enigmatic remarks, would go away.

"It's a damn pity in a way," he said, covering his feelings, to appease Backhouse, to get him on side.

"You seem to be enjoying it, George."

Backhouse was a strange fish.

Intelligent enough, but one was never really sure that he was *agreeing* or just listening for his own private meanings. He asked more questions than he ever printed in his paper. What did he do with all the information he got? Where did it go? He never let on whether you had convinced him. He never voted on anything.

He then said to Backhouse, without reserve, because of the irritating presence of Backhouse, and because he felt strong from having the commission, "God, you're right. Yes, I am enjoying it. Yes."

And went on with the drenching. That, oddly enough, seemed to please Backhouse. The admission of the enjoyment.

"Watch out, George—I'm not part of the contents—I'm not to be burnt." Some kerosene splashed onto Backhouse's shoes.

The house had not been connected to the town electricity. Crowhurst always said he liked the "soft" light of gas and the lantern, and that electricity gave "hard" light. No amount of talking could change his mind.

He drenched the three single beds in the three separate rooms.

The women's clothing in the wardrobes, some dating from the turn of the century, hanging there since the death of the sisters.

"That's enough, George—they're hellishly old. They'll burn well enough."

George ignored Backhouse and threw some more kerosene over the women's clothing.

He emptied the drum and went outside to the Chev to get the third drum. He did the inside walls, the wallpaper coming clean as the kerosene carried away the dust.

Then he and the police sergeant—Backhouse declining to assist—lugged in bales of straw and placed one or two in each room against the walls, drenching them also with kerosene.

Outside he saw some shaking of heads.

George knew of the bad feeling about the burning. A deputation from the local Labor League and a union official from the city had tried to get an injunction. Talk about giving the house to an unemployed family.

No one appreciated the effect of the Depression and its causes more than George. He had organised a debate on the matter in town quite early. He had used the word Depression when it became necessary. He'd set the Spend for Employment Scheme rolling at Rotary. He'd built a warehouse when his judgement told him to wait a year. It had however turned out well except that he could not get the staff and others to call it "the warehouse". They all called it the shed.

As for the house and the will, George was governed, he felt, by this view: I have been given a commission: I have to carry it through to execution against all obstacles: others may feel it their duty to create obstacles: my duty is to overcome these: I am irrevocably deputed.

I am irrevocably deputed.

He told the Labor League that when one carried out a commission, one could not consider and weigh the complete chain of implication, the full stretch of possibilities. People who did achieved nothing, intimidated by the unforeseen. Frozen in their tracks. All activity, he told them, had consequences which could not be foreseen. Tradition, law and experience guarded against consequences which could be foreseen. One had to know, within tradition and law, when to stop consideration, have the courage to proceed into unforeseen consequences—in a word, to get on with the job.

They had not been convinced.

There'd been a story about town, too, that the house contained money, which would be burnt. There was no money. And he would not burn money.

The fire brigade, out of breath, and in pieces of uniform, pulled their reel up the hill to the house. The water pressure, anyhow, too low, as it always was at the end of summer.

They couldn't have done much if the house did get out of control. Still, they stationed themselves about the grounds with beaters.

Crowhurst had been a stamp collector through his life, and had specifically stated that the collection too was to be burnt. It was considered, in conversation about the town, to be the most valuable thing in the house. He and Backhouse leafed through the thousands of stamps, right up to date with a complete set of the new German stamps.

George placed no value on stamp-collecting—misspent time. You could not eat it nor hang it on a wall.

He told Backhouse his thoughts about it, and Backhouse seemed to give the opinion some credit.

To the detail. As the last act he sloshed the kerosene over the stamp albums, opened to allow easier burning. Opened at random pages, the kerosene running over the impassive faces of monarchs, dictators, emperors, triangular stamps, brightly coloured from islands of the South Seas.

The faces of aviators, generals, and explorers.

The twenty or so albums lay on a bench, the meticulously fixed stamps glued there by Crowhurst the schoolboy and then Crowhurst the old man, representing the power and the glory of all the nation states.

Backhouse left at this point, saying that he didn't want to watch any more.

George finished the drenching and came out for fresh air, away from the kerosene fumes, wiping his brow with his sleeve. The small crowd were talking with the firemen, children playing with the useless fire-hose reel.

He went to the sergeant. "About ready, Herbert," he said seriously. "Hot work."

They smiled at the unintended joke.

He spoke to the captain of the brigade, who got the men back to their places with their beaters.

He opened all the windows for draught.

He was rather pleased with the crowd, although it had been

intended that there should be no spectators.

He went to the car and got out the blow-torch, which he had decided would be the most suitable method of lighting the house.

He put on his coat.

He'd given it some thought. It was, after all, an official act.

He lit the blow-torch and pumped it until it roared.

He looked across at the firemen and the sergeant and nodded. They nodded back.

The crowd stopped talking.

He pulled out a piece of paper from his side coat-pocket and read, "I, George McDowell, executor of this estate, hereby consign this house and all its contents to ashes in accordance with the wishes of the late Herbert Charles Crowhurst as expressed in his last will and testament."

The blow-torch roaring.

Backhouse, he noticed, had not gone but was standing one foot on the running-board of his car, in a pose of dissociation.

George moved into the house, the roaring torch in his hand, touching the bales of straw and other well-soaked places with the blue flame of the torch. He stopped at the stamp albums and held the torch to them, burning a black hole straight through the faces of the monarchs, dictators, emperors, page after page curled away into ash.

Through the bedrooms and the women's clothing. The house filled quickly with crackling and smoke.

He realised he was lingering in the house. The house, dry from summer, was igniting around him. The paintings on the walls were aflame. The dining-room table was alight, the fruit bowl burning.

He was lingering. Run. He almost had to instruct himself to run.

He was held there in the igniting house, as if testing his invulnerability.

Run. He instructed himself again.

He came out the front door, eyes watering, and pulled himself stiffly together. Brushed ash from his clothing.

The firemen had stationed themselves too close and now moved back. The crowd oo-ahed as the flames came fingering out the windows, and they too moved back. George decided to move his car. So did Backhouse.

Woomph, perhaps a lantern exploding.

The house roof shingles began to fall in.

In all, the house and contents took two and a quarter hours to burn to the ground. All that remained was a blackened cement washtub, a bath with four squat legs. A Bega stove and the chimney.

The intention was that the rubble would be carted away and the land was then to be auctioned, with the proceeds going to Lodge Abercorn, of which Crowhurst had been a member.

No trace would be left of the Crowhurst family, which had lived in the town almost since it was incorporated as a municipality.

Later, George could not remember when his body had been more alive, the conflagration raced through him as through the house. It left him burned out, tired, and he went to sleep for a few hours, something he had never done before—sleep during the day. Never.

He felt it somehow indecent to talk about it now that it was over and done, but he did say to Thelma that very few men in a lifetime had the opportunity to burn the home and possessions of another human.

He considered it had helped to burn away his shyness, although it was a rule and practice which one could not put on the list. The burning of the house, together with his meeting with Paul Harris, founder of Rotary, made 1936 a memorable year and one of both public and personal progress, although, Thelma said, some people thought he'd become hard and unyielding because of the burning.

The enterprising spirit of the Anglo-Saxon race

THAT next bright morning he called around to the motel to collect Becker and take him to the Lookout—this visiting American he'd met at Rotary the previous night and who knew his daughter Terri in the city.

The American was bemused.

"No," he said to this Becker, "you must see our Points of Historical Interest."

He liked visitors. They filled the time he had, it seemed, these days.

"After all we are, or I was, in the same business, Mr Becker. I was making soft drinks before you were born. Now, of course, retired. Would you believe there were independent cordial-makers in every country town before you chaps came along with your Proprietary lines—Coca-Cola, Jusfrute, Schweppes. Still that's Progress, I suppose."

I suppose. That's Progress. How you believe in something and it changes like a stick into a snake. Cherished beliefs turn and bite you. Competition. Good for the winner, bad for the loser. And always more losers than winners. That was why people became socialists. Socialism was a system for losers. But for the life of him he couldn't see whether he'd won or lost now, now that it was the final round. Some words were only made clear by the events that arose and followed in and around and behind the word.

"Situations and people's subsequent behaviour make the meaning of some words clear," he said.
"Sorry, sir?"
"Just thinking aloud. No matter."

School of Arts—Tap-dancing, Tues., Thurs., Sat.

"That was where the Science Club used to meet before the war. These days they use it for Housie—the Catholics. I suppose we have the answer to everything now. This has always been a brick town. Weatherboard towns don't trust themselves. I've always said a brick building was a statement of faith."
"Brick, sir???"

Street Light, Weathered-grey Ironbark Blackened with Creosote at the Base

"Believe it or not, that's our first street light—still standing. Not that it is a Point of Historical Interest. I just mention that in passing. I can remember when it was our only street light. It was a carbide light, before I moved a motion that we have a row of electric lights in the street run off the generator from sunset to midnight, except on moonlight nights—we were a bit tight, that council. I made one of the speeches on Switch-on Night from the back of Carberry's Fiat motor-lorry. . . .

How do we get up on the lorry, Henry! Didn't anyone think of steps? What about the Ladies? A butter-box or something! Do I always have to think of everything myself?

"We had a potted palm on the lorry and a table draped with the Australian flag. Coloured lights. I have always said Australians don't know how to put on a Show—have a proper ceremony. I was telling you last night about the St Louis Rotary Convention. Now, you Americans, you people know how to put on a Show."
"Yes, sir, you did tell me."

Electricity is used extensively in America and Europe, and seven towns now have electricity in New South

Wales alone. The approach to this town could be a White Way of Electricity—a proclamation of this town's belief in the Scientific Future. No city parliamentarians came. Some of the locals were peeved. I was not. Towns should be masters of their own affairs.

I have always avoided bowing and curtsying to politicians, which is not to say anything against Harry Bate.

"Towns should be masters of their own affairs and powers unto themselves. I have always avoided this bowing and scraping that goes on with city parliamentarians. I remember thinking at the time that electricity power and its conveniences might equalise the country and the city and keep the young from leaving the town. We failed to keep our young. My two daughters have gone."

There were those opposed to the spending of the £8000. Council could go too far and ride the good horse called Good Times into the ground. There were those on council who would always have you budget for bad times. I have always budgeted for better time ahead.

"Ironbark poles—all ironbark poles and many still standing."

An unnatural extending of the daylight. 'The moon and the stars are good enough for God,' Old Holdstein, the Lutheran said. We all grinned behind our hand and winked at each other.

"One old chap I remember said that it was extending daylight unnaturally. Most people, he said, didn't want to be moving about at night. But we are go-ahead down this part."

'You are living in the unscientific past, Mr Holdstein,' I said. 'And you, George McDowell, are an arrogant man, dazzled by mechanical fabrications and unable to have proper fear of their implications.' The others were having a bit of a laugh behind their hand.

"I replied that we have to go where Science takes us. That's the destiny of our Times. He said that he knew very well where Science was taking us."

"Do you mind if I smoke, sir?"

"No, by all means."

He pulled out the ashtray for the American. "I myself have never smoked and did not take alcohol until I was fifty. Both my daughters smoke, I don't know why. I always believed though, privately, that I could become a heavy drinker if I ever had let myself go."

Tutman's Ice Works—"Safe and Pure" —Two Shillings in the Slot

"Now there's an interesting story. My childhood friend, the late James Tutman, built that ice works and it's still going. He was a pioneer of ice-making in this country. First to make block ice, or one of the first. I once predicted that it was finished. Now his son's put ice in plastic bags for service stations and hotels."

I show James the advertisement from Popular Mechanics for the Tyrell Institute Formula, and we agree to write away for it and try it. It says that it will "magnify your energy, sharpen your brain to razor edge and put a sparkle in your eye". I tell James that we get no answer to our letter, but, in fact, we do and I take the powder but do not tell James. I do not want to share the secret. I should not have done that. I'm sorry, James. I'm sorry. It did not work anyhow. I felt no different.

"We were great friends and business associates and fellow Rotarians. Do you know what my greatest mistake was?"

"No, sir. What was your greatest mistake?"

"I decided against going into ice-cream manufacturing. The coast is ideally suited. Milk, butter, cheese. I decided against ice-cream. Why? I thought domestic refrigeration would spell the end to commercial ice-cream. I thought every woman would make ice-cream in her home. I was wrong. Throughout my life I have underestimated the laziness, lack of initiative, lack of resourcefulness of the human race."

"H. L. Mencken once said, sir, that no one has ever gone broke underestimating the public taste."

On the balance, things are for the best rather than for the worse. "Where is the proof of that?" I ask Teacher.

"Sit down, George, and get on with your work."

"Where is the proof?"

"Don't be insolent, George."

Sit down.

Sit down.

I wanted it to be proved, I wanted it to be true.

Dr Trenbow's Former Residence with Wireless Aerial

"Am I boring you with all this talk of the old days?"

"No, not at all. But sooner or later I have to get on with my calls."

"That stone residence is where old Dr Trenbow lived. He, too, was an advanced thinker. He had the first wireless set in this town and formed a Radio Listening-in Club. It was in 1924 when F. P. Naylor, representing the Associated Radio Company of Australia, visited this town.

F. P. Naylor rises to speak. "It is with great pleasure that I come here this evening to address your listening-in experiment organised by your Science Club. For those of you new to wireless the method of use is as follows: the family gathers around a table on which the wireless receiving apparatus is placed. A selective switch is turned—this ebonite knob—to get the correct strength of sound, this other ebonite knob is turned. The best artists in the city travel through the ether at 186,000 miles per second, thus annihilating distance. The apparatus literally takes the broadcast programme 'out of the air'. For family listening a trumpet is used to distribute the sound equally up to a distance of 200 yards. For private listening the ear receiver is used." Dr Trenbow and I had spent the afternoon rigging up the aerial from the chimney to the pine-tree. The doctor had purchased a Burgusphone wireless receiver. Thus annihilating distance.

"The wireless annihilated distance. I'll tell you a funny thing. They used to say that until we had wireless, this town was always about ten minutes behind the world. The town clock was always slow by about ten minutes. Every time someone went up to the city, they found their watch slow. When wireless came, we could set the clock by that."

"That's intriguing, sir."

McDowell's Cordials and Aerated Waters
—Tru-frute Flavours—
Now Demolished Except for the Brick Front which Still Stands

"I built that factory in 1925, lived in it until I married. Get out, we'll have a look around. You'll be interested, being in the soft-drink business, yourself."
>The Business.
>Business Card.
>Letterhead.
>Printed Invoice.
>Painted Sign.
>Printed Label.
>Advertisements.
>All bearing my name. A person becomes a business entity. An address. A telephone number. A letterhead. There was something fine about it. Something of a special pleasure in a letterhead. A registered business name. The Eckersley Carbonator will be here on Tuesday.

"This is where the Eckersley Carbonator was—over here—and the Progressive bottle-washing machine here. And this here was my office, this slab here was my office."
>My office.
>And these are my tears and this is my aching heart. This was my office and this was my factory. I didn't sell my factory: I sold my works and days.
>Economic factors and economy of scale.

"Economic factors and economies of scale. That was where the men's shower was."
>Where are the men? What is the future of the country town? We could all live in a single skyscraper. One town in a single building instead of spreading houses over good acres. Soon, anyhow, the town will be nothing more than a refrigerated outlet for frozen merchandise from the city. The country merchant and the country manufacturer are disappearing.

"Soon towns will be just refrigerated outlets for frozen products made for us God-knows-where by people we've never met. Soon we won't even bake our own daily bread."

204

Tears.

Tears.

"Morning, George, sentimentalising again, I see."

Sentimental George? Yes, he was a very sentimental person. Ben Backhouse, queer fish. A good town editor. Stuck by the town.

"Our editor, Ben Backhouse, this is Mr Becker from the United States."

Local papers disappearing. Owned by people you never see. People you can't argue with in the street, can't put a case to. This Max Newton. What happened to Frank Hanley, always working here on some paper on the coast?

"Ben, whatever happened to Frank Hanley?"

"Can't remember, George."

"What happened to Boot? I met Boot once with my father. He had the paper at Tilba and then Cobargo."

"That's a long way back, George."

Time. George. My second daughter died of pleurisy. Wouldn't happen now. I placed an advertisement in the local paper thanking the nurses at the Cottage Hospital and thanking Dr Trenbow. Don't see that now. I own all the shops in the arcade.

"I own all the shops in the arcade, which was my idea. How many towns do you know that have an arcade? But it's not the same, not the same as being a manufacturer. Why, I'm just a collector of rents now."

"You've done very nicely, George. No one is going to listen to your whingeing."

"I was telling Mr Becker that I was in soft drinks myself until two years ago. No one to take over things. No son. Of course, I'm a rich man. My eldest daughter has done very well—a headmistress. I often ask myself these questions..."

What questions?

I once had plans for a political party of Makers and Growers. This country is run by financiers, real-estate men, trade unionists, and public servants—who all make nothing. I was quite a reader. I was once quite a philosopher in my own way, and a world traveller.

"In my own way I was once quite a philosopher. You'd agree with that, Ben?"

"Oh yes, George, you were."

"I have always said the small town is the answer to our problems. We will one day have to return to the small town. I was against *small-mindedness*, but always for *small towns*. It's not how many square miles in a country that makes it great: it's how many square people. I see, only recently, a young fellow from the university agreed with me about the towns. He said the future is in small communities. I cut the piece out. His name was McGregor. Or was it Craig. I held high hopes for the country way of life, Ben. You'd agree with that. I once wrote the Creed. Do you remember the Creed, Ben? You printed it. The point of ever larger cities eludes me. This is where the men's showers were, where I'm sitting now."

Where are the men?

Triple-filtered water was the answer to impurities in the local supply. I didn't use Blue Ark essence for many years. Made everything myself. All my drinks were 15 parts pure fruit juice. No one noticed when I stopped doing it myself. People don't basically care. Or appreciate. People have never cared as much as I have. Why was that? No one ever commented. I didn't sell my factory: I sold my works and my days.

"George?"

"Ben. Have you met this American chap from Coca-Cola?"

It's enough to make you weep. Tears of the out-of-business man.

"Come on, George, you'd better get up."

"What time is it, Ben?"

"Nearly eleven."

"Nearly eleven, and we haven't begun our tour of the Points of Historical Interest. Haven't been to the Lookout. Something could happen yet to make this town go ahead. Remember Dorman Long and Co., and what they did for Moruya. Granite for the Sydney Harbour Bridge."

"Maybe, George. But this town's doing OK."

A man fell down a mine-shaft and drank his own blood to stay alive for six days. As a boy I was attacked by a sow, and my nose and right arm were broken. Tutman lost a finger. That chap in the garage at Nowra lost an eye when the car battery exploded. Reeves broke his wrist cranking a car. We all lost something or broke something in those days. Life wasn't as safe as it is now, it seems, looking back.

"Ben, I've seen the flower of this town leave."

"George, come along, I'll drive you home. Here wipe your eyes."

"I'm not crying, Ben. Nothing wrong with my eyes. Why, look, everywhere you look—McDowell Cordial bottles, broken glass. I tell you who I saw the other day. Can't bring his name to my lips. He was with the Coastal Steamship Company. I think he was on the *Benandra* when it sank on the Moruya Bar. Crying? Yes, I'm crying. Why shouldn't I damn well cry?"

"George, come on, stand up, old fellow."

"What did we pay for the Lookout? How much did it eventually cost the club?"

"Oh, I don't know, George. It was a long time back. Seven hundred pounds, I think."

"There could have been economies."

Economies of scale and economic factors, and the events and behaviour and personal feelings behind words revealed by the turn of events.

I never spoke to her again after that one unfaithful act. She pleaded. "But, George, it has never been this way for either of us. We were as we had never been."

"We were like animals, and I do not wish to be that way."

They had become like animals on the dirt floor of the Showground Pavilion. She died, impaled on a burning branch in a bushfire. Going away from the town.

"Will you help me, Mr Becker? Give me a hand, and we'll get George over to the car. Come on, George. Stand up."

Stand up.
Stand up.
The class will sing
Advance Australia Fair
Blue Bells of Scotland
Dear Little Shamrock
The Song of Australia
Rule Britannia
One two three
George will speak on The Enterprising Spirit of the Anglo-Saxon Race.

I must dig out those accounts. They must be in a box somewhere.

I never had an experience like it with anyone else before or since. It remains singular and alone.

All right, children,
one, two, three.

In those days one could not afford the risk. You can never be certain. Never trust your memory.

"My recollection, Ben, is that it cost more than £700."

"Give me a hand. Come on, George, over to the car. Steady now, he's quite a weight."

"He seemed to be in good spirits when he called for me at the motel. Obviously the demolished factory and all."

"Come on, George, you can't sit here in the rubble."

"I think, Ben, I'll start again from scratch. It's my view that there'll be a swing back to country-made things. I'll start again from scratch."

"Come on, George. Here wipe your eyes. No one is going to listen to your whingeing. You've done very nicely."